PRAISE FOR *Time After Time*

'Heart-warming ... an enjoyabl[e] ... welcomed by fans of Australian romance writing.' — *Weekly*

'Karly Lane has a way of dragging you in and making you feel like you are a part of the story ... It is a wonderful read.' —Beauty and Lace

'Lane vividly evokes Australian rural communities, and gives due recognition to its challenges, especially for farmers. Written with the warmth, humour and heart for which Lane's rural romances are known, *Time After Time* is an engaging read.' —Book'd Out

PRAISE FOR *Wish You Were Here*

'A comely rural romance that encapsulates the heart and emotions of Australian country life ... You can't go wrong with a Karly Lane novel and this latest one was no exception. —Mrs B's Book Reviews

'It's always a great day when a new Karly Lane book is released ... *Wish You Were Here* has all the small town country vibes you could want in a closed door romance with a whole lot of heart.' —Noveltea Corner

'... a fabulous rural romance, the perfect book to snuggle up with on the recliner! Loved it.' —Mrs G's Bookshelf

'With the magic of country atmosphere, a cast of incredible characters . . . true community spirit and a relatable romance, it has all the contents of an engaging read. You can smell the way of life, feel the weather and breathe in the fresh air as Karly's inviting storytelling comes to life from the pages.' —HappyValley BooksRead

PRAISE FOR *A Stone's Throw Away*

'Fans will not be disappointed and new readers are likely to be converted . . . those looking for romance, suspense or contemporary novels will all find something to enjoy.' —Beauty and Lace

'With its appealing characters, well-crafted setting and layered storyline, *A Stone's Throw Away* is an entertaining read.' —Book'd Out

'Karly Lane has delivered a wonderfully immersive novel with a highly engaging plot, gripping suspense and compelling twists. *A Stone's Throw Away* is a story of courage, resilience and a passion for the truth.' —The Burgeoning Bookshelf

'I'm always highly impressed by Lane's ability to write compelling, entertaining and emotional storylines and weave some of Australia's history through her stories . . . an absolute treat.' —Noveltea Corner

PRAISE FOR *Once Burnt, Twice Shy*

'Well written, and bravely done . . . *Once Burnt, Twice Shy* is Karly Lane's best yet, celebrating the power of community working to support one another in terrible calamity.' —Blue Wolf Reviews

'Karly Lane gives it her all in *Once Burnt, Twice Shy* . . . a story of faith, courage, strength and future prospects, Lane's eighteenth novel is a sizzling summer read.' —Mrs B's Book Reviews

'This book has a huge amount of hope after loss, a wonderful read.' —Noveltea Corner

'Heart in mouth stuff, readers. You won't be able to put the book down till you know what happens to Jack and Sam.' —Australian Romance Readers

PRAISE FOR *Take Me Home*

'Full of romance, humour and a touch of the supernatural, this is another engaging tale by the reliable Karly Lane.' —*Canberra Weekly Magazine*

'Such a fun read . . . Karly has smashed the contemporary fiction genre with *Take Me Home*.' —Beauty and Lace

'*Take Me Home* is a delight to read. I loved the change of scenery while still enjoying Karly Lane's wonderful, familiar storytelling.' —Book'd Out

PRAISE FOR *Something Like This*

'Another unmissable rural romance story of pain, loss, suffering and the power of love . . . Karly Lane is firmly on my must-read list.' —Beauty and Lace

'There is more to this narrative than rural romance; this is a multi-faceted exploration of loss, grief, families, second chances and courage . . . I loved this!' —Reading, Writing and Riesling

'An engaging story, set at a gentle pace, told with genuine warmth for her characters and setting, *Something Like This* is a lovely and eminently satisfying read.' —Book'd Out

PRAISE FOR *Fool Me Once*

'*Fool Me Once* is a guaranteed perfect light read . . . Karly Lane has woven a delicious tale of lust, love, betrayal, consequences and chasing dreams.' —Blue Wolf Reviews

'With its appealing characters, easy pace and happy ending, I found *Fool Me Once* to be another engaging and satisfying rural romance novel.' —Book'd Out

'Karly Lane's affinity for the land shines through in her stories . . . *Fool Me Once* is a feel-good story not to be missed.' —The Burgeoning Bookshelf

Karly Lane lives on the beautiful mid-North Coast of New South Wales, and she is the proud mum of four children and an assortment of four-legged animals.

Before becoming an author, Karly worked as a pathology collector. Now, after surviving three teenage children and with one more to go, she's confident she can add referee, hostage negotiator, law enforcer, peacekeeper, ruiner-of-social-lives, driving instructor and expert-at-silently-counting-to-ten to her resume.

When she isn't at her keyboard, Karly can be found hanging out with her beloved horses and dogs, happily ignoring the housework.

Karly writes Rural and Women's Fiction set in small country towns, blending contemporary stories with historical heritage. She is a passionate advocate for rural Australia, with a focus on rural communities and current issues. She has published over twenty books with Allen & Unwin.

ALSO BY KARLY LANE

North Star
Morgan's Law
Bridie's Choice
Poppy's Dilemma
Gemma's Bluff
Tallowood Bound
Second Chance Town
Third Time Lucky
If Wishes Were Horses
Six Ways to Sunday
Someone Like You
The Wrong Callahan
Mr Right Now
Return to Stringybark Creek
Fool Me Once
Something Like This
Take Me Home
Once Burnt, Twice Shy
A Stone's Throw Away
Wish You Were Here
Time After Time

For Once in My Life

For Dave
In My
Life

KARLY LANE

For Once in My Life

ALLEN & UNWIN
SYDNEY · MELBOURNE · AUCKLAND · LONDON

First published in 2023

Copyright © Karlene Lane 2023

All rights reserved. No part of this book may be reproduced or transmitted in any form or by any means, electronic or mechanical, including photocopying, recording or by any information storage and retrieval system, without prior permission in writing from the publisher. The Australian *Copyright Act 1968* (the Act) allows a maximum of one chapter or 10 per cent of this book, whichever is the greater, to be photocopied by any educational institution for its educational purposes provided that the educational institution (or body that administers it) has given a remuneration notice to the Copyright Agency (Australia) under the Act.

Allen & Unwin
Cammeraygal Country
83 Alexander Street
Crows Nest NSW 2065
Australia
Phone: (61 2) 8425 0100
Email: info@allenandunwin.com
Web: www.allenandunwin.com

Allen & Unwin acknowledges the Traditional Owners of the Country on which we live and work. We pay our respects to all Aboriginal and Torres Strait Islander Elders, past and present.

 A catalogue record for this book is available from the National Library of Australia

ISBN 978 1 76106 612 2

Set in 12.5/18.25 pt Simoncini Garamond Std by Bookhouse, Sydney
Printed and bound in Australia by the Opus Group

10 9 8 7 6 5 4 3 2 1

 The paper in this book is FSC® certified. FSC® promotes environmentally responsible, socially beneficial and economically viable management of the world's forests.

To all the women who still get a shock when it comes to saying your age out loud and wondering how it's possible to suddenly be this old! Pause for a moment and take in everything that's come before: the first loves; the marriages; the children; the first school days; the tears and the teenage tantrums. The endless running around and fixing everyone else's problems. The divorces, the heartaches and the grief. The losses and the victories. The friends we've made and the ones we've lost along the way.

Now look forward and don't be afraid. This is our time to find the things that truly matter to us. Be proud. Be fierce. Be true to yourself. The greatest times are still ahead.

One

Jenny Hayward flopped down on the lounge chair, kicked off her shoes and closed her eyes as she let out a slow breath. Home. The silence of the house was like a soothing balm to the hectic pace of the hospital. It'd been a long day—a long *two years*, if she were being honest. That was when her husband of twenty-seven years had announced he was moving out.

Lost in the shock and pain of his betrayal, Jenny had turned the house into her sanctuary, doing a clean-out of anything she didn't find comforting or calming. Her best friend, Beth—dark-haired, Italian-Maltese—became a slightly more intimidating version of the decluttering queen, Marie Kondo, as she held open a garbage bag and barked, 'Does it bring you joy? No? Well chuck it!' In a couple of days, they'd transformed the house. It had been nothing short of a miracle.

Jenny had never been a big believer in the whole crystals and energy hocus-pocus the way Beth was, but weary and heartsick, she couldn't have summoned the strength to protest even if she'd wanted to when Beth had told her to 'leave everything to me'.

As far as makeovers went, there hadn't been anyone better qualified for the job. Beth had always had a knack for decorating and had done a course, intending to one day turn her talent into a business. She'd filled Jenny's house with soft furnishings, scattered soothing colours about the rooms and added little touches—a plant here, a Buddha statue there and, of course, her signature crystal-infused candles, which she'd begun making during Covid and had become a booming success.

'When you've been knocked down, bloodstone will pick you back up,' she'd said, then had placed little pottery bowls of tourmaline near the front and back doors and lit a candle, carrying it through the house like a priest performing an exorcism. 'This will flush out all the negative vibes and allow the good stuff back in,' she'd explained as a delicious scent of sage, black tea and bergamot filled the room. In Jenny's bedroom, she'd scattered amethyst, informing her that it would relieve stress and anxiety and promote a chill vibe for sleeping.

And there'd been more. Beth had placed her candles infused with their healing crystals in every nook and cranny, and as much as Jenny—a level-headed, science-based nurse—wanted to scoff at the ridiculousness of the idea, she'd found herself noticeably calmer and the house, which had always been full of the eggshells she'd been walking on, suddenly felt like a *home*. Of course, the candles smelled gorgeous, but maybe there *was* something in the whole crystal thing, because now her house was a haven and she loved coming home to it at the end of a long shift.

Sometimes it seemed hard to believe the split had been that long ago. Austin had been her life for so long. They'd had a reasonably happy marriage, getting married young and starting a family. Jenny had always wanted a brood of children, but Austin—ever practical—had declared that two kids were all they could afford. Deep down, she'd known he was right. After all, she'd had her hands full with an almost-two-year-old and a newborn. As the girls grew older, she'd learned to ignore the little whimper inside whenever they passed by a baby in the shopping centre. It was silly—she was far too busy for any more children, she'd remind herself.

After Brittany started school and she only had Savannah at home, Austin began to hint at Jenny going back to work. His income as a salesman in a white goods store wasn't stretching all that far and raising two children on a single wage was never going to get them where they were hoping to go. The only job she'd ever had was as a check-out chick in a grocery store from when she'd left school up until going on maternity leave with Brittany, and as much as she'd enjoyed the job and the people she'd worked with, it had been almost five years and everyone she'd known had moved on. She wanted to do something different, only she wasn't sure *what* exactly. Austin hadn't been overly sympathetic when she'd brought up her concerns. 'It's not like you've had any burning ambitions to have a career or anything. We just need something that brings in a pay cheque.' Which she had to grudgingly admit was true, but it did nothing to still that growing restlessness she was noticing inside. All she was any good at was having babies. She loved being a mother, but unfortunately, you didn't get paid for that, so she knew she needed to start thinking seriously about what would bring in a pay cheque—and what she'd enjoy doing.

In the end, the answer had arrived in the form of her aunty, who'd commented on how short-staffed the hospital system was and that Jenny should think about becoming a nurse.

'But I didn't even finish high school,' Jenny had said.

'You can go in as a mature student. Do a bridging course and enrol in university. You'd make a great nurse.'

Jenny had chewed the idea over in her head for a while. It hadn't crossed her mind before. She wasn't sure why; her aunty was a nurse and she had multiple cousins who were nurses, but she'd always considered herself not quite smart enough to do anything that would require getting a degree.

She'd brought it up with Austin, who'd laughed, then sobered at the look on her face. 'How would we afford university? That's a lot of money for something you didn't even want to do before today.'

'I wasn't planning on enrolling right now,' she snapped, hurt by his lack of encouragement, which immediately caused all her insecurities to resurface. 'It was just an idea.'

She handed her resume to the local supermarket the next day and managed to pick up a few hours a week. She put Savannah into day care for the days she worked, hating every minute of it. Guilt became Jenny's constant companion. She felt guilty that she was putting her child in day care when she should be at home looking after her. She felt guilty that she resented her husband for making her go back to work so early when she knew the money would help out enormously. She felt guilty for hating a job she was lucky to have when there were people who didn't have one. The guilt went on and on, draining her energy and making her miserable.

Eventually, she'd brought up the nursing idea over coffee with Beth, who'd encouraged her to enrol in a bridging course so she could think about university in the future if she still wanted to. Jenny didn't tell Austin. What if she failed? What if she couldn't even get over this first hurdle?

What if you can? her little voice of reason piped up helpfully.

Jenny studied and submitted her assignments and, to her surprise, she was passing—not only passing, but doing better than she'd ever done at school. She discovered she was enjoying it. *Her! Enjoying* study? It was crazy. Managing to keep her newly acquired diploma a secret, by the end of the year she'd worked up the courage to apply to university to see what happened. To her shock, Jenny was accepted into a nursing degree.

Telling Austin hadn't been as bad as she'd been anticipating, at least not once she'd assured him she could get a student loan to cover her fees, and so there she was, sitting in a lecture room, surrounded by other people like her—some older, most younger—but other people excited to be taking this next step and forging themselves a bright path into a new career. She'd never felt more alive.

It'd been a crazy time, juggling two small children and study, but she'd managed with Beth lending a hand to babysit and cheer her on. Her graduation had been the proudest day of her life, with her family travelling to be there and Austin accepting all the congratulations and admiration about how difficult it must have been for them all to have taken such a huge thing on. She'd put aside her irritation, deciding not to bring up the countless arguments they'd had over the time, when he'd occasionally had to cook his own dinner or heaven forbid, find his work clothes in the folding when she'd been struggling to meet a deadline.

Jenny gave a small smile. Back then she'd had so many big plans.

After that, life finally started to get easier. The girls were a little older and both in school. She loved her job and the people she worked with and the extra income—nothing outrageously wonderful—but enough to allow them to move into a bigger house with a backyard and room to grow. Austin had scored a job with a large firm and had his sights set a lot higher than being a white goods salesman. He seemed happier than he'd been in a long time.

Then one day she found herself staring down at two red lines on a pregnancy test.

It wasn't that she didn't *want* another baby, it was just that their lives had moved on from nappies and toilet training. Brittany was eight and Savannah was six and now she'd be going back to breastfeeding and sleepless nights after taking for granted the fact that she'd finally got both children sleeping in their own beds.

If she hadn't been so caught up in everything going on, she probably would have realised that it was at this very point in time that her marriage had begun its downhill slide.

'You can't be pregnant. Take another test,' Austin had said after staring at her for what seemed an eternity.

'I took two,' she told him dully. But at his insistence, she did a third test and watched his face fall as the twin stripes appeared in the window.

'I knew I should have got that bloody vasectomy years ago!' he growled, getting to his feet to pace the room.

'I didn't stop you,' she pointed out.

'You didn't make the appointment though, did you?'

It wasn't her place to do it, she thought irritably. He was a grown man more than capable of booking his own doctor's appointment and yet maybe he had a point. Had she been the one who'd wanted him to have the vasectomy, she would have definitely booked it in and seen to all the arrangements, but she was beginning to suspect that perhaps she hadn't felt entirely comfortable with their options being so . . . final, despite the fact she wasn't exactly over the moon about the news either.

'We should never have trusted the pill. How did it even happen?'

'I don't know,' she said, sinking to the edge of their bed. 'It was probably when the kids were sick a few weeks ago. I had a touch of it—an upset stomach,' she said.

'You're supposed to be a bloody nurse. How did you not realise you wouldn't be protected?'

'I don't know!' she snapped irritably. He was right, she should have suspected that diarrhoea, even a slight case of it, could have affected the pill's protection. It hadn't helped that they'd also had sex unexpectedly. Their sex life had been as dismal as their budget over the last few years, with her exhausted from shift work most of the time, and him travelling with his new job so much. She simply hadn't thought about any consequences—hadn't for so long that she'd almost forgotten about sex being linked to babies and stretch marks!

Eventually, shock had turned into acceptance and Jenny found herself becoming excited about baby number three. Everything would be fine. They'd manage—they always had in the past, they would again.

Chloe had been the perfect baby—adored by her two older sisters and managing to wrap her father around her little finger from the very first moment he'd laid eyes on her. The initial concerns about having another baby seemed to have been forgotten and life settled into a new rhythm. Everything *seemed* to be fine-ish. But she'd felt Austin pulling away. At first it hadn't been that noticeable—his work took him away on conferences and training seminars, so it was normal that when he was getting home she was heading out on a night shift, like ships passing in the night. Then it was *her* job causing issues. She needed to do casual shifts after her maternity leave in order to keep her registration, so she was often stressed and tired, looking after a young baby on top of the odd work hours. Intimacy had naturally taken a back seat for a while. She noticed, of course, but she wasn't too concerned—in a year or two things would settle down and they'd reconnect and get back on track . . . Only they hadn't. Nothing went back to any kind of old normal. Instead, they settled into some *new* normal that was only ever supposed to be temporary.

Over the next ten years or so, the investment apartment in Sydney they'd bought so Austin didn't have to pay for accommodation on his numerous trips eventually became his full-time residence—for work. Then he'd dropped his bombshell on her: he'd been seeing someone down there for two months. He'd seemed surprised when Jenny had been shocked.

'You barely even notice I'm gone,' he'd accused when he'd come home to announce he wanted out of their marriage.

'That's because you're never here,' she'd thrown back.

'Because I was working. To give you and the kids a better life.'

'And I haven't been?'

'My career has always been the one that allowed us to live the lifestyle we have. Do you honestly think you'd be living in this house or that the girls would have got a new car for their birthdays if it wasn't for my job? Your pay cheque wouldn't cover half of this stuff.'

She'd been stunned, truly shocked by his remarks. She shouldn't have been—she'd always known Austin was ambitious. When they were first married, he'd lay awake at night and tell her all about his plans for making his first million. She'd always let him dream big without trying to pop his bubble—she'd never cared about the money side of things, she had everything she'd ever wanted: healthy children, a stable marriage and a house to live in. But Austin had never been satisfied with what they had for long, always striving for more. And she took offence at his belittling her career. She hadn't become a nurse to make a fortune. She loved her job, despite the fact it was stressful and nurses were underpaid and often under appreciated. She did it because she cared about people and wanted to look after them. And she was good at it.

She still loved her job, Jenny thought as she pushed herself up off the lounge and headed for the black tourmaline candle on the sideboard, lighting it with a decisive strike of a match. There was no room in this house for bad energy anymore. She took a long breath in and let the spicy citrus scent fill her senses.

She wasn't sure why she'd felt a need to let the past intrude on her thoughts like this. She'd spent the last few years learning how to be herself and she had to admit this newfound independence thing could be quite exhilarating. It was time to stop looking back and focus on the future.

Two

The sound of the front door opening and voices chatting drew Jenny's gaze to the living room entryway. She smiled as a small human cyclone came running across the room towards her.

'Nanna!'

'Sophie!' Jenny gathered the grinning toddler in her arms and hugged her until she squirmed and wriggled to be put down. It was hard to believe that in, three short months, her only grandchild was going to be two.

Brittany, Jenny's eldest daughter, had moved back home six months earlier when rental prices skyrocketed in the area after Covid sent the real-estate market through the roof. As a single mother who worked as a teacher's aide in a small school, it had become impossible for Brittany to afford rent. While most of Jenny's friends looked forward to their children moving out so they could redecorate their empty nest, Jenny was happy to have hers living at home again. The house had been quiet with only herself and her youngest, Chloe, living there.

Shortly after Brittany and Sophie had moved in, Savannah had come home from backpacking overseas to pick up a bit of work before meeting up with some travel friends. The six weeks had turned into an open-ended kind of arrangement. Now, with her three grown daughters back home, it felt like a bunch of flatmates living together, only Jenny still had to play referee and break up arguments over who was hogging the bathroom in the morning. But most of the time she enjoyed this new adult companionship.

'Leave the cat alone!' Brittany called after the toddler, who was gleefully chasing the cranky old tabby that simply wouldn't die. The damn thing had to be close to twelve and was still going strong.

'How was your day?' Jenny asked as Brittany dropped a bright pink Bluey backpack on the table followed by her own huge tote bag. She often wondered where her girls had gotten their height from—certainly not from her. Brittany, dressed in a flowy maxidress that would have bunched on the ground if Jenny was wearing it, her long black hair pulled back in a thick ponytail, always looked so graceful—something Jenny had never been able to pull off.

'Long. How about yours?'

'Yep. Same.'

'One more day to go till Friday,' Brittany said, coming to a stop beside her as Jenny stretched her arm out and fist-bumped her.

'We got this,' she said with a determined nod.

'You'd better go and get ready,' Brittany said.

Jenny fought back a sigh. Damn it. She'd forgotten.

Once a month, they went down to the markets. Jenny loved the night markets—they were breathing fresh life into Barkley and always had such a great vibe—but she was finding it difficult to summon up the energy to get dressed and leave the house again. Once upon a time, between kids' activities, work and sport, she'd barely stayed at home. Nowadays, however, nothing gave her more pleasure than an early night curled up in her PJs, watching a chick flick with a glass of wine. But that was not going to happen tonight.

Jenny got out of the shower and wrapped the towel around herself as she walked into her bedroom, noticing Savannah sitting on the end of her bed, curly blonde hair cascading over her shoulder, wide blue eyes studying her mother thoughtfully. Her middle child was the most outgoing of her three children. She was Jenny's little adventurer. And the one she seemed to worry the most about. She'd left university—or rather, 'put it on hold for a bit', as Savannah described it—to go and travel for a year. That had been about five years ago and, other than the compulsory return home after her visas ran out, she'd pretty much been working and backpacking the entire time.

'What were you planning on wearing tonight?' Savannah asked as she leaned back on her arms.

Jenny raised her eyebrows at her daughter's sudden interest in her fashion choices but shrugged nonchalantly. 'Jeans and a top, I suppose.'

'That's what you always wear,' Savannah said dismissively, then pushed herself up and walked across to her wardrobe. 'How about this?' She held up a teal and brown dress. 'With those tan boots you bought. And maybe a belt.'

'Don't you think that's a little dressy for the night markets?'

'You should start dressing up more. You don't want to become one of those women who let themselves go.' Savannah draped the garment on the bed and bent down to place the boots on the carpet beneath it, giving it a firm nod of approval.

'I hardly think my seventy-odd dollar jeans and the ninety-nine-dollar blouse I just purchased is letting myself go.' She'd recently found an online boutique she loved and had been splurging a little more than usual on new outfits.

'Oooh,' Savannah said, her eyes brightening as she ducked into her mother's walk-in wardrobe and produced a garment. 'This denim jacket you got would look awesome over the top.'

Jenny shook her head wearily, giving up trying to protest. Part of her wanted to see what the outfit looked like. She'd had no idea what she was going to wear the jacket with, wasn't even sure why she'd bought it in the first place, only that it had looked too nice *not* to buy. Maybe she did need to cut back a bit with the online shopping.

'Okay, fine. Get out and let me get dressed,' she mumbled, snatching up the clothing from the bed.

'And do your make-up,' Savannah threw over her shoulder.

'Make-up? It's just us and Beth going to the damn night markets,' she said, exasperated by this sudden bossiness. They tried to do something with Beth every few weeks when her husband, Garry, a fly in, fly out worker, was away.

'Will it kill you to wear some make-up once in a while? Seriously, Mother.'

I'll give you seriously, Mother *in a minute*, Jenny thought, but eyed her reflection in the mirror critically. Lately she'd been ignoring the faint crinkles in the corner of her eyes. They were laugh lines, she reminded herself, before reaching for the foundation she hardly ever bothered wearing. Maybe she could go and get her eyelashes and brows tinted again soon. It seemed like a waste of time and money when she rarely went anywhere, but if the kids were beginning to notice she was giving up on the maintenance, did that mean her age was starting to show?

She was fifty. Fifty! When the hell had that happened? When she was a kid, fifty had been ancient—incomprehensible, really. Suddenly, though, she was staring down a very confronting barrel. She was a fifty-year-old divorced woman with adult children . . . and a grandchild, she reminded herself. Crap! *She was a divorced grandmother!* God, that sounded even worse. *Stop it*, she told herself firmly as she applied eyeliner and eyeshadow. *You're being ridiculous.*

When she headed downstairs to the living room a few moments later, she found the others waiting and it crossed her mind that it was a little odd that she wasn't the one calling to her three daughters to hurry up and get ready. Even Beth had already arrived.

'Are we ready, then?' Jenny asked after she'd kissed Beth's cheek. But she paused when she realised no one else was following her to the door.

'What's going on?' she asked.

'Okay, so don't be mad,' Brittany started, and dread filled Jenny. Nothing good *ever* started with that phrase.

'The thing is, Mum,' Savannah said, picking up from her sister, 'we kind of *did* something.'

'Did what?' Jenny asked as real panic began to set in.

'We're not going to the markets,' Beth said. 'Well, *we are*,' she corrected, glancing at the other girls, 'but *you're* not.'

'What Beth's trying to say'—Brittany once again took the baton and ran with it—'is that we've organised a date for you.'

'You've *what*?'

'There's this app—a dating app—and we kind of set you up on it,' Chloe said excitedly.

Jenny had a million questions racing through her head but not a single one of them would come out as she stared with growing horror at her children and best friend.

'We thought it might take a while to get a response so we didn't say anything, but the notifications have been going off all day, so we accepted,' Chloe continued with a small squeal and clap of her hands. Her honey-blonde hair was pulled back in a high ponytail that was swinging like a cheerleader's.

'You accepted a date *for* me? Without asking if I even wanted to go on it?'

'You would have said no,' Savannah said.

'Of course I would have. This is insane.'

'Jen,' Beth started in the calm, let's-talk-the-crazy-woman-down voice she'd had plenty of practice using on Jenny over the years. 'The girls just thought this would be something fun for you to do . . . you know, get out of the house a bit.'

'You thought it was too,' Savannah reminded Beth, clearly not about to be thrown under the bus alone.

'Well, you can just go and *un*-accept and explain what happened.'

'We can't,' Brittany said with a slight wince. 'He's on his way over.'

'What!'

'It'll be fine,' Savannah said, airily. 'We checked him out; it's not like we'd set you up with some weirdo.'

'*How* did you check him out?' Jenny asked, suddenly concerned.

'We've been chatting online to him,' Chloe said.

'So, he's perfectly happy to be set up on a date with someone's mother? This doesn't scream *weird* at all?' Jenny asked, searching their faces frantically.

'Well, technically, he thought he was chatting to *you*,' Brittany admitted.

Jenny opened her mouth to yell, but nothing came out. She couldn't seem to manage a single coherent word as she stared at her best friend and daughters, lined up like a football team's front row, staring her down determinedly.

'You can't be serious.'

'We are. It's all been arranged.'

'But I don't *want* to go on a date.'

'We've waited patiently for you to take the first step back out into life again, and you haven't done it. We can't sit by any longer and watch you wither away,' Brittany said.

'You're too young to be an old, lonely woman,' Savannah said with a shrug.

'An old, lonely . . .' Jenny let the sentence fade away as she stared at her daughter in shock. 'I'm *not* old!'

'Well, you're not getting any younger, either, Mum,' Chloe pointed out.

'Now hold on a minute—'

'Jen, it's all right to acknowledge that you're not as *fun* as you once used to be,' Beth soothed.

Okay, that one hurt. She was still fun, damn it! 'I am *not* ready to be sat down in a rocking chair with my knitting just yet, thank you very much,' she informed them bluntly, then narrowed her eyes as all four of them displayed sporting, smug smiles. Too late, she realised she'd walked into a trap. Maybe she *was* losing her edge a bit—once upon a time she'd have never fallen for something that obvious.

Brittany nodded. 'So you agree, then, that you're not ready to give up and you should be out there enjoying life.'

'I don't see why dating has to be the thing that's going to save me from a life of dreary boredom,' Jenny shot back.

'Because you're still young and attractive and you need to get back out there and find someone to have fun with again,' Savannah said.

'Among other things,' Beth added with a wink.

'Eww,' Chloe said, with a dramatic shudder.

'Well, what did you expect was going to happen if you set your mother up on a date with a man?' Beth asked, seeming genuinely confused by the reaction.

'I was trying to *not* think about it, that's all,' Chloe answered.

'Would you two stop?' Brittany cut in before turning back to Jenny. 'Ignore them. Look, you don't have to rush into anything—'

'Good. So, I don't have to go out tonight then,' Jenny said.

'You do. That bit's already been arranged. But you don't have to feel *pressured* into doing anything more than going out to dinner, if that's what you're worried about.'

Until that point, she hadn't even thought about what more could be involved than going out for dinner and now she *was* worried. Considerably. Surely this person wasn't going to expect *sex? Tonight?* She hadn't even shaved her legs, for goodness' sake!

'Uh-oh . . . I think we're losing her,' Beth murmured.

'Nope. I'm not ready for all this.' Jenny shook her head and backed away.

'You are. At least, you will be,' Brittany assured her. 'You're never going to feel ready unless you get out there and do it. Remember what you always told us? Whenever we were nervous about doing anything new, you used to tell us to just wing it. Get in there and just do it.'

Well, that seemed like stupid advice now.

'Yeah,' Chloe piped up, nodding encouragingly at her older sister. 'When I had that meltdown about a class presentation I had to do in year seven, you made me go in and do it . . . Actually, you pretty much dragged me into school that day, when all I wanted to do was hide in bed.'

'This isn't the same thing . . . that was school and you *had* to do it,' Jenny said, sensing a touch of malicious revenge in her daughters' pep talk.

'Think of this as something just as important. You can't hide in bed every time something scary happens and you don't want to face it,' Savannah replied.

This time, Jenny was positive her children were enjoying the opportunity to fling their mother's advice back in her face. No one told you what to do when your great and wise parental advice came back to bite you on the arse years later. She'd brought this on herself by being such a brilliant mother. 'Oh, for goodness' sake,' she muttered.

'Mum, if you can't do it for yourself, then do it for us. Be the role model you've always been and show us what a brave, independent woman looks like,' Brittany said, using a motivational tone that Tony Robbins would have been proud of.

Fuck. There was no getting out of this—not unless she wanted to admit that everything she'd used in the past to try and mould these kids into responsible, well-adjusted humans could be ignored once you were an adult.

'Fine,' she said tightly. 'But this is the one and only time. You take me off that stupid dating app and *never* do this again.'

'So, about that . . .' Brittany winced—actually winced, as though in great pain. 'You've kind of got a few more dates for the rest of the weekend.'

Jenny stared at her eldest daughter. She thought she'd already been shocked as deeply as a person *could* possibly be shocked . . . but nope, now she was shocked into speechlessness.

'There's *more* men I'm supposed to be seeing?' she finally managed. Who the hell did that, lined up multiple dates with different people all weekend?

'Well, they all responded to your profile and we didn't want to risk turning any of them away in case they were, you know, "the one",' Savannah told her, making little quotation marks in the air.

'"The one" . . .' Jenny shook her head, trying to dislodge the absolute insanity she was hearing. 'This stops now. I'm not some piece of . . . meat you get to hold out as bait to catch a bunch of crocodiles with.'

'Seriously, Mum,' Savannah said, eyeing her pityingly. 'This is why you needed a push. You have no idea how the world of dating works. You'll thank us for stepping in and navigating all this for you so you didn't stuff it up.'

A knock on the door cut short her scathing reply, which was partially a relief since she wasn't sure she could keep to the 'no swearing out loud' rule, as panic quickly settled in.

'It'll be fine. His name's Derrick and he's an accountant,' Beth said in a pacifying tone as she walked—or rather frog-marched—Jenny to the front door. 'He lives in Hamwell. And smile,' Beth ordered in a sugary sweet tone, as Brittany opened the door to a man who looked to be in his late fifties. He was dressed in a pair of impeccably ironed navy trousers and a crisp white shirt.

'Jenny?' he asked, as his gaze shifted between the five women smiling at him—well, four smiling and one frozen in a terrified, caught-in-the-headlights kind of expression.

'This is Jenny,' Beth said, thrusting her forward so that she almost staggered into the poor man's chest.

His face did a quick change from surprise to delight before he stuck out his hand. 'Derrick,' he said, as Jenny automatically shook it. They stood there staring at each other awkwardly until Beth stepped in again.

'Well, you two kids have a great time,' she chirped, pointedly ignoring Jenny's dangerous glare.

Three

As the door shut firmly behind them, Jenny forced her stiff limbs to move, feeling like a robot as she followed Derrick to a dark sedan in her driveway. The car looked exactly like something an accountant would drive: sensible, well kept and also a lot more expensive than her dependable old hatchback in the shed.

'So, where are we going?' she asked, forcing cheeriness into her tone.

Derrick looked up from clipping in his seatbelt, his expression a little odd. 'I booked at the pub in town that you suggested when we spoke—well, *chatted*,' he amended, 'online.'

'Oh. Right. Sounds great,' she said with forced enthusiasm. Her head was spinning as she tried to piece together everything that had happened in the last half an hour or so.

Derrick, on the other hand, seemed completely at ease with the situation. And why wouldn't he be? No one had surprised *him* with any of this.

Barkley was on the outskirts of the bigger regional town of Hamwell, around a forty-five-minute drive away. It had been Jenny's idea to move to Barkley from Hamwell when the town grew from a charming large country town into a less charming mini city in the space of a few years. Jenny had grown up in a small town similar to Barkley, with its wide streets and rolling farmland, and she had wanted that same close-knit community upbringing for her children.

'Do you come from here?' Jenny asked. She didn't think she'd ever seen Derrick around. He could easily have been one of the new blow-ins from the city. It felt like Covid had convinced everyone to move to the country, and what started as a trickle of newcomers had turned into a deluge. Now Barkley suddenly had something it had never had before—a growing population

'Ah, no. Hamwell,' he said, a slight frown on his face. 'I'm pretty sure I mentioned it when we first started chatting.'

'Oh, right. Sorry,' she said, tapping her forehead. 'It's been a busy week.'

'Tell me about it. We're in the lead-up to tax time and things are only going to get busier,' Derrick said, before explaining at length what his next few months were going to entail.

They drove through the wide, quiet streets, passing the federation-style brick houses and brick-fenced yards. It was getting cooler as autumn crept in, and the grass in front yards and along the footpaths was starting to fade from green to varying shades of browns and yellows. The beautiful Japanese maple, Chinese pistachio and liquidambar trees planted along the median strips and in front yards were on beautiful display, with their bright yellow, red and orange leaves creating a tapestry of colour to replace the fading hues of the landscape. Derrick pulled up outside their destination, the two-storey heritage-listed pub. The Coach House had undergone renovations over the last few months and the disruption to the main street during its facelift had been a constant source of complaint from some of Jenny's older patients. She hadn't been here since they'd reopened but had been hearing good things about the food.

Jenny looked around as she walked inside and found herself pleasantly surprised. The new management had completely rebranded the old pub into something almost yuppified. The architecture of the original hundred-and-twenty-year-old hotel was still intact but there was a vibrant, modern look to the furnishings, with beautiful teal lounge chairs scattered in front of an open fireplace and tall floor lamps strategically placed around the room adding a sophisticated touch that probably wouldn't be expected in Barkley. Rustic timber frames hung on one side displaying Barkley in its early years, and a large mural, of the pub in its heyday, dominated the far wall.

'It isn't as bad as I was expecting,' Derrick murmured beside her, and even though she wasn't exactly a regular in here, something about his pompous tone made her a little defensive. 'Would you like a drink?' he asked.

Jenny opened her mouth to answer, but he'd already turned away. 'Allow me to choose a wine. You pick a table and I'll be right back,' he told her, walking towards the bar.

Jenny bit back a flicker of irritation at the assumption that he knew what she'd like to drink, and looked around for a table, spotting one on the far side of the room. It would do fine—was hopefully inconspicuous enough so she wouldn't be recognised by anyone who may come in and spot her.

Derrick returned, carrying two glasses of pale-looking wine.

'Try this and tell me what you think?' he instructed as he placed the glasses on the table and peered at her.

'Oh,' she said, realising he wanted her to try it right *now*. She gave him a weak smile before bracing herself. She knew she was going to hate it; she only drank moscato—lolly water, as Beth often referred to it. The moment the dry, crisp wine hit her taste buds, Jenny felt her body preparing to launch into a compulsive shudder but reined it in with remarkable effort.

'It's a sauvignon blanc,' he informed her. 'They don't have the range here that my usual restaurant has, of course,' he said, his chin tilting a little arrogantly. 'But this is passable, I suppose.'

Jenny fought back a grimace as she forced herself to swallow the sip. She gave a noncommittal, 'Hmm.'

'All your children still live at home with you?'

Jenny nodded. 'Yes. It gets pretty rowdy sometimes,' she said smiling faintly as she recalled the usual chaos at breakfast and dinner. Before Brittany and Sophie had moved back in, she'd almost forgotten how full-on those times were with a toddler. 'Do you have children?' she asked. Maybe this was where they'd find something in common.

'I have a son.'

'Oh, lovely. Does he live at home with you?'

'God, no,' Derrick said, looking horrified by the thought. 'He's twenty-seven. Thankfully he's out of my hair and doing his own thing now.'

Out of his hair? Jenny raised an eyebrow slightly.

'I see . . . you're one of those types,' he said bluntly, catching her expression.

'What type would that be?' She was trying to be pleasant, she really was.

'The ones who wrap their kids in cotton wool. Too many people aren't being firm enough with their kids today. They need to fly the nest and learn how to take care of themselves the way we did. How are they supposed to appreciate the value of a dollar when they don't have to live in the real world?'

'It's a little bit tougher out there nowadays than it was when we were that age.' Besides, she didn't wrap her kids in cotton wool—she would if she could, but hers were too independent. One had jumped feet first into a relationship and became a single mum and another was happiest flitting around the damn globe. God only knew what grey hairs Chloe was going to add in the coming years.

'It's all comparable. Everyone's just gone too soft. It's no tougher than it used to be.'

She was no statistician, but she was fairly sure that wasn't entirely true. 'I actually don't mind having my children and grandchild living back home. I like the company.' It was nice to have the empty rooms filled with the daily sounds of family life once more.

'I downsized the house so that wouldn't happen,' Derrick said dismissively. 'So, classical music?' he continued, leaning back in his chair and eyeing her over the top of the wine glass as he swirled it idly.

'Sorry?' She was still processing his authoritarian parenting practices.

'You mentioned in your profile that you enjoyed classical music.'

She had? Why on earth would her profile say that? Her kids knew for a fact she only listened to eighties music and a bit of nineties country. Obviously this was all part of Operation: Give Mum a Makeover. 'That was a mistake. It was meant to be . . . well, to be honest, anything else.'

He frowned. 'So you *don't* like classical music?'

'Not particularly, no.'

'Oh,' he said, sounding far more disappointed by the idea than she thought he should be. 'There's a concert coming up in the park. I was thinking that would have been a nice next date.'

'You didn't even know if *this* date was going to work out and you were planning the second one?'

'Well, your profile had sounded promising,' he said, clearing his throat.

'Do you do this often? Meet people on the app?'

'When there's anyone interesting on there. It's sometimes difficult to find women of a certain . . . standard.' He sipped his wine.

'Standard?'

'Sadly, the majority of these apps are designed to find a quick hook-up.'

'Oh. I see.'

'You will,' he assured her blandly. 'If you spend enough time on there, you'll understand.'

'Yes. Well. I don't intend to be spending much time on there.'

'That's what I keep telling myself, too.'

'Are you ready to order?' a tall blonde asked, coming to a stop beside their table.

Jenny looked up and smiled, vaguely recognising the face but unable to put a name to it. The waitress appeared to be around the same age as her two eldest girls and she suspected that's where she knew her from. Yes, she wanted to order—the faster they got through their meal the sooner she could get back home again. She picked up the menu, scanning the items quickly. She found herself quietly impressed. This was a huge step up from the rather bland pub food that had been on offer previously. 'I'll have the bacon-wrapped pork tenderloin, thanks.'

'Is the barramundi fresh?' Derrick asked, without lifting his gaze from the menu.

'It is. We have it delivered daily.'

'That's what they all claim,' he said curtly, and Jenny narrowed her eyes slightly at his tone. 'I'll have the cacciatore,' he finally decided, but held on to the menu as the waitress reached out to take it. 'Is it freshly cooked?'

'Any fresher and the chicken would still be clucking,' the blonde answered with a straight face.

'That will be all,' Derrick said dismissively without so much as cracking a smile.

Jenny chuckled and the waitress smiled as she collected the menus and sauntered away.

'You'd be surprised how many so-called restaurants use frozen meals.'

'Well, I heard they'd gone to a lot of trouble to employ the new chef, so I'm sure they cook everything on site.'

Derrick grunted, sipping from his glass.

'So, tell me about your job,' she asked and forced her wine down, concentrating on the warming sensation it created in the back of her throat as Derrick found the one topic he enjoyed talking about. His monologue lasted until the blonde returned carrying two plates.

Her meal looked like something out of a food magazine. For a moment Jenny could only stare at the artistic presentation. The investment into a proper chef certainly looked like it was paying off. There had always been considerable doubt as to whether Tony, the previous cook, had any actual qualifications—word was that he'd learned most of his cooking skills from a stint in prison during the eighties and nobody had ever been game to ask him.

'Thank you,' Jenny finally managed, glancing up at the waitress. 'This looks amazing.'

'Yes, well, even pubs have to lift their food standards nowadays if they want to stay relevant. We've had a number of top Sydney chefs relocate to Hamwell over the last year or so,' Derrick informed her with a small sniff, then began a new line of conversation about the effects on bottom lines from Covid shut-downs in regional areas. This had the advantage of allowing Jenny to dig happily into her food, only having to give the occasional nod or grunt in agreement as she ate.

'I'll order more wine,' Derrick announced, slipping it in partway through a particularly boring lecture about God-only-knew-what, almost causing Jenny to miss it.

'No. I'll get this round,' she said, getting to her feet before he could argue. She was eager for a moment to herself. Something harder than white wine wouldn't go astray, either.

Jenny weaved her way through the tables but stopped when she came to a group of four elderly people, who waved at her.

'We thought that was you,' one of the women said, smiling as she held out a hand.

Jenny took the hand and squeezed it gently. 'Hello, Nola. I didn't see you over here.'

'Well, you were too busy with your . . . *friend*,' Nola said, lifting her eyebrows slightly as she searched Jenny's face eagerly.

Nola Jenkins was a regular at the hospital. Jenny had grown close to her a few years back when her husband had started having health problems that led to frequent stays.

Nola and Betty, who was also at the table, worked in the hospital cafe and were tireless volunteers of the Hospital Auxiliary, who raised valuable funds for the hospital and were as much a part of the hospital family as the doctors and nursing staff. As dearly as she loved these women, Jenny was under no illusions that whatever she said here would be spread around the hospital before she even had time to start her next shift.

'Oh, that's just an old family friend. He's passing through town and wanted to catch up,' Jenny said with a dismissive wave. Seeing the disappointed faces before her, she realised, to her surprise, that her bluffing skills must have been on point.

'We were hoping it was a new man,' Betty said in an overly loud whisper.

'Sorry. No men—new or old—on the horizon,' Jenny said, forcing a bright smile. Not if she could help it, at least.

'A good catch like yourself?' Errol, Nola's husband, chimed in, shaking his head. 'The blokes around here should be lining up.'

'Tell you what,' Ted, the other man at the table said, 'if I was twenty years younger and not already married—'

Betty snorted loudly. 'Twenty? More like forty,' she scoffed.

'Now, now, pet, you know I only have eyes for you,' he said, sending her a wink.

'You're half-blind, you silly coot,' she retorted, before rolling her eyes at him.

'I'd better go order our drinks. It was lovely to see you.' Jenny waved and made her getaway while they were all busy insulting Ted's shortcomings.

At the bar, Jenny rested her arm along the countertop and surveyed the glass shelves before her, waiting for the bartender as he moseyed his way down from where he'd been talking to two men. She didn't recognise him, not that she'd ever spent much time in the local pub. She found herself a little distracted by the slow, easy smile on his face as he came to a stop before her.

'Can I get a scotch and ginger ale, please? Actually,' Jenny said abruptly, 'can you make it a double shot of scotch?'

'Going that good, huh?'

'Sorry?' Jenny eyed him warily.

'Your date,' he said, tilting his chin at the table behind her.

'Oh. No. It's fine,' she said, sending a weak smile to Derrick as she followed the bartender's glance and found him looking at them. 'It's been a long day.'

She watched as the bartender took a tumbler and tipped two generous glugs of the amber liquid into the bottom and added a splash of ginger ale. 'You want ice with that?' he asked, lifting an eyebrow.

'Sure.' She was probably going to need something to water down the burn.

'And for your date?' he asked, after sliding her drink across to her.

'Same as before, I guess. And he's not my date . . . I mean, I guess he is, technically . . . but I didn't know he was going to *be my* date until he turned up on my doorstep.' *Why* she felt the need to justify herself to the bartender, she had no idea.

'So a guy you didn't know just knocked on your door and asked you on a date?' he asked, kinking an eyebrow.

Jenny let her gaze roam across his wide forehead and down to a set of rather nice eyes, before she answered. 'My daughters and my best friend decided to set me up on a dating site. They just didn't tell me about it until tonight.'

'Bold,' he said with an appreciative nod.

Jenny took a healthy swig of her drink and squeezed her eyes shut as she clamped down on the coughing fit that threatened to erupt.

'Here you go,' he said.

She cracked an eyelid open to take a tentative breath, relieved to find she could do it without coughing. The wine for Derrick sat on the bar in front of her. Jenny tapped her card on the top of the machine the barman held out, before taking the two glasses and bracing herself as though heading back into battle.

'You got this,' she heard the bartender say with a hint of amusement. She looked over her shoulder, but he was already walking towards his next customer.

Nick Mason glanced back over his shoulder, watching thoughtfully as the brunette walked away.

'Was a real shame what that mongrel ex-husband of hers did to her.'

Nick turned and saw Bill, a white-haired regular, speaking to his two drinking companions.

'Yep,' agreed Claud, another of the pub's permanent fixtures, in his slow, drawn-out fashion.

'What did he do?' Nick asked when the conversation appeared to have run its course, leaving everything hanging.

'Left her for some kid—same age as her daughter. Caused a big stir a few years back.'

Nick looked at the table across the room to where the woman in question sat, trying her best to look suitably impressed by whatever the guy across from her was saying—and failing.

'So who's that guy then?' Nick asked, nodding at her date.

'No idea. Not from around here, I reckon,' Bill said, downing the last of his schooner and waiting for another.

'Doesn't look like someone Jenny would be interested in. I wonder who he is?' Joyce added, wandering across from the poker machines to join in.

As the speculation continued, Nick realised most people seemed to know the woman from their hospital visits and for some reason it was a surprise to see her out on a date. Why, he couldn't understand. She was attractive and apparently single. But this date was a disaster, especially if she felt a need to dull the experience with scotch. Not a good sign.

This wasn't the first time he'd found himself embroiled in a gossip session. He actually found them quite helpful for getting to know his customers. Sometimes he found out a little bit *too* much information, but on the whole, it was handy to be armed with some intel in order to make contacts and keep himself from making too many blunders.

It was yet another quirky small-town thing he had to get used to since moving from the city. Kind of like the way people here referred to shops and places around town by their names or owners from fifty or more years earlier. For the first week he'd lived here, he'd spent three days trying to find Smiths' Furniture Shop, which was also known as the two-dollar shop and the cheap shop, but was actually called Mega Save Bargains. All he'd wanted was somewhere that sold liquid chalk to write on the sandwich board he put out on the footpath. Such a simple thing had become a major pain.

Still, he wasn't complaining too much. He'd bought his dream pub and life right now was good. *Maybe it could be better, though*, he thought, as he rested his hip against the bar and took one more look at Jenny.

Four

Jenny wondered what on earth Beth and the girls thought she would have remotely had in common with this man. Clearly, they'd been excited—even surprised—that someone had responded in the first place and weren't willing to turn away *any* candidate. She took another sip from her glass and let her rising indignation block out whatever the hell Derrick was going on about that involved unencumbered security or some such shit.

'So, I was thinking if you didn't want the night to end yet...'

Oh, how she did want this God-awful night to end. 'Actually,' she said quickly, trying her best to soften it with a suitably regretful smile, 'I've had a really long day at work and I think I should probably head home.'

She did feel the slightest stab of guilt as his face fell momentarily, but then he opened his mouth and his droning voice brought forth a fresh urge to stab him with a fork, so she squashed the guilt back into its box and stood up.

Unable to do anything else except follow her lead, Derrick fluffed about for a moment before heading across to the front desk to settle the bill.

'Calling it a night so soon?'

She jumped at the voice behind her. She'd been admiring some of the prints of the early days of the pub that lined the wall and turned to find the bartender doing the rounds of the tables, collecting dirty glasses.

Jenny cleared her throat and mustered her most formidable look, the one she usually reserved for drunken misbehaving youths who staggered through the doors of Emergency in the early hours of the morning. 'It's getting quite late.'

'Yeah, I guess so. It's almost . . . wow, nine,' he said in a deadpan tone that didn't match the slight twinkle in his eye.

Nine? Was that all it was? Crap—she'd thought for sure it had to be getting close to eleven. She *felt* like it had to be close to eleven. 'Yes, well it's . . .'

'Been a long day,' he finished for her, nodding. 'I hear ya. No judgement here.'

Oh, but there *was* judgement coming from this slightly-too-long-haired man who seemed to be finding everything about her date amusing. Who even asked him? So what if he had bad-boy vibes and looked really good in black jeans and a white T-shirt that seemed to hug his torso like a second skin. Not that she was taking any notice.

She smothered a silent groan. Why on earth had she told him about being set up on this stupid date? It was embarrassing. It was bad enough she'd agreed to it in the first place, without a complete stranger knowing about it as well.

'Ready to leave, Jenny?' Derrick asked, turning to beckon to her.

''Night, Jenny,' the bartender murmured as he walked past carrying his load of glasses. He didn't look back.

She wasn't sure why this guy was bothering her so much—she didn't know him from a bar of soap—but there was something about that cocky little grin he'd been wearing most of the night that annoyed her.

Nothing about this night was doing anything constructive to change her mind about her current relationship status. She'd been single for two years and she quite liked it. She didn't have to worry about fitting in with a man's plans. Didn't have to remember to buy his mother's birthday, Mother's Day and Christmas gifts. Didn't need to run any of her purchases or shopping trips past him. And certainly didn't have to worry about shaving her legs on the off-chance someone might need to be that close and personal. She was more than happy with how single life was going and tonight had done nothing to sway her into giving it up.

The air was a little cooler now than it had been earlier and as the door of the pub shut behind them, the chatter from inside became muffled, barely breaking the quiet of the now almost empty main street. Night life was not Barkley's forte. They didn't have the late night cafes and multiple restaurants that Hamwell boasted, but they did have country charm—in bucketloads.

As Derrick's voice continued to drone, Jenny saw her street sign come into view and relief surged through her at the thought of closing the front door and heading up to her comfy bed.

'Are you sure I can't tempt you into a little nightcap or something before we call it an evening?' Derrick asked, turning his face towards her hopefully.

'God, *no*,' she breathed under her breath automatically.

'Pardon?' he asked, sending her a quick glance.

Jenny sat up straighter in her seat. She hadn't realised she'd spoken out loud.

'Unfortunately, no,' she said, clearing her throat quickly, her gaze willing her house to come into sight faster. 'I had a very early start. I'm not much of a night owl.'

'Of course. Well, never mind. Next time maybe you can have an afternoon nap so you'll be bright-eyed and bushy-tailed,' he said with an encouraging grin.

Did he seriously just suggest she needed a nanna nap?

As Derrick made to get out of the car when they pulled up, Jenny quickly stopped him.

'No, don't worry about getting out. Thanks so much for a lovely dinner. It was very nice to meet you.' She leaned across, intending to place a quick peck on his cheek in a friendly manner, only to have him turn his head at the last minute and latch onto her lips with surprising force. The sensation felt like a very strong octopus sucking at her face—and not in a good way . . . if ever there *was* a good way for that experience to occur.

Jenny pulled away, silently shuddering at the smack of suction which followed, and groped blindly for the door latch to exit the car with as much dignity as one could, even as she was scrambling.

Yuck, yuck, yuck! Her inner fifteen-year-old was making gagging noises. 'Night,' she called, not game to look back as she walked briskly up the driveway.

The outside security lights came on, momentarily blinding her, and she swore as she stumbled. She kept meaning to tilt that stupid spotlight up a little higher so it didn't hit you square in the eye. Yet another job to add to the to-do list. Though if a potential burglar came along and set it off, blinding them could be handy.

Closing the door behind her, Jenny let out an audible sigh as she kicked off her shoes and dropped her handbag on the hallway table. Thank God that was over.

The TV program that had been playing suddenly muted and four pairs of expectant eyes homed in on her as she entered the room.

She frowned. 'What are you all still doing up?'

'What are you doing home so early?' Brittany countered.

'I told you he sounded boring,' Savannah said with a sigh.

'He was all we thought we had to work with at the time,' Chloe reminded her sisters.

'What on earth did you think I had in common with him?' Jenny demanded.

'Don't look at me.' Savannah put her hands up defensively. 'I said he looked like a weirdo.'

'He did *not* look like a *weirdo*,' Beth cut in. 'And to answer your question,' she continued, turning her gaze onto Jenny, 'he had an impressive career, a solid income and was financially independent.' She held her fingers out as she ticked off the points. 'I checked his credentials out personally. He came with glowing reviews on his website.'

'Which would have been fantastic if I'd been going to him to get my taxes done,' Jenny said with an unimpressed glare. 'I hope you've all got that out of your systems now,' she snapped.

'That was just a practice run,' Beth dismissed blithely. 'We've since honed our skills and we think the next one will be a better match.'

'Absolutely not.'

'Come on, Mum, this will be good for you. You need to get back out there again,' Savannah said.

'No. I don't. I'm quite happy with things the way they are, thank you very much.'

Brittany shook her head sadly. 'I never thought I'd see the day my mother would turn into such a quitter.'

'How can I be a quitter if I wasn't even the one who started it in the first place?'

'Semantics.' Brittany waved away Jenny's argument impatiently.

'Oh, come on, Mum. I promise, this next guy seems much better. Please?' Savannah asked, batting her eyes pathetically. 'You can't give up so soon.'

'If I do this,' she said, eyeing them sharply, 'you have to promise that will be the end of it.'

A chorus of enthusiastic agreement filled the room.

'And I'm taking my own damn car this time. Did it not even cross anyone's mind that I was getting into a car with a complete stranger?'

'He drove an Audi,' Chloe said with a shrug.

Jenny rolled her eyes at her youngest. 'Because I'm sure serial killers are too broke to be able to afford a luxury car.'

'Mum's right. That *was* a really stupid oversight on our part,' Savannah admitted. 'Sorry, Mum. Although we did take his rego and Brittany got a call to say you'd arrived at the pub, so we knew you were okay.'

'You got a phone call?'

The women swapped a quick glance before Beth said, 'Oh, come on, Jen. As if you would have agreed to go if we gave you the option of driving there. Besides—everyone loves the old-fashioned, come to the door and collect you thing, right? How long has it been since anyone did that for you?'

Well, never to be honest. Austin had never really been into flowers and dates even in the early days. Jenny shook her head and gave an annoyed groan. It was one weekend. Surely she could do this if it meant *never* having to go through it all again? It couldn't get any worse than tonight's disaster.

Five

Jenny stared at the contents of her wardrobe in despair. She had no idea what she was doing.

'Mum?' Chloe called, sticking her head into Jenny's bedroom. 'How do you make fairy floss?'

Jenny frowned, attention momentarily distracted as she turned to look at her daughter. 'Fairy floss?'

'Yeah. I'm babysitting Sophie tomorrow and I've decided we're having a rainbow picnic.'

'I don't think it's a simple thing to do without a machine.' The thought of Chloe's usual mess in the kitchen when she cooked something as simple as scrambled eggs—let alone something as fiddly and messy as fairy floss—had Jenny's eye twitching more than a little bit.

Chloe gave a disappointed pout. 'I thought that would be fun. She loved it at the show.'

'I believe your sister also banned any of us from ever buying it for her again when she was still bouncing off the walls till close to midnight,' Jenny reminded her pointedly.

'Rules like that don't apply to fun aunties,' Chloe declared. 'What are you doing?' She tilted her head slightly as she took in her mothers' bare feet and bath towel–wrapped body.

'Trying to work out what to wear to this stupid date.'

'Oh! Can I pick out something?'

'I could use the help,' Jenny said, stepping back and waving a hand towards the closet.

She watched as Chloe started pulling out clothes, holding them up against other items and silently considering before discarding each one.

'I haven't really had a chance to talk to you lately,' Jenny said.

Her youngest was very different in temperament from her other two children—she'd sometimes gotten lost among the arguing and squabbling of her older siblings since they'd returned.

'About what?' Chloe asked.

'Nothing really. Just what you've been up to. How you're feeling about uni. Time seems to be flying. You'll be heading off soon.'

'Yeah. I can't wait, to be honest.'

'To leave?' Jenny asked, feeling a little hurt by the remark.

'Well, yeah. I mean, I'll miss you and everything. And, as much as I love Soph, it's been a little hectic with a toddler getting into everything over the last few months and Savannah has been a proper bit—'

'Okay.' Jenny quickly held a hand up, cutting her off. 'I get it. I know it's been a bit of an adjustment with everyone back home. I'm sorry we haven't had as much time to talk the way we used to though. I feel like I haven't even seen you in ages.' Jenny sometimes missed the nights when there'd been just the two of them.

'It's all right. You've had a lot to do and work keeps me pretty busy. I need all the extra hours I can get before I leave.'

'We'll have to go to Hamwell for the day and get you some new clothes and bits and pieces for your room down there. Maybe let me know when you've got a day free and I can swap a shift with someone.'

'Sure. I'd like that, Mum.' Chloe smiled, and Jenny felt her heart squeeze painfully in response. Her last baby was growing up and moving away.

'Don't go getting all soppy,' Chloe groaned, then smiled sheepishly. 'You know you won't be getting rid of me forever. Look at your other two kids. Chances are I'll be back again at some point too.'

'And if you are, that's fine. Your home is always going to be your home, no matter how old you get or how far away you move.'

'I know, Mum.'

Jenny did her best to swallow past the lump of emotion in her throat and wrapped an arm around her daughter, giving her a squeeze. 'So what am I going to wear?'

'I think when we go shopping in Hamwell, we need to update your wardrobe too,' Chloe said, shaking her head dismally. 'This is going to be a tougher job than I anticipated.'

Alan reminded her of an owl. A shy, very nervous, owl. He had a habit of blinking every few seconds, which made it difficult for Jenny to hold his gaze for any length of time while he spoke.

When she'd arrived, she'd apprehensively walked into the pub and braced herself. She could do this—this time she was prepared. She'd be direct and tell him it was going to be an early night. Jenny had paused briefly to admire the staircase as she passed by, taking the time to appreciate the craftsmanship that had gone into building things when all this had been new. *The stories this place could tell*, she'd thought, shaking her head, before letting out a resigned breath and continuing inside.

She'd spotted her date immediately in the throng gathered at the bar for after-work drinks. He stood out like a sore thumb, dressed in an expensive suit amid the sea of denim and hi-vis work shirts.

He had obviously seen her profile photo, recognising her straight away, and stood quickly from his seat at the table he'd selected, sending the salt and pepper shakers rocking.

Jenny focused on his face, which had momentarily looked terrified before settling into mildly petrified as he shot out a hand and leaned forward, bumping into his chair again and almost tripping.

'It's nice to meet you,' Jenny said, shaking the dampish hand and resisting the urge to wipe her palm on her skirt as she slipped into her seat, hoping if he sat back down he'd avoid knocking anything else over. She'd dealt with nervous people before—usually big, tough footballer types, and usually when they were about to get an injection, but she hadn't seen this level of nervousness in a long time.

'Would you like a drink?' he asked, making to stand up and almost tipping the table in the process.

'It's fine. I'll get them.' There was no way those drinks would make it back to the table from the bar in one piece if he went. She asked him what he'd like and prayed the night would get better.

'Back again?'

Jenny bit back a groan as the same bartender from the night before sauntered over. He was going to think she was . . . Well, she had no idea what he'd think she was, but after coming out on another date with a different man two nights in a row, it was definitely not going to be something good. Not that she even *cared* what some stranger thought, she told herself with a silent scoff. That cocky smile was back on his face again—the one he'd worn last night. The one that made her feel decidedly warm in places she hadn't felt warm in way too long.

She felt the tip of her tongue poke out and lick her lip nervously, then she swallowed hard as she watched his eyes narrow slightly as they followed the action. *Stop it! Get a grip, woman.*

'A glass of the house wine and . . .' She searched the shelves behind him for inspiration. Alcohol had not been her friend this morning when she'd had to get up early. It was pathetic really just how much of a lightweight she'd become over the years. 'Do you have anything non-alcoholic that isn't boring?' she asked.

'Non-alcoholic, huh?' he replied slowly, before reaching under the counter and bringing up a laminated menu to hand over. 'Anything on here take your fancy?'

Jenny took the card he held out and cleared her throat as she forced her eyes to disengage from his. This was seriously getting ridiculous. Her eyes skimmed the menu and she found herself sighing inwardly at the names. Virgin Margaritas, Virgin Tequila Sunrise, Hot Lips . . . 'Cuddles on the Beach,' she read out loud, raising a doubtful eyebrow.

'Yeah, when Sex on the Beach is ruled out, you can still cuddle,' he said, the corner of his mouth twitching just enough to emphasise his otherwise solemn expression.

'Fine. I'll have one of those, thanks,' Jenny said briskly, hoping to discourage any further conversation. She was *not* interested in any kind of flirtatious banter with the bartender. How old was he anyway? Not that she cared but it was hard to tell. He certainly didn't look like any of the men she knew around her own age. No greys were starting to work their way through his hair—he still *had* hair, so that was another giveaway right there. Austin's hair, she'd noted the last time she saw him, had been receding faster than an outgoing tide. She probably shouldn't enjoy that fact quite as much as she did.

'I reckon that poor guy needs something a bit stronger than wine to settle those nerves,' he said, nodding towards the table she'd come from and tearing her away from her thoughts. 'I'm beginning to think your kids don't like you, if these are the guys they're setting you up with,' he continued lightly, his eyes crinkling a little at the corners in a way she definitely *did not* find attractive . . . at all. But the man had a point.

'Apparently there's a limited supply of eligible men in my preferred age range,' she said clearing her throat.

'You don't look like the kind who's after a sugar daddy.'

A sugar da— What the actual hell? They were *her* age. 'Hardly,' she told him, with a sharp glare. Was this guy the *only* bartender this place had?

'There you go,' he said, sliding the drinks across the bar as she tapped her card to pay. 'Good luck with contestant number two, Jenny.'

She sent him an unimpressed frown, but he was already taking the order of the person beside her.

'Here we go, whoops,' she said, as Alan reached for the glass as she was about to set it down and almost sloshed the contents down the sides. *For the love of God, man, take a freaking breath and calm the hell down.* She watched as he lifted the glass to his lips and took a hefty sip, almost downing the contents in one go. Whoa.

'I'm a little bit . . . nervous. You could probably tell,' he said, managing a weak smile.

Blind Freddy could tell, she thought dryly. 'That's okay. These things are a bit nerve-wracking.'

'They are.'

'So why do you do it?' she asked.

'My mother,' he said, and looked down into his glass mournfully.

'Excuse me?' Jenny asked, certain she must have missed something.

'My mother's been trying to marry me off for years,' he said, shaking his head. 'I think she's sick of me living at home.'

'If you don't mind me asking, how old are you again?' Jenny asked hesitantly.

'Fifty-four.'

'And you're a . . . ?'

'Town planner,' he supplied.

'You don't want your own space?' *At fifty-freaking-four years old?*

'Oh, there's plenty of room at my mother's. My father died about twelve years ago and she lives in the house all by herself. It's too much for her to handle on her own,' he said, taking another sip of his drink, smaller this time. 'Lately she's been talking about downsizing and moving into a retirement village, but that's such a waste of time. I mean, why would you?'

'Maybe she's craving the community that those places have. You know—making new friends and having people her own age around her.'

'I don't know why. She's got plenty of friends.'

But Jenny dealt with the elderly on a daily basis and suspected there was more to the story than Alan was letting on. 'Maybe she doesn't get to see them as often as she'd like. Does she still drive?'

'No. She never had a licence—Dad always drove.'

'In a retirement village she wouldn't have to depend on anyone driving her places. They often have community transport and most of their entertainment is onsite. It might give her a bit more independence than she's getting at the moment.'

'I don't know how she thinks I'll be able to find a place if she sells up, with the housing market the way it is at the moment,' he grumbled.

And there was the crux of the problem. 'I'm sure you'll find somewhere,' Jenny said, taking a drink.

'Anyway, she's given me an ultimatum to find a girlfriend or she's putting the house on the market immediately. She wants to make sure I'm happy before she makes any final decisions about the house.'

More like she wants to make sure she palms you off to someone else so you're their problem and not hers anymore, Jenny thought, almost wishing she hadn't gone the non-alcoholic route as she sipped at her drink and looked around for the waitress. *Come on, people, let's get this shit show on the road. The sooner it's done, the sooner I can go home.* Thank God she'd brought her own car.

'Shall we order?' she asked, reaching for the menu.

After a few minutes, she noticed Alan was still studying the list. He had changed his mind at least three times so far.

'I can recommend the pork tenderloin. I've heard the steak is pretty good too.' The food was the only thing worth remembering about her last date here.

'I'm pretty fussy about how I like my steak,' he said cautiously.

'The chef seems amazing. I'm sure if you tell the waitress, she'll let him know.'

'I don't think I'd like to chance it. That's quite a significant amount of money to waste on an overdone steak.'

Shoot me now. 'Maybe the pork then?' she suggested helpfully.

'I don't eat pork. Bad experience once.'

'The chicken?'

'Still don't trust that they don't pump them full of hormones.'

Oh, for the love of Christ. The waitress was walking towards them with a bright smile and Jenny wished she could warn her about what she was walking into.

'Cassie, isn't it?' Jenny said, greeting the young woman from the previous evening. 'You went to school with Brittany.'

Cassie smiled. 'That's me. Nice to see you again, Mrs Hayward.'

'Please, you're all grown up now, call me Jenny. And I think we're ready to order . . . or at least one of us is. Alan might need a little bit of help though.'

'No worries,' Cassie said. Over the course of the next five minutes, she expertly walked Alan through the entire menu and both of them learned far too much about the man and his many gastrointestinal issues.

Yeah, nah, I can't do this, Jenny thought as irritation began to rise inside her. This man had absolutely nothing in common with her. It was beyond depressing. 'I'm sorry, I just need to use the ladies for a minute,' Jenny said, standing abruptly before making her way across the room.

She pushed the door open and stepped inside. From memory, the old restroom had been a tiled, cold and fairly basic area, but was now transformed into something surprisingly opulent. A small chandelier was suspended over a sitting room area with deep grey walls and furnished with two armchairs upholstered in a pale shade of pink. Through an inner doorway was a sleek sink. The overall feel was extremely elegant for a country pub. Jenny sank into one of the armchairs and let out a satisfied sigh. She kicked off her heels to wriggle her toes in the fluffy pink mat that graced the floor between the two chairs. Maybe she could just stay in here for the rest of the night. Her ears were loving the sudden quiet after the music and chatter outside.

The door swinging open made Jenny jump slightly and she dragged her shoes closer to her feet to put them back on, feeling awkward at being caught out enjoying the peace and quiet.

'Oh. Sorry. I didn't mean to interrupt,' Cassie said, noticing her on the chair. 'Is everything okay?'

'Everything's fine,' Jenny said, putting a smile on her face. 'I just needed . . . a minute.'

'Are you sure everything's okay?' Cassie asked slowly, hesitating and then taking a seat opposite her.

'I guess I'm just not used to this whole dating thing. You might have realised this is the second one I've been on in two days,' Jenny said, twisting her mouth wryly.

'I think it's great you're getting out there.'

'Do you? My darling children and best friend ambushed me with it. I didn't even pick the men. Would you do that to your mother?' she asked as an afterthought.

'Probably not, since she kind of likes my dad and they're still married,' Cassie said with a grin.

'Oh. Well. No, you probably wouldn't want to do that.'

'I know Brittany and I'm sure they're all just trying to help. Maybe these dates are a way for you to see what you *could* have? If you don't particularly mesh with any of these guys then maybe you'll know what you *do* want from someone else?'

'Hmm. So far, I'm fairly certain it'll be the opposite of what they've found me.' She eyed the younger woman curiously for a moment. 'Are you back for good? I remember you moving away a while back.'

'I did. But I've recently come home. Mum hurt herself, and I came back to help Dad with the farm. But she's on the mend now.'

'That's good. You should get in touch with Brittany, I'm sure she'd like to catch up. She doesn't really get out that much with Sophie to keep her on her toes.'

'She's a good mum. She seems happy.'

'She's a great mum.' Jenny smiled fondly as she thought about her eldest daughter. 'She's doing so well—considering she's working full-time and raising a little one. But I worry that she's a bit lonely. She doesn't really have much of a social life. Most of her friends from school moved away. It'd be nice for her to have a friend around again.'

'We'll be meeting up soon,' Cassie promised. 'I've really missed being back home. I guess Brittany and I have that in common—we've both moved back in with our parents.'

'Well, if your mum and dad are anything like me, I'm sure they're happy to have you home. But I suppose I better get back out there before my date breaks into another cold sweat over something.'

'Good luck.'

Jenny slipped her heels on, took a silent breath and counted to five before resolutely standing and making her way back to her table. She only had to get through the meal and then it would be over. How bad could the second half be, after all?

'So, astronomy?' Alan suddenly asked, as they finished some small talk about the weather. Jenny looked at him quizzically. 'Your profile listed astronomy as an interest.'

'It did?' *What the actual hell?*

'It's one of mine, too.'

'Oh. Right. Yeah.' She didn't know a damn thing about astronomy. She was going to seriously kill those kids of hers. *And Beth*, she added as she pictured their smug faces.

'What's your favourite planet?' he asked.

Again, Jenny stopped eating to look at him and realised she needed to do a quick memory check of primary school and early science lessons. 'Ah, Pluto,' she said, coming up with the name triumphantly.

'Very funny. Pluto was declassified as a planet.'

'Really? Well, that's weird. What is it now?'

'It was officially classed as a dwarf planet back in two thousand and six.'

Dwarf planet . . . so it's technically still a damn planet then, she thought irritably. 'Well, if they're going to go and change everything we've already learned, shouldn't they at least bring it up with the times and rename it a "planet of short stature"?' she asked lightly. 'You know . . . politically correct terminology and all.'

The stern expression on his face told her he did not find her joke funny at all.

'What's your favourite planet?' she asked quickly.

'Saturn,' he said without hesitation.

'Why Saturn?' she asked, somehow suspecting he had a ready-made list on the subject that wouldn't require any kind of participation from her—hopefully long enough that she could finish her meal and just nod at appropriate times.

She was right.

'You probably should have worn a helmet for this one,' the bartender commented dryly as he brought over their post-dinner coffees and Alan excused himself to go to the gents briefly.

'Sorry?'

'I would never have suspected a fork could fly that far across a room until I saw it happen tonight.'

Jenny bit back an unexpected chuckle as she recalled Alan's earlier incident when he'd somehow managed to hit his fork with an elbow and send it hurtling off the table, narrowly missing her and causing a surprisingly loud clatter as it disappeared under what sounded like several tables. More than a few heads had turned in their direction.

'Yes. Well, he's a little bit nervous.'

'Just a tad. Although I can't see how you'd be considered so terrifying.'

'I think it's the situation,' she said.

'I'm Nick, by the way.'

She almost preferred it when she hadn't known his name—the entire situation seemed even more humiliating now they were introduced. 'Jenny,' she said, almost grudgingly.

'I know.'

Of course he did.

'Well, keep your head down,' he advised as her date appeared in the distance. He walked back to the bar.

If only she could.

❖

This time when Jenny arrived home, she ignored the curious faces waiting up for her and headed for the kitchen to retrieve the ice cream from the freezer.

'I seriously think you're doing this for some kind of evil payback,' Jenny said to the girls, who had followed her to the kitchen. She propped her hip against the kitchen bench as she dug into the mint-flavoured dessert she'd been thinking about all the way home as a reward for surviving date number two.

'We're doing this because we care about you,' Savannah said.

'I find that very hard to believe after what I've sat through. You all suck at picking dates.'

'We're only working with what we've got,' Chloe replied, evoking a stern glance from her two older sisters. 'Well, it's true! Between the age group, location and weeding out the creepers, it narrows down the field considerably.'

'And what's with the pub? I've been there with two different men in twenty-four hours. They're going to think I'm some kind of—'

'Lucky woman who's playing the field,' Brittany cut in.

'Isn't that a bad thing?' She eyed her daughters curiously.

Savannah took a scoop of ice cream from the container with a spoon of her own before giving an offhand shrug. 'Guys do it all the time. Why can't women have a bit of fun?'

'But it's not fun,' Jenny pointed out.

'You have to break a few eggs to make an omelette,' Brittany said wisely.

'I really don't think that saying applies here.'

'Sure it does,' Chloe assured her. 'You have to sort through the rubbish to find the treasure.'

Jenny had had enough of the metaphors. 'Tonight was another disastrous date. Let's just call Sunday's off. I'm not sure I can do this again.'

'No!' Savannah almost shouted. 'I picked this guy. I promise he'll be more to your liking.'

'And what amazing things does this one think I'm into in my spare time? Lion wrestling, maybe?' Jenny asked dryly. 'Why on earth would you have put all that stuff on my profile? What else is on there I should know about?'

'Nothing. We just zhuzhed you up a bit,' Beth told her.

'Well un-zhuzh me. In fact, show me this stupid profile so I can do it myself.'

'You managed to send a conversation we had about that cute new doctor from the hospital *to* the cute new doctor on Facebook, remember?' Beth said. 'Are you sure you want to be let loose on a dating app?'

Dear God, the cute doctor incident. Jenny felt the swift rise of heat on her face as the memory resurfaced. 'We vowed never to speak of that again,' she hissed in a mortified whisper.

Beth chuckled. 'It was kinda funny. We can look back on it now and laugh about it.'

No. No, they could not.

It was humiliating. Beth had sent her a link to the hunky doctor's Facebook account late one evening and the two women had been admiring his handsome attributes, which would have been completely fine, until somehow Jenny managed to bump something and the stupid touchy mouse had highlighted the entire conversation and sent it as a message to the doctor.

'Fine. I don't want to see the profile. But there better not be any more stupid surprises.'

'Everyone stretches the truth on their dating profile. Just relax, Mum,' Brittany said, waving a dismissive hand. 'Go with the flow. Enjoy going out.'

'Out. Let me guess . . . we'll be having lunch at the Coach House? Again? Why there?' An image of the young bartender flashed through her mind and she quickly pushed it away.

'Remember Cassie Reynolds? From high school?' Brittany asked.

Jenny nodded. 'I spoke with her tonight actually.'

'Well, we asked her to keep an eye on you for us.'

'You had her spying on me this whole time while I've been on these dates?' Could Jenny's mortification get any worse?

'Not spying, as such,' Savannah hedged, looking a little insulted.

'We just asked her to keep an eye out for any red flags. You know . . . if he tried to slip anything into your drink while you went to the toilet, or how he treated the servers—you can tell a lot by how someone treats the wait staff,' Chloe said.

'And what's she supposed to do if she thinks something's not right?' Jenny asked, surprised by her daughters' scheming.

'She'll step in and handle it.'

'Well, I suppose that should make me feel marginally better, considering you set me up with a complete stranger . . . *again*.'

'We wouldn't leave you stranded on a date if the guy tried anything with you.'

She wasn't sure whether to be terrified that there was a possibility someone might try and drug her or to be touched that her kids had a plan in motion in case it ever happened.

Six

Jenny braced herself as she opened her car door and got out to greet her date. This was the last one, she told herself firmly.

'Hi,' she said, pinning the fake smile in place as the man greeted her in the carpark where she had been waiting, before feeling it melt into something almost genuine. Craig was . . . not too bad.

'Jenny,' he said. Was that a note of relief in his voice she detected as well?

She nodded. 'Nice to meet you.'

Craig was surprisingly easygoing—at least compared to overconfident Derrick and nervous Alan.

She glanced at the white four-wheel drive he'd just locked with his remote. 'Nice car. How long have you had it?' she asked.

He sent her a wide smile. 'A little over a week. She's my pride and joy.'

'It's really nice.'

'Yeah. I've got lots of camping trips planned and a few four-wheel drive tracks I've been wanting to try.'

Camping. She knew the guy had to have something wrong with him. It was too good to be true. She let him continue to fill her in on all the great camping spots he liked to go to as they headed indoors. *You can do this.*

The lunchtime crowd seemed a little more laid-back on a Sunday. A guy with a guitar sat in the corner playing live music, adding to the relaxed vibe of the place. The place was beginning to grow on her. She really should make an effort to come back here on a weekend—without a date. Since the weather was nice, they chose to sit outdoors under the pink bougainvillea, the mouth-watering scent of delicious meals filling the air around them.

'And you're a teacher?' Jenny said once they were settled and looking at each other, hoping to find some common ground—any common ground, really.

'Yeah. Maths.'

Oh God. Still, it could have been worse—he could have been a PE teacher. She had an even worse history with PE at school.

'But I trained as a PE teacher.'

Of *course* he had.

'I've been training for an upcoming marathon next month. Your profile said you jog?'

Son of a— 'I, ah, did some muscular damage a while back,' she said, schooling her face into something she hoped resembled vast disappointment. 'Sadly, I had to give up running.' They'd *promised* her there wasn't any more weird shit on her profile. Why had she believed them?

'Wow . . . that's terrible.'

She felt a tinge of guilt as the guy's face fell. Like, actually crumpled in dismay.

'Yeah, but it's okay . . . I barely miss it any more, I keep pretty busy.'

'Oh, yeah? Doing what? What other sports do you do?'

'I, ah . . . yoga,' she said, and his face instantly brightened.

'Me too!' He grinned. 'There's a sunrise hot yoga work out over in Hamwell on a Sunday morning. It's amazing, you should come along.'

Right. Getting up before sunrise on a Sunday to do yoga. Sounds freaking amazing—*not*. She managed a weak smile and had never been so grateful to be interrupted by the tall but still disconcerting bartender, who suddenly appeared beside their table.

'Are you ready to order?'

'You're doing table waiting now, too?' she asked, lifting a surprised eyebrow.

'I do whatever needs to be done,' he said, sending her a polite, innocuous smile that was ruined by the gravelly tone that slithered down her spine all the way to her toes. How the hell did he do that? Surely he didn't mean to be this stupid-sexy, and yet, by that look in his eye, he *knew* he was putting a double meaning in his words.

'I think I'll have the T-bone, but hold the potatoes. Just a side of steamed veggies, thanks,' Craig said, completely oblivious to the tension that zapped between Nick and Jenny.

'Watchin' your carbs, mate?' Nick asked, tearing his gaze away from Jenny to regard her date.

On their previous encounters, there'd always been either a bar between them or at least some distance, and this was the first time he'd actually been close enough for her to touch him . . . Not that she would, she hastily reminded herself, in case she did something stupid like reach out and poke the rather nice biceps peeping out from under his tight shirt to see if they were real.

Jenny let out a small, shaky breath. It was physically impossible for a mere look to actually spear you, but she was struggling to explain how it suddenly felt as though there was nothing holding her upright now that he'd taken his gaze away from her. *Oh, for the love of . . . .* This was ridiculous. He was just a guy, a hot—okay, *incredibly hot*—younger-than-her guy . . . Maybe this was some weird menopausal symptom. Was she too young to be going through menopause yet? She'd never been remotely interested in younger men before. He may not be young, as in her kids' age kind of young, but he was definitely younger *than her.*

'Jenny?' Craig's concerned voice interrupted her thoughts, and she snapped her head up.

'Sorry?'

'Are you ready to order?'

She scrambled to pick up the menu, which she knew off by heart now.

'Or do you need more time?' Mr Sex-on-Legs put in smoothly, and she lifted her gaze to meet his, instantly regretting it when she caught that smouldering look once more. Yes, she needed more time! Away from him. To work out what the hell was wrong with her.

'I'll have the same . . . with potatoes,' she said. Maybe a good dose of carbs would help soak up some of the weirdness going on inside her.

'Well, it's not like you need to watch your carb intake,' Craig said, his gaze roaming over her from across the table.

'Oh,' she said, caught off guard by the remark and the somewhat approving expression.

'I actually like women with a few extra curves,' he added, lowering his voice.

Extra *curves?* she thought. As far as compliments went, she supposed that one was meant to be taken as a good thing, but it occurred to her that despite the decidedly sexy look in his eye, it didn't stir her blood. Jenny glanced at the bartender somewhat self-consciously, and noted that he was sending Craig a look she couldn't quite decipher. It definitely wasn't hospitable, that much she knew. Maybe the *extra curves* hadn't been a compliment after all?

'Anything else?' Nick asked. His voice had dropped a few degrees in temperature.

'I think that's all?' Craig said, giving her a questioning glance, and Jenny nodded.

'I'll send over drinks?' Nick asked, lifting his eyebrows slightly at her and she nodded.

'Just a soda water for me, thanks,' Craig said, 'and wine for the lady.'

She managed a polite smile at her date. 'I'm fine with a soft drink or something too.'

'Nonsense, just because I'm not drinking doesn't mean you shouldn't. It helps you unwind,' Craig said with a wink.

She looked quickly at Nick.

'You don't have to have wine,' he said calmly.

'Wine will be fine, thanks,' she said, suddenly feeling uncomfortable under the weight of his heavy stare. Since when did the bartender become the sober police? She could have one wine and still drive without it being a problem. For the first time in this whole terrible nightmare of dating, she was actually beginning to think maybe, just maybe, Craig might not be a complete write-off and she didn't need the bartender butting in to derail the whole thing.

'I really do like your curves, you know,' Craig said when they were alone again. 'Bigger women are my weakness.'

Bigger women? What the actual hell? Okay, she wasn't a size ten, but seriously, she was within a normal weight range—at least, she'd always thought so. Any remaining interest in Craig instantly fizzled out. If there was one thing that annoyed her the most about men, it was this idea of perfection some of them had; the fact a woman had to look like the women in magazines or on the big screen. Maybe it was a leftover hang-up from her husband dumping her for a younger woman—who, yes, did look like a freaking Kardashian, with her long hair and fake nails and fake eyelashes. But that's what the whole thing was—fake. Anyone could get hair extensions and fake eyelashes glued on and fillers pumped into them, but it wasn't real. Although, Christy *did* have youth on her side, so there was that. But still! What happened to being able to see the natural beauty in someone? Maybe she was too old and jaded to be dating.

'So, have you had much luck on the dating app?' he asked, leaning back in his chair.

'No, not really. You?'

'Yeah, a bit. It's good for finding some company—you know,' he said, sending her a look across the table that she was sure was supposed to be smouldering but only added to her irritation.

A tall glass of sparkling liquid was placed, with a touch more force than seemed safe, in front of Craig, then Nick was at her side, placing her glass more gently on the table before walking away without comment.

'You haven't found anyone interesting so far, then?' Craig continued without batting an eyelid at the interruption.

'So far, all I've found are people who seem as disappointed in the whole process as I am.'

'The trick is to not look for anything other than a good time, you know? It's just a bit of fun.'

'I think some people are looking for a little more than a bit of fun,' she said, taking a large sip of her wine. 'Some people are genuinely looking for a relationship.' Jenny had had enough of him already . . . but that steak sounded really good and she was starving.

'Is that what you're after?' He looked a little less sultry-eyed now.

'I'm not sure yet,' she said with a disinterested shrug and another sip. 'Maybe.'

'Yeah, nah. I'm not up for anything serious.'

She paused. Something about the edge of nervousness she detected made her pay a little more attention to him. She'd spent long enough poking and probing discreetly to prise out information about a patient's life and background as she took a medical history to recognise the signs of something fishy going on. 'I'm sure I read something different on your profile,' she said, deciding it could be entertaining to watch this guy start to unravel.

'No. It says, "not looking for anything serious". The same as yours,' he said pointedly.

Really? Not that she particularly cared—after today there'd be no more dating app for her, but she supposed when the girls were setting up her profile, the option of 'looking for a relationship' might have been considered overstepping boundaries. She gave a silent snort—yeah, right. Her kids and best friend had taken a running jump and left any boundaries in the dust. 'I probably should change that,' she murmured, downing the last of her drink.

'Why don't we just start with a bit of fun and see where that goes?' he suggested, slipping back into Mr Charming again and sending her a smile that drooped a little as his phone dinged on the table. He didn't check it.

Wow, yeah, she knew exactly how a bit of fun would end after this. He'd be deleting her number and blocking her in case she turned out to be some clinging desperado. *In your dreams, mate.*

Jenny watched as Craig caught Nick's eye at the bar and snapped his fingers. Within moments, a young waiter arrived and Craig ordered another round of drinks. Before she could protest, the waiter had gone. She fought back an irritated growl. When the drinks arrived a few minutes later, Jenny did a double take at the tall, brightly coloured cocktail in front of her then swung her gaze to the bar. Nick was watching.

'I ordered wine,' Craig snapped, eyeing the concoction before her and probably wondering how much it would add to the bill.

'The bartender said this was the lady's favourite,' the young waiter stammered, and instantly Jenny's annoyance was replaced with relief. Nick had made her a mocktail so she wouldn't have to drink any more alcohol.

'This is perfect, thank you.' She beamed at Craig so he wouldn't make a scene and secretly enjoyed his irritation as he sipped at his boring soda water. She forced a smile to her face and asked him a bunch of questions about his upcoming marathon as she enjoyed the fruity mix of cranberries, orange and peach, letting him talk about himself until their food arrived.

This time it was a young girl who delivered their meals and despite the knob across from her droning on about nutrition and athletic diets, Jenny found her appetite was thankfully still intact. When his phone continued to ding and he sent yet another frustrated look at it, Jenny sent him a bored glance.

'You know, if that's important, feel free to answer it.'

'No. It's—' He stopped mid-sentence and paled slightly, moments before he leaped to his feet. 'Give me a minute,' he stammered, leaving the table to head inside.

Jenny followed his progress with interest as she continued to eat, spotting him heading off a woman who'd just barrelled through the front door.

'What's that about?' Nick asked, coming to a stop beside the table, holding another mocktail.

'I have no idea,' Jenny said. 'Why are you plastering me with non-alcoholic mocktails today?'

He frowned. 'So your date doesn't get you plastered with alcoholic ones,' he said, looking back inside the pub.

Jenny followed his gaze and saw the woman was now waving her phone about wildly and Craig was doing his best to try and catch hold of her to stop her heading outside to the beer garden.

The phone on the table started to ring and a photo of a woman with a toddler flashed up on the screen. The same woman Craig was currently inside with.

Jenny's mouth dropped open. *That lying, cheating, absolute bastard!* She was furious with herself and, quite frankly, the entire world right now for putting her in this stupid predicament.

Nick swore under his breath, then grabbed the phone on the table and headed towards the door with determined strides. He intercepted the couple pushing open the glass door and held out the phone to Craig, who was tripping over himself trying to keep up with the woman.

'You left your phone at the bar, mate,' Nick said, blocking the woman from walking any further into the outdoor area.

'Where is she? Who were you here with?' the woman screeched, then turned her furious gaze upon Nick, demanding, 'Where was he sitting? Did you see him with anyone?'

'The phone was on the bar,' Nick said, holding his hands up in defence. 'I'm just returning it.'

'I told you, babe, I just stopped in for a drink. I'm on my way home. Come on, let's get out of here.'

'I've got your bill ready if you want to tap your card, mate, before you go,' Nick said, as he produced a card-reader from the nearby bar and held it out.

Craig fumbled for his wallet and hastily tapped a credit card, then ushered the slightly subdued woman out of the pub—never once looking back at the table where Jenny sat.

'Are you okay?'

Jenny stared up at Nick, mortified. She was an adulterer. No better than Austin and Christy.

'Hey, it's okay.'

'It's not. I was just on a date with a cheating husband.' Her head suddenly began to feel light.

'I take it you didn't know he was married when you accepted?'

Jenny sent him a withering glare. 'Of course I didn't. I'd never do something like that.' Her anger had at least momentarily pushed aside her dizziness.

'Then it wasn't your fault, was it? This was all on him.'

'How did you know what was going on?' she asked as he started clearing the plates from the table.

'I've seen my share of cheating men getting caught out and I didn't want a scene going down and scaring off my customers.'

Jenny squeezed her eyes shut as she imagined what would have happened if the woman had worked out who Craig had been sitting with. Her cheeks flared with heat. She would have had to have left town—there would be no other way to deal with the embarrassment, she thought, as she imagined being accused of sneaking around with a married man in front of the whole town. She'd never live it down. The humiliation of what could have happened made her feel nauseous once more.

'Hey,' Nick said, 'you didn't know.'

'I feel so stupid,' Jenny said, pressing her hands against her hot cheeks. She'd thought for a moment Craig might even be the one who could change her opinion of online dating.

'Least I made the bastard pay for it—and all the drinks. Maybe he'll think twice before he sneaks off again and does it to someone else. You okay out here?'

'Yeah, I'm fine. Thanks,' she said with a distracted air as she searched through her handbag and pulled out her phone. 'I have a call to make,' she said in a low voice as she listened to it ring.

'Hey! Aren't you supposed to be on date number three?' Beth asked when she answered.

'It's over. I want you to get on that app and delete me,' Jenny said, 'right now.'

'Why? What happened?'

'He was married, Beth.'

'Married? What? No way.'

'Did anyone bother to check that out?'

'How could we have possibly checked that out?'

'Exactly!' Jenny snapped. 'You don't know anything about these people. They could be axe murderers.'

'I don't actually think that's a thing anymore . . . I mean, when was the last time you actually heard on the news of anyone being murdered with an axe?'

'Beth! I'm serious.'

'Sorry. Yeah, that would have been a shock. Are you safe there?'

'What? Oh. Yeah. It's fine. He left.'

'You want me to come down?'

'No. I want you to make sure that's the end of all this stupid dating business. I'm done. I mean it, Beth.'

'Okay, Fair enough. We'll stay out of it.'

Jenny hung up and fought back a rush of emotions. Anger was the loudest, but it was closely followed by embarrassment and shame. Why had she ever thought humouring Beth and her kids would ever have been the right thing to do? She should have stood up to them and just said no.

Jenny made her way towards the exit, but inside she made a detour and went to the bar instead. She climbed up onto a bar stool and frowned at how ridiculously uncomfortable it was. She didn't feel like going home yet and she was still too angry to see any of the others right now. 'Never again,' she said, firmly.

'I was wondering when you'd finally work out those guys you've been seeing were all wrong for you.'

Jenny's head jerked up. She stared at Nick. 'Excuse me?'

He sent her a lopsided grin as he continued to stack glasses behind the bar. 'You've been on how many dates now?'

'That's none of your business.'

'Nope, you're right, although I kind of feel as though I've been part of it.'

'They haven't all been *that* bad,' she said, moving uncomfortably in her seat.

He sent her an arched eyebrow.

'Well, okay, they were disasters,' she admitted. 'But the others were nice men,' she said. Why was she even explaining herself to this man?

'Maybe so, but they weren't right for you. You're too young to be settling for some of those old blokes.'

'Too young? How old do you think I am?' she asked.

'Mid-thirties?' he said, tilting his head slightly.

Jenny let out a surprised chuckle. 'Seriously?'

'Absolutely. Why?'

'Either you're blind or just a terrible liar.'

'I'm neither.'

'Well, I'm not in my thirties, either.'

'Huh,' he said, leaning back slightly as he studied her. 'Was I close?'

'Not even,' she told him blandly. 'Try fifty.'

'Really?'

Jenny rolled her eyes. She was *so* not going to fall for fake flattery. 'Anyway, it doesn't matter now. I'm deleting my profile so there won't be any more dates.'

'Well, that's a shame,' he said, placing both hands on the bar as he gave her his full attention.

'I'm sorry I'll be taking away your entertainment.'

'I didn't consider any of that *entertainment*, trust me,' he said with a wry twist of his lips. 'Maybe a trainwreck,' he added.

'And yet you were happily standing by, watching. Why? Are you that hard up for excitement around here that you need to resort to spying on your customers?'

'I wasn't spying. It's part of my job to keep an eye on things.'

'The other part is pouring drinks, so, if you don't mind, would you do that for me, please? A real one,' she tacked on quickly. This constant back and forth between attraction and annoyance with this man was really confusing.

'Yes, ma'am.' He touched an invisible cap on his head and took a glass out with a smirk.

Jenny found herself following his movements. Her gaze lingered on the rather nice fit of his jeans and the stretch of his shirt . . . the fabric looked soft and comfy. He'd had a haircut recently, she decided. His dark hair had been on the shaggy side and had kept falling into his eyes, then she was surprised she'd noticed.

He turned and grinned as he caught her looking at him and she immediately snatched her gaze away from those annoying, laughing, hazel eyes, giving herself a mental shake—she hadn't taken *that* much notice.

'Your drink, my lady,' he said with an exaggerated bow of his head as she held her card up, waiting to tap it on the machine. 'It's on the house. After your dating marathon, you deserve it.'

'Does your boss know you give away his alcohol like this?'

Again, with that cocky grin that both irritated, and well . . . no, just irritated her really.

'He's pretty easygoing.'

'Well, thanks, I guess.' She didn't like the way he could make her feel so off-centre.

'You're welcome. So, what now?' he asked as she took a sip of her drink.

'What do you mean?'

'You said you were giving up on the dating site, so what are you going to do now?'

'Nothing. I guess. I'll go back to enjoying my life the way it was before.'

'Which was?'

Boring. Jenny paused with the glass halfway to her mouth. No, it wasn't. Was it? 'Uneventful,' she said, realising he was still waiting for her reply.

'Uneventful?' Doubt coloured his voice. 'And you're happy living an *uneventful* life?'

Well, when he put it like that . . . 'I'm happy living a stress-free life, which lately, being thrown together with strange men, it definitely has *not* been.'

'Then maybe you should take control over it. Pick your own dates from now on.'

'Maybe I will,' she said with a sudden burst of defiance. Maybe she'd go straight home now and do just that.

She sipped her drink as she pondered this new course of action. Choose her own dates? She could do that. Surely she couldn't do any worse than the girls had?

She glanced at her watch and realised it was getting late. She could be doing a million other things than sitting alone at a bar, ogling men—or rather, one man in particular. Could she *get* any more cougar-like? Who was she? She barely recognised herself lately. She just needed to put everything back the way it was before and it would all be fine.

Seven

Nick watched the woman until she disappeared from sight.

He wasn't sure why he'd felt a need to watch over Jenny like some guardian angel—or stalker, he supposed, depending on how you wanted to look at it—but she'd been distracting him for the past two days and he'd possibly become a tiny bit fascinated by her. She brightened up his workday. Maybe he enjoyed taking the mickey out of her and those ridiculous bloody dates a little too much, but they were an absolute joke. What wasn't a joke was the way he was beginning to wait for Jenny to appear. She'd surprised him earlier when she'd told him her age—there was no way the woman looked fifty. And yet the knowledge took nothing away from the attraction he seemed to have for her. She was a feisty, funny, sexy as hell–looking woman and there was no denying he definitely wanted to get to know her a lot better.

He'd caught Jenny watching him over the last few days and had to admit he enjoyed the fact he somehow made her uncomfortably aware of him. He wasn't big-noting himself; he wouldn't say he was *Men's Health* magazine material, but he wasn't too shabby, all things considered, and the way she looked at him from time to time gave his tired, overworked ego a pat on the back it sorely needed.

When she'd first told him about the blind dates, it all started to make sense, and—if he were being honest—he was kind of relieved. It was obvious she'd been bored out of her brain and that the guy hadn't stood a chance for a second date, which made him feel a lot better.

Then she'd returned the next day with another fella who wasn't much of an improvement on the first one. There was simply no way this woman had anything in common with any of the blokes she'd been out with.

Today, though, had taken the cake. Gone was the amusement at her doomed dates and in its place was a serious need to punch date number three in the face.

It'd started before the guy's angry wife had stormed into his pub. The guy had been leering at Jenny across the table—practically licking his lips at the prospect of what he'd like to be doing to her after their meal. Nick hadn't expected it to bother him so much, but it had. A lot. He'd seen this type of guy before and knew the game: he'd buy Jenny a few drinks and loosen her up then whisk her away and do . . . well, probably everything that had been running through Nick's own mind over the past few days. He gave a silent grunt, acknowledging that that made him not much better than the dickhead she'd been out with. Only, Nick didn't have a wife hidden away, and Jenny wouldn't be some casual one-night stand he'd fling aside when he was done.

That thought made him stop stacking glasses and straighten. When had he become interested in a relationship? He wasn't. He didn't do serious relationships. He didn't do desperate dating apps just to find a willing body, either. For the last two years, he'd been too busy putting together his business proposal, sorting out finance and renovation plans and selling his soul to the devil.

He began packing the dishwasher with glasses and had to force himself to calm down as the clink of glass got a little loud. It still stung. He'd wanted to do this thing himself—he'd been dreaming of this for the better part of the last decade and then, at the last minute, just when it looked like his dream might not happen, he'd been faced with a choice: Buy the pub with a partner or lose the opportunity completely.

He knew most people would think he should be grateful that he had a partner who had come forward to help him, and, maybe, if it'd been anyone else who'd offered to help, he would be. But it wasn't anyone else. It was Susie.

Closing the dishwasher and turning it on, Nick's eyes swept the room and, satisfied everyone seemed happy, went upstairs to the office and his living quarters. He loved old pubs—old anything really; he was a sucker for heritage buildings in any form, but pubs had always held a special place in his heart. He'd always been able to see a long-term plan, but lots of his mates hadn't. They used to joke about his budgeting and investing strategies, though he'd never found it difficult—he was a man of simple tastes. He drank in his early days, probably too much, but then he settled down. He figured out how much he was wasting on nights out each weekend and realised if he was serious about buying a pub one day, he had to save. The army wasn't exactly a high-paying power job, but that only meant he had to be smart and find ways to invest in things that would give him the highest return. He'd surprised even himself when he discovered he had a talent for investing. Not enough talent to do it as a full-time career, like his sister had urged him to do—he'd rather poke his eye out with a stick before he took on a job in a city office and have to dress in a suit all day. He'd had enough of uniforms and ceremony, now he just wanted his own life and his own business.

The staircase, with its solid, red cedar balustrade that curved in a majestic sweep up to the second floor, was just one of the hotel's heritage pride and joys. They didn't build things like they did back in 1885. He still had to pinch himself that he owned a place with ties to the town's very beginnings. During the renovation, he'd unearthed some pretty amazing things—old bottles and newspapers; a few secret hidey holes that he assumed had been installed for some rather suspect reasons he'd yet to discover; and the most exciting thing of all: a door under the staircase that led to a room that had been sealed off for God only knew how long.

At the top of the stairs, he turned into the first doorway and tossed a bunch of receipts he'd brought with him on the desk under the window. The view was nothing fancy—it overlooked the main street—but it matched the framed photo of the hotel he'd hung when he'd first bought it. If you swapped the cars for horses tied up outside and bitumen for dirt, the view of the town was exactly the same as it had been almost a hundred and forty years ago. He liked the wide-open space of the countryside out here—the constant change of colours the further west you drove. He'd grown up in the city, but there was something about small towns that fascinated him. Maybe he missed the community spirit the army had provided and was craving that sense of belonging to something bigger than himself again. Maybe it was just the way he felt lighter—like he could breathe deeper, the further into the countryside he went, that made the decision to move here a no-brainer.

He'd never been to Barkley before, but the moment he'd seen the old hotel during his research, he'd known this was the one he wanted to buy and this was the town he wanted to live in. His mates had thought he was crazy; so had his sister. She'd done her best to talk him out of it and yet, he hadn't been able to shake the feeling that this was where he wanted to be. When the pub had eventually come up for sale after a few years being caught up in a deceased estate and family court battle, it felt like a sign. Nick was out of the army and ready to buy. It had been fate.

It had also threatened to be a bottomless pit of endless renovations and expenses, which had jeopardised his dream more than once in the last twelve months. Nick sank into the chair behind his desk and tilted his head back to stare up at the ceiling. The damp patch in the shape of a lopsided snowman stared back down at him and he gave a weary sigh. Fixing the roof was the next job on the long and growing list. Each time he crossed off a job, another replaced it. At this rate he'd never make any kind of profit—not if everything he made just went back into the building.

He pushed aside the million other thoughts racing around in his head and focused instead on the one job he could get out of the way now. He reached for the invoices. The paperwork wasn't going to do itself.

Eight

Life, for the most part, returned to normal after Jenny's weekend misadventures in extreme dating—it had kind of felt like the *Hunger Games* and *she* had been the one running with a target on her back.

She was packing the groceries into the back of her car at the supermarket later that week when she felt someone stop beside her.

'Excuse me, are you Florence?'

Jenny looked up quickly. 'Ah, no. Sorry.' She smiled. The man seemed vaguely familiar, but she didn't know his name. His stocky build was cloaked in flannel and dusty jeans with a rip in one pocket.

'I'm sure it's you.'

'Excuse me?' Jenny straightened.

'I've seen you before. Your profile. You're Florence_71 on the Date Me Now app.'

Jenny gaped at the man, before a surge of embarrassment and anger swelled up and threatened to burst forth. 'I'm sorry, you have me confused with someone else,' she snapped, slamming the boot of her car and hurrying to the driver's door. She'd told Beth to take the stupid thing down! This was why online dating in a small town was such a crap idea.

She scrolled to Beth's number and waited for her to answer.

'Hey, what's up?' Beth's cheery voice sounded in her ear.

'Apparently, my dating profile . . . that's what. I was just approached by some random guy who recognised me from my profile! I told you to delete it.'

'Really? Was he good looking?'

'Beth! I'm serious. This has to stop.'

'Okay, I get it—sorry. I tried to delete it but I couldn't remember the password we made, then I got side-tracked and I forgot all about it. I promise I'll do it tonight.'

'Don't worry. I'll take care of it myself,' Jenny told her, before giving a huffy goodbye and dropping the phone back into her bag. If you wanted something done right you had to do it yourself. How hard could it be?

Jenny carried her glass of wine upstairs and sat down at the small desk across from her bed, opening her laptop calmly. She'd always loved that the master bedroom was such a strange shape, more long and narrow than the usual square shape. It had always seemed cluttered before her overhaul. Maybe it had just felt that way because Austin had always been such a larger-than-life figure. He took up room . . . not physically, he wasn't tall or muscular, it was more his personality. He was confident—overly so, now that she looked back at it with the benefit of distance and maturity. Once all his clothes and stuff had been removed from the cupboards, the room had felt bigger. It shouldn't have made that much difference—he'd already been moving his belongings out bit by bit before the break-up—but with all traces of him removed, the room had seemed to double in size, as though it too could finally let out a big breath.

She'd had a reading seat built beneath the window that overlooked the backyard and dragged out her sewing machine to knock up a seat cover and set of cushions in shades of pink, red and grey. She found a small timber writing desk on the side of the footpath during a council pick-up run, and dug out an old wooden dining chair that had been left over from their very first dining table and gave them both a coat of white paint before adding them to her new bedroom décor. Jenny splashed out and bought new bed covers and sheet sets, as well as curtains, and ripped up the carpet to install timber flooring. The transformation had been nothing short of remarkable. Afterwards, she'd felt rejuvenated and, little by little, she'd been turning her hand to renovating other bits and pieces of furniture, adding the little touches that made the place her own.

She took a sip of her wine and typed in the website for the dating app, then signed in, checking the sticky note with the information scrawled across it that she'd managed to extract from Brittany. Username: Florence_71. Password: getmumlaid. 'Charming,' she muttered under her breath. She hit the keys with a little more force than was probably warranted and sat back as her profile loaded.

And there it was. In all its glory.

Where the hell had they found that photo of her? she remembered the day it was taken: she'd been held up at work and was hurrying to get ready for an awards night for Austin's company. In the rush, she'd accidentally spilled tomato sauce from the bolognese she'd been cooking to leave Chloe for dinner across the top of her dress and had ended up wearing one of Brittany's because she was already late and Austin had been furious. In the photo, the soft jersey fabric of the blood-red dress was clinging to, well, pretty much *everything.* She'd never have chosen to wear it in a million years. Austin had given her an incredulous look as she'd tugged on her heels, his only comment something muttered under his breath and a quick shake of his head as he hurried her out to the car. She'd felt ridiculous and spent the entire night uncomfortably pulling at the dress like a fidgeting child.

She stared at the image. She'd been neatly cropped out of the original photo, which had been taken of a group of people—Austin and some of his employees. Thanks to the camera angle, the dress didn't actually look as terrible as she remembered. She tilted her head. How strange. At the time she'd felt like some frumpy, overdressed woman trying to compete against the younger, leaner women who worked in her husband's office. But the woman staring back at her from this photo didn't look as bad as she'd felt.

She flicked through the rest of the photos. *They didn't!* She gaped at the next photo. On a dare, she had dressed as a sexy nurse last Halloween for a party the girls had thrown. It had been in her own house and the only people at the party were a few work colleagues, Beth, Garry and a few of the older kids' friends. Why on earth would they put up that photo of her? She groaned aloud and quickly searched the page for the delete button. This had gone on long enough.

Almost ten minutes later, after accidentally clicking on profiles and somehow initiating a few likes and mutual 'into you' invitations—whatever the hell those were—she accidentally stumbled upon her inbox. She saw the opened messages between the girls and her previous disaster dates and clicked her tongue irritably. How naive had these men been? The person they'd thought they'd been talking to had really been *four people*! And *this* was why the whole online dating thing was so ridiculous. You could be talking to anyone on here—or in this case, *four* anyones!

Still annoyed, but curious about some of the unopened messages, she cautiously clicked on one.

Hi, I'm Paul. I'm after a one-night stand—no strings. Hit me up if you're keen to meet.

Yeah, nah, thanks, Paul. At least he was upfront about what he was after, Jenny supposed.

She opened the next one and clicked on the profile picture, shrinking away from the screen as an image came up of a shirtless, long-haired man who looked to be somewhere in his sixties, covered in dirt and dust as though he'd just come in from working in his backyard. *Clearly too much effort to take a photo after you'd had a shower*, she thought, closing the profile.

Clicking on the next one, she shook her head. At least this one was cleaner. Very clean, since he was standing in a shower, naked. Maybe Beth and the girls had been a bit more selective than she'd given them credit for.

Jenny scrolled through the list of accounts that were deemed, God only knew how, to be her perfect matches and felt any hope she might still have had completely drain away. This was depressing. Surely to goodness these were not the only single, available people in her age group within a three hundred kilometre radius?

She let out a bitter snort as she paused on one profile of a man claiming to be forty-nine. 'In your dreams, pal,' she muttered. There was no way the grey-haired man in the photo was anything under late fifties. Why did these men think they had to resort to lying about their age? Unless they weren't *looking* for women in their own age bracket. She gave a shudder and went back to the messages.

Albert. Fifty-one. She studied the not-too-shabby image of a bald, neatly dressed man in the small photo. Hobbies: Beach walks, movies, dining out. *Seems safe enough*, she thought, opening the message attached to the profile photo.

Hi there, beautiful lady. You're hot. I really want to—

Jenny let out an indignant gasp and clicked delete. Did men honestly think they had a right to say these things to complete strangers? Worse yet, did they actually expect women to respond? He'd looked halfway normal too!

As she was about to shut the page, her computer dinged and an envelope emoji popped up on the screen. *Caffeine_Addict wants to chat!* it announced excitedly, and the little envelope jumped and jiggled about on the screen.

Aww.

Stop it, she told herself sternly. *It's not cute. It's creepy.*

And yet, for some reason, she didn't continue her search for the delete button. With an irritated sigh, she reached over and clicked on the envelope then picked up her glass to take a sip.

There was no photo on the page that opened and Jenny went to delete the message, but she hesitated when the cursor started flashing, indicating that whoever had sent the hello was continuing to type. Well, it was kind of rude to delete a message while someone was in the middle of writing something, she supposed, and clicked on the profile tab to see if there was anything worthwhile reading while she waited for the little cursor to stop jumping.

Easygoing, polite, laid-back with a good sense of humour. No photos as discretion required by employer and occupation, she read. Discretion, huh? Well, that was something that most people on here didn't seem to think about very often.

The message box popped up and she paused before putting her glass down.

Caffeine_Addict
Hey, Florence . . . as in Nightingale, I presume . . . or perhaps not exactly . . . the original Florence Nightingale didn't look quite that good in uniform, to be honest.

That bloody fancy dress outfit! *Oh, you knew her?* she typed back, then gave a disgruntled murmur. Why was she even encouraging this?

Caffeine_Addict
Not well . . . she was always off somewhere doing something heroic like tending the ill and wounded. No time for fun, that girl.

Florence_71
How inconsiderate of her.

Caffeine_Addict
Exactly. I like your profile. It seems to list an impressive number of extracurricular activities. Hiking, rock-climbing, visiting museums, the theatre . . . dining out and pottery. You're a very versatile woman.

She rolled her eyes. Thanks, kids . . .

Florence_71
Yours, on the other hand, seems very mysterious. Discretion required by employer and occupation? Curious.

Caffeine_Addict
Well, you know the drill . . . I could tell you but then I'd have to kill you.

Real original, Jenny thought sarcastically.

Caffeine_Addict
So, Florence, how's my competition on here? Any other likely contenders?

Florence_71
Nope. None.

Caffeine_Addict
None? Wow you must have some pretty tough standards.

> Florence_71
> Not that there's any lack of interesting choices. It was a difficult decision to say no to the guy who just now invited me over to join him in a shower. Tempting, since I hadn't even replied to his hello. I'm no expert, but I suspect he could possibly be a serial killer.

> Caffeine_Addict
> What? And you knocked him back?

> Florence_71
> I know. Shocking.

> Caffeine_Addict
> So what can I maybe tell you that would save me from the dreaded swipe of doom?

You could tell me what your occupation is, she found herself typing back.

> Caffeine_Addict
> Maybe you could try and guess . . . That way if you do, I technically didn't tell you, hence, I won't have to do away with you.

Jenny bit the inside of her cheek as a smile threatened to emerge, which was ridiculous because this was stupid.

> Florence_71
> You're an ASIO operative?

> Caffeine_Addict
> Nope.

> Florence_71
> An undercover cop?

Caffeine_Addict
Nuh-uh.

Florence_71
A celebrity? Someone famous pretending to be one of the simple folk for a laugh?

Caffeine_Addict
Well, that would make me a bit of a jerk.

That wasn't a no . . . she replied, her eyes narrowing as she waited for an answer.

Caffeine_Addict
Nothing that exciting, unfortunately. The truth is, I was kinda stalked once. And yeah, I know that makes me sound completely lame and unmanly.

Florence_71
Haha! I found you!!

She stared at what she had typed and realised maybe he was actually serious and could potentially be suffering from some kind of trauma.

Florence_71
Sorry, that sounded a lot funnier inside my head.

Caffeine_Addict
Nah, all good. That was kinda funny actually.

Jenny winced, wondering how to proceed.

Florence_71
That must have been scary.

Caffeine_Addict
It wasn't much fun, to be honest.

Well, this conversation has turned south rather fast. She'd almost been enjoying the banter and now she felt like she owed it to the poor guy to hang around a little longer and make sure she hadn't offended him. Maybe she could try to turn the chat around.

Florence_71
Well, technically, you still haven't told me what you do for a job.

Caffeine_Addict
That's true. I'm self-employed.

Wow, this was like pulling teeth.

Florence_71
Doing?

Caffeine_Addict
You sure don't give up easily do you?

Florence_71
Neither, apparently, do you.

Caffeine_Addict
Nothing too exciting. I get businesses up and running and set them up to sell. Lots of paperwork.

Florence_71
That sounds impressive. I hear you on the paperwork, though. There's nothing too exciting about that.

Caffeine_Addict
So am I still in with a chance?

Florence_71
To be honest, the fact you can string a sentence together is pretty impressive.

Caffeine_Addict
Anyone with reasonable grammar is a standout on here.

Florence_71
Mind you, if you had turned out to work for ASIO you would have been a ten for sure, just sayin'.

Caffeine_Addict
Maybe I'm using a cover story to protect my identity?

Florence_71
Maybe I'm choosing to humour you and believe your cover story so I don't end up in concrete boots.

Caffeine_Addict
I think you're confusing us with the Mob. We don't use concrete boots. That was sooooo seventies.

Jenny did smile at that. This was . . . She shifted in her chair uncomfortably. Okay so *maybe* it was a *little* fun . . . and *maybe*, when you managed to actually connect with someone, it could be a somewhat pleasant way to pass a few minutes if you were bored.

Caffeine_Addict
Favourite colour, flower and season?

Jenny considered her answer for a moment.

Florence_71
Pink, hydrangeas and winter.

Caffeine_Addict
Nice. Why winter?

Florence_71
I have a slight boot and jacket addiction.

Caffeine_Addict
Gotcha. Enough said. I too have a fashion addiction.

Florence_71
Oh? You buy too many pairs of boots too?

Caffeine_Addict
Socks and sandals.

Florence_71
Oh. No. That's . . . so wrong.

Caffeine_Addict
Really? You're not a fan?

Florence_71
SO WRONG. On so many levels. I think I've found
the reason you're still single.

Caffeine_Addict
You think? Wow. Maybe I'll switch up my footwear
next time I go out on a date and see what happens.

Florence_71
On behalf of everyone with taste—I sincerely
hope you do!

Caffeine_Addict
Jeez, okay, it's not like I have feelings or anything.

Florence_71
Sorry, but it's for your own good. Trust me on this one.

Caffeine_Addict
Well, on that note, I need to get to work. It was nice chatting to you, Florence . . . I hope to do it again soon.

Florence_71
Me too.

The chat ended and Jenny reached for her glass, tipping it to her mouth only to give a huff when she realised it was empty. Her disappointment of course was entirely about that and not that the conversation was over.

Maybe she'd look for the delete button tomorrow.

Nine

Nick rubbed his hands over his face and chuckled. He'd been working on the books for hours when Jenny's face had popped into his mind and he'd wondered what she was doing. He hadn't seen her since the weekend and had found himself glancing up hopefully each time the door opened—which was stupid, since he'd only seen her for the first time last week; chances were slim she'd be popping in unexpectedly for a mid-week drink. *Slim, but not completely nil*, a small voice reminded him optimistically.

He wasn't sure what it was about this woman that was having such a strange effect on him. Maybe he'd been working too hard. Maybe it had been a long time between drinks when it came to women. Not that this town didn't have its share of good-looking women. He'd been given a few opportunities since arriving, but he'd had too much at stake to take any of them up on their offers.

Then Jenny Hayward came barrelling into his life with her ridiculous dates and big brown eyes and tonight, while he'd been sitting at his desk thinking about her, he'd had a sudden urge to check out her profile for himself. He hadn't even been sure he'd be able to find her—he was only on one dating app and he hadn't used it in a long time—so long, in fact, it had taken him three attempts to try to remember his password, but once he was in, it hadn't taken him long to locate her. There was no doubting the profile was hers when he came across it. He'd given a small snort at her account name: Florence_71. He'd skimmed through the pictures, his eyes almost popping out of his head when he came across the one of her in a very short nurse's uniform, which he was fairly sure was not her usual working attire. Then he felt his eyes widen further as he saw the little green light that signalled that she was currently online. What if it wasn't her but her kids trying to set her up on another date? Maybe he'd just feel it out and see. Last time they spoke, she'd been fairly adamant they wouldn't be messing with her love life online anymore.

This is a bad idea. The thought had echoed through his head even as he opened the chat window, but he'd pushed it away and forged on.

Any remaining apprehensions dissipated when the little bubbles began bouncing at the base of the screen and he read her sassy comeback. He was lost—completely and utterly lost as her droll sense of humour gave way to playful banter and he became even more intrigued than he was before. There was no way this could be anyone *but* Jenny.

He hadn't started out wanting to keep his identity a secret—he'd fully intended to tell her who he was—only he was enjoying their chat so much and the moment passed by and then it felt like he'd gone too far to reveal the truth without it seeming weird. Her reaction to the whole age thing the other day and the fact that she thought he was some lowly bartender suggested she probably wouldn't react well if he revealed his identity. It wasn't like he was intending to lead her on or anything—it was just a bit of harmless fun.

But then a twinge of guilt elbowed Nick sharply in the gut and he realised he'd probably taken the whole fake identity thing way beyond what he'd intended. He knew he should put a stop to it. He'd meant to tell her who he was—he really had—but then she'd been so cute trying to figure out his occupation and the chat was unfolding so naturally that he didn't want to ruin it. When he did end the conversation, it had been reluctantly. He could easily have sat and talked to her all night, learned all her secrets and listened to her playful comebacks until the sun came up.

He closed the app, putting his phone in the desk drawer so he wouldn't give in to temptation again. If the army had given him anything, it was the ability to dig deep and find that self-discipline he needed to stop himself doing anything more stupid and to focus on finishing the payroll.

Jenny was cooking dinner when Savannah came inside, calling out a hello.

'I'm in the kitchen,' she called back, stirring the mince in the frypan.

'Is that what I think it is?' Savannah asked, coming over to kiss her mother's cheek and glancing at the ingredients on the bench.

'Yep. I figured since it was such a rainy, miserable day, we needed comfort food.'

'Yes,' Savannah groaned. 'Mum's hug mince. I was thinking about this all day today. If you hadn't already started dinner, I was going to make it.'

The hearty gravy, turmeric, pasta and mince stew was the winter meal of choice around the Hayward table. Jenny had been making it since the kids were small and it always made her smile to know how much they still loved it. The girls had named it 'Mum's hug mince' because apparently it was the next best thing to a hug from Mum when they'd had a crappy day.

'There's a parcel for you on the hall table. When I left for work today there was a pick-up card in with the bills.'

'Oh, thanks,' Jenny said, racking her brain for what it could be. She hadn't made any purchases lately except for—*Oh shit*. Her heart rate spiked momentarily as she remembered exactly what was inside the parcel. That one time she clicked on a post out of curiosity . . . She'd cringed at the sight of every conceivable pleasure device known to mankind. Most of them had seemed anything but pleasurable and some were downright terrifying. She'd worked in emergency long enough to have seen all kinds of things that had 'accidentally' gone into places they weren't designed to go, so she was rather jaded about the whole thing, and yet her hand had hovered over the 'buy now' button. It was just all the sudden interest in her love life the girls had been stirring up that had her thinking about how long it had been since she'd had sex. With a living, breathing human man, not a laughably exaggerated silicone mould. Another thing her years as a nurse had given her was an insight into how unrealistic these plastic phalluses really were compared to the average man. And yet, she'd thought it would be one way to avoid all the endless drama that went along with finding a real man.

'Mum?'

Jenny snapped her head up to look over at her daughter. 'Sorry? What?'

'You're burning the mince,' Savannah said, pointedly looking down at the frypan.

'Oh. Bugger.' Jenny scrambled to turn down the heat and deftly moved the meat around the pan. Managing to avoid too much damage, she finished adding the rest of the ingredients and left the pan to simmer.

'Are you okay?'

'I'm fine,' Jenny said quickly, her thoughts back on the parcel sitting out in the hallway.

The sound of the front door opening and closing was followed by Chloe calling out a hello, moments before she appeared and joined them in the kitchen.

'Mum, you got a parcel,' she announced, holding up the rectangular package, inside a prepaid postage bag. 'What'd you order?'

'Ah . . . I'm not sure.'

'Want me to open it?'

'No!'

All eyes turned towards her and Jenny felt the colour drain from her face before it quickly began to rush back in again. 'It might be that early birthday present I ordered, a while back,' she said, hastily.

'For who?' Chloe asked hopefully.

'Your sister. I like to be organised.' She reached out for the package, trying to remain cool. *Please don't look at the sender information . . .* Surely the company wouldn't put their actual name on it?

Inwardly breathing a sigh of relief, Jenny managed a smile as Chloe relinquished the parcel and headed to the fridge to find a drink. 'Can someone set the table and you can serve yourselves? I'll be right back.'

She forced herself to walk from the room, despite the fact every nerve in her body was screaming to run. What would happen if her daughters discovered what was inside the box? Why the hell had she bought it? This was utterly mortifying. Where was she even going to put the damn thing? Oh my God . . . what if she died suddenly and the girls had to clean out her bedroom and they found it? Why the hell didn't she think of all this before she ordered the stupid thing? She'd throw it in the bin the next time she was home alone. Until then, she'd have to stash it somewhere no one would accidentally find it.

Jenny eyed the bedroom and bit her lip. She couldn't keep it in her closet, it was like a department store with the girls constantly raiding her wardrobe for clothing. Likewise her bathroom—someone was always hogging the main bathroom and hers was often being used. Her bedside table . . . it was just asking to be found there. She continued to scan the room until she spied the dirty clothes hamper. Perfect. The one place no one would stumble across it. Heaven forbid anyone except she would think of doing laundry around here.

Satisfied her dirty little secret was safely hidden at the bottom of her hamper, Jenny composed herself. It was a simple lapse of judgement. A moment of weakness. Tomorrow she'd dispose of it and everything would be fine.

It hadn't been the best morning at work. Jenny let out a weary sigh as she sat down for the first time since her morning shift started and wiggled her toes inside her ugly, but very practical and comfy, work shoes. It was so good to be off her feet. She opened the *Paw Patrol* lunchbox she'd had to borrow from Sophie, who had an extraordinary number of lunch containers for a two-year-old. She'd been too tired the night before to search for the lid to every other container she'd pulled from the cupboard.

As she ate her tuna salad, she flipped through the magazine on the table disinterestedly. There seemed to be a lot of celebrities with way too much time on their hands, Jenny thought, as she scanned the photos of some multimillionaire's kid at a party that had got a bit out of hand on a yacht in some exotic location.

Her phone beeped and she dragged her gaze from the turquoise water and white sandy beach to look at the screen.

New message from Caffeine_Addict.

Jenny dropped her feet from the chair across from her and wiped her hand on a napkin before clicking the link to the app. *This is new. Don't these only open on my laptop?* she thought, timidly reading the message. Then she muttered beneath her breath as she recalled opening a number of things in her search for the delete profile thingy last time she'd logged into the app. God only knew what she'd managed to activate—clearly receiving messages on her phone, for a start.

Caffeine_Addict
Hey. Whatcha up to?

Florence_71
Just having lunch. How are you?

Caffeine_Addict
Same. How goes the search?

Florence_71
I've decided online dating is not for me.

Caffeine_Addict
No. You can't give up that easily.

Florence_71
I think I've gone through enough. If the only men available are the ones coming up on my match list, I think I'd prefer to stay single.

Caffeine_Addict
Yet you're still on the app?

Florence_71
Well, occasionally I get interesting conversation from some guy on here. So I guess it's worth keeping for that.

Caffeine_Addict
Interesting, huh?

Florence_71
Considering the low bar from other conversation on here.

Caffeine_Addict
And here I was thinking I was being all witty and stimulating.

Florence_71
You are. It brightens up my day.

Caffeine_Addict
And nights? Come on, I must feature in some of your dreams, surely?

Florence_71
Bold of you to assume I dream.

Caffeine_Addict
Everyone dreams? Don't they?

Florence_71
If I do, I don't remember them the next morning.

Caffeine_Addict
Maybe you need to relax a bit more before you go to sleep.

Florence_71
Oh, let me guess. You know exactly what would relax me, right?

Caffeine_Addict
As a matter of fact, I do.

Here we go. This was when the one person online she actually kind of looked forward to talking to was going to turn out to be just like all the other men on here.

Florence_71
I'm sure.

Caffeine_Addict
Meditation. It's great for increasing melatonin and serotonin, reducing heart rate and decreasing blood pressure.

Huh. That wasn't the sleazy comeback she was expecting. Jenny stared at the screen and narrowed her eyes.

Florence_71
You almost sound like you're in the medical profession . . . allied health, maybe? Are you sure you're a businessman?

Caffeine_Addict
Bold of you to assume a business owner can't be open-minded enough to embrace new age thinking.

Florence_71
My apologies. Meditation, huh? Maybe I'll give that a go.

Caffeine_Addict
Let me know how it goes. I gotta go. Talk soon.

Jenny put her phone back on the table and fought the disappointment that followed. She had no idea who this guy was, or what they were actually doing, but she was enjoying their banter and it was refreshing to talk to a man and not have it end in some disaster of a date. She quickly finished the rest of her lunch and washed the container before heading back out, hoping that the afternoon wouldn't be as crazy as the morning had been.

Ten

Jenny closed her eyes as the meditation podcast started on her phone. 'Breathe in . . . and out,' came the sleepy-sounding male voice. Obediently, Jenny did as she was told, willing her body to unwind and relax. She'd been trying, unsuccessfully, to master meditation on and off over the last year. She wanted to wrestle her racing thoughts and stress into submission, but for some reason her thoughts never stayed in 'the zone'. It wasn't for any lack of trying—she desperately wanted to float on that bloody fluffy white cloud this guy kept talking to her about, but within a few minutes of starting, her mind would wander and she'd forget to listen to the next step and end up still awake by the end of the track. *Twenty minutes to blissful sleep meditation, my arse.* She reached over and turned off her phone, lying on her back to stare up at the ceiling with a frustrated huff.

Just go and open it. The thought came loud and clear, making her frown. *You know you want to. The curiosity is eating at you.* Jenny refused to turn her head to the doorway of her ensuite where the laundry basket stood. 'Absolutely not,' she growled.

The chat with her online buddy resurfaced and, not for the first time, she wished he had a profile photo. She had no idea what he looked like and that really should have been a huge red flag, only it wasn't. Without an image in her mind, their conversations felt . . . different, somehow. He could be anyone—maybe he was a three-hundred-kilo housebound computer geek; maybe he was just an average, everyday shy guy with a dad bod and low self-esteem. Still, she couldn't help but wonder. A sudden image of a brown-haired, hazel-eyed face flashed through her mind and she caught her breath. She had to admit she kind of missed seeing Nick. Somehow he'd managed to get under her skin and she often found herself thinking about him. She'd even been tempted to head to the pub just so she could possibly bump into him again, but she always chickened out.

Orgasms make you sleep better—do it for your stress levels and insomnia.

Okay, so maybe there was *some* scientific evidence behind this theory, and lord knows she was sick and tired of lying awake at night stressing . . . *Oh, for goodness' sake.*

Jenny threw back the covers and stomped across the room to retrieve the box from the laundry hamper. Despite her reservations, she found herself taking out the small device. It didn't look all that scary; maybe she'd ordered the wrong thing?

She'd shied away from the disturbing array of intimidating-looking penis-shaped objects the site had offered. She didn't particularly fancy walking funny for a few days after using one of them. This one had looked far less intimidating, like a computer mouse.

Placing it on the bed beside her, she opened the instruction sheet, which folded out to the size of an enormous road map of Europe and was filled with every conceivable language except, it seemed, English. *The Stimulator*, the brochure boasted, *is a powerful advancement in pleasurable stimulation. Whisper-quiet and discreet. Designed to stimulate with unlimited possibilities.*

Well, that sounded . . . promising. She located the right instructions, but they were completely unhelpful as to exactly *how* you were supposed to use the stupid thing.

Well, it can't be rocket science.

After a moment of investigation, she worked out how to turn it on, then gave a snort at the irony.

A low hum sounded and a gentle vibration ran through her palm. *That's not too bad*, she thought, lying back against her pillows and pulling the blankets up under her chin. At the first contact with the sensitive area that had definitely not had any significant contact for a long time, Jenny jumped. *Okay, so far so good.* She pressed the button on the side again and the vibrations got a little stronger, as did the sound. Footsteps on the staircase alerted her to one of the girls coming up to their bedroom and she quickly pressed the button to turn the device off, only for the gadget to speed up more. What the hell? She pressed it again and the speed of the vibrations increased and the hum grew even louder. *What the actual f—*

The footsteps halted and Jenny frantically continued to press the button—it was the power switch, but apparently it had to go through a complete cycle of speeds before it could be turned off. *Shit, shittity, shit!* The hum had now turned into the sound of a small engine revving for take-off and Jenny sucked in a startled breath as the vibrations suddenly hit something rather unexpectedly pleasing as they continued to speed up. 'Mother F—' Jenny gasped, as one hand grasped the blankets and the other frantically hit the power button.

'Mum? Are you okay?' Brittany's concerned voice sounded at the door.

Click, click, click. How many freaking modes did this bloody thing have? Jenny clasped her thighs together tightly in an attempt to muffle the noise, but it only intensified the vibrations, which led to a sudden explosion of stars before her eyes as a soundless cry of pleasure escaped, leaving her body sagging like a rag doll. Then, with one last click, everything went blessedly silent, just as the door cracked open the tiniest bit and her daughter stuck her head in.

'I thought I heard you calling out?'

'No. No . . . maybe I was having a dream or something,' Jenny said, pushing her hair out of her face as she scrambled to sit up, grateful the only light coming into the room was from the hallway. 'Everything's fine.'

'Okay then. Goodnight.'

''Night,' Jenny called, before collapsing back onto her pillows and letting out a long sigh. *Discreet? Compared to what? A fighter jet landing inside the house?* Jenny squeezed her eyes shut, feeling humiliated. How utterly embarrassing it would have been to get caught by her daughter doing . . . *that*. The nurse side of her gave a disappointed roll of her eyes at her priggish reaction. Women's sexual health was something she often had to educate patients about, and yet, sneaking about, ordering things off the internet and hiding them, felt anything but normal or natural. She'd throw it away tomorrow, she decided with a determined nod and closed her eyes.

When she woke up the next morning, Jenny realised she'd had a solid eight hours' sleep. That never happened. Her gaze lingered on the basket in the corner and she gave a small grunt. It could have been a fluke. The only logical thing to do was to try it again and test the results to make sure. Maybe throwing it out *was* being a little hasty. Maybe she'd hold off for a few more days . . . just to see.

Eleven

Jenny slid into the office chair at the nurse's station to finish filling out the never-ending paperwork for her last patient, but looked up as she heard the conversation at the front desk. Normally their ward clerk, Tammy, wasn't easy to rattle—she could hold her own against the vocal, entitled patients who, nine times out of ten, were either there for something that could have easily waited until they could get into their GP or were intoxicated young males who liked to puff up their chest when they were brave with alcohol—so hearing her somewhat strained tone put her on immediate alert.

'Jen!' Tammy called, pressing the button to open the security door across from them to admit someone on the other side.

Jenny didn't bother to ask any questions as she slid her pen into the pocket of her work trousers and crossed the room to meet whoever was about to come through the door.

She faltered as she recognised Nick, but quickly turned her attention to the young guy he was supporting, one hand clamped over the kid's arm, which was wrapped in a red cloth. On closer inspection, she realised the cloth was a once-white tea towel now saturated with blood.

'Get him in here,' Jenny instructed, indicating an empty bed. She was concerned by the amount of blood and its bright colour.

'What's your name, mate?' she asked the boy, briskly but calmly.

He was leaning heavily into Nick and didn't seem to hear her.

'What's his name?' she asked Nick.

When there was no immediate response, Jenny looked up to see Nick looking distant.

'Nick! What's his name?'

Her tone seemed to snap him back from wherever he'd just been.

'Dylan,' he replied.

As Nick helped the semiconscious young man onto the bed, Jenny pulled on a set of gloves and slid on a pair of plastic goggles from a nearby trolley, calling out for the other RN. The guy looked to be in his early twenties and was clammy and pale.

'What happened?' she asked, mentally cataloguing the damage.

'He was cutting meat and got caught in the bandsaw at work.'

Jenny flinched inwardly but focused on what needed to be done. She nodded for Nick to remove the pressure he was still applying and removed the towel to find a torniquet had been applied and the arm was wrapped adequately, if roughly.

'It didn't go right through, but close enough,' Nick told her as she unwrapped the bandage. 'There was significant bone damage and some arterial bleeding. I packed the wound as best I could to try and stem the blood loss.'

Jenny sent him a quick glance before looking back at the damaged arm, noting that the wound had indeed been expertly packed with gauze, which, along with the tourniquet, was doing a good job of slowing the amount of blood Dylan was losing. A small trickle was still pulsing in the corner of the wound above his wrist and she quickly applied more gauze and pressure. She was worried about the circulation to his hand and the fact he was beginning to lose consciousness. His blood pressure was dropping. The care he'd received at the scene had saved his life so far, but the small amount of blood pumping from the wound worried Jenny more than she cared to admit. He'd definitely hit his radial artery.

'Where's the doctor?' Nick asked from beside her but standing a respectful distance away to avoid getting in the way.

'We don't have one full-time here. This is a multipurpose hospital and I'm the resident nurse practitioner.'

Donna, the other registered nurse, had begun gathering the supplies they'd need. She and Donna had developed a solid work partnership over the years and she was glad they were rostered on together today.

Jenny accepted the crystalloids and volume-expanding fluid Donna placed on the tray between them, needing the plasma and saline to replace some of the fluids Dylan had already lost in lieu of the blood bags that their smaller hospital simply didn't have on hand.

'Tammy, can you call through for a flight out of here ASAP. I'll talk to them once you get them on the line,' she called out to the ward clerk as she and Donna worked to stabilise their patient, keeping a close eye on his stats.

'Hey, Dylan, can you hear me?' Jenny asked, eyeing the young man's drowsy expression and rubbing his other arm to try and stimulate a response. He hadn't been able to tell her anything coherently since coming in. It was a race against time to get him out of here and into an operating theatre.

It was the smell of the hospital that interrupted the firm hold Nick had had on his emotions since the moment he'd heard the commotion in the kitchen and run in to find Dylan hunched over the bandsaw, screaming in agony.

His training had clicked in automatically—he hadn't even stopped to think about what he was doing before he'd grabbed one of the kitchen's well-equipped first-aid kits. The veil of calm that descended upon him blocked out the rest of the commotion. He'd thrown out orders more to keep everyone else busy. Someone called an ambulance while another took the rest of the staff out into the main bar, making more room to work and defuse some of the panic and alarm while Nick focused on saving the kid's life. There'd been no time to wait for the ambulance—since it would have had to come from Hamwell.

They'd carried Dylan to his car and Nick drove with single-mindedness and determination, barely recalling the short trip to the small, sprawling building on the outskirts of town that housed the local hospital.

He was still operating on adrenalin and training when he walked inside and although he registered that Jenny was there, he hadn't been able to react—the smell had already started to chip away at his emotions. He hadn't batted an eye at the blood or the chaos going on around him—even the kid's sobbing and gut-wrenching groans hadn't shaken his steely control—but one whiff of that bloody antiseptic, sterile hospital, and it all started crumbling. He remembered the fluorescent lights flashing as he jogged beside the stretcher being wheeled towards the operating theatre, then staring at the dried blood on his hands as he listened to the doctor deliver the news that Richie hadn't made it.

He stepped away from the edge of Dylan's bed and let the two nurses work. Their hurried yet measured movements gave him some much-needed comfort and he felt the heavy memories subside as the sounds of the emergency room slowly began to filter in.

Before he knew it, they were moving again.

Jenny had left the room briefly to take a call and the next minute they were wheeling the bed out of the room and looking skyward as a speck grew larger as it drew closer and the helicopter landed. Jenny greeted the young doctor who jogged across the landing pad to the double swinging doors of the Emergency Department and gave him a quick handover of Dylan and his injuries, then they were rushing Dylan out to the waiting chopper. Nick stood inside the hospital, watching as the helicopter lifted off and flew away to save Dylan's life.

Fuck this day.

❖

Jenny turned to Nick and lightly touched his arm. 'Come on, I want to make sure you're okay.'

'Me?' he replied, looking at her. 'I'm fine.'

'Yeah, but let's just get you something to drink.'

'I work in a pub, remember,' he said, with a wry twist of his lips.

'Not that kind of drink.' She grinned back briefly before leading him to the small common area used for the maternity ward. At the moment they had no babies due and it was quiet.

Jenny pulled out two plastic cups and dug out some coffee, sugar and biscuits then put the jug on to boil.

'That was pretty impressive,' Nick said as she handed him a coffee.

'It was bloody scary, is what it was,' Jenny said, making an effort to sound matter of fact rather than weary. Now that her part was over, the adrenalin that had been pumping through her earlier was beginning to ease, leaving her exhausted and a little shaky.

'You stayed calm and handled it like a pro,' he said with a note of sincerity.

'He wouldn't have made it this far if you hadn't been at the scene and did what you did. *That* was impressive,' she said. The statistics she'd learned years ago replayed in her head: if the radial artery was severed, a person could lose consciousness in as little as thirty seconds and die in around two minutes. Time was absolutely critical. She was still a little stunned that they'd somehow kept Dylan alive this long, all things considered. 'Not many people would have known to pack a wound and apply a torniquet like that.'

'Training,' he said simply.

'As what?'

'I was in the army.'

'How long were you in for?'

'Nineteen years.'

'From the army to bartending,' she said. 'What made you make that kind of change?'

'It was time to get out. I wanted to do something different.'

'Were you trained as an army medic?'

'I did a few courses—mostly field training in combat first aid. It came in handy when I was deployed.'

'You were in Afghanistan?' she asked, even more curious about him now.

'Among other places, yeah. Feels like a lifetime ago, though.'

'And now you're a bartender?'

He held her gaze but gave nothing away. 'Yep.'

'You didn't want to go into some kind of medical career once you left the military?' She'd worked with a few ambos who'd been in the army, and they knew their stuff. After today, it was clear Nick had skills he could be using.

'Nope.'

Interesting, she thought, detecting a distinct cooling in his demeanour. Clearly this was a subject matter he wasn't comfortable talking about. 'Well, Dylan was lucky you were there. I didn't realise kitchens had bandsaws,' she said, frowning a little. Sharp knives and mincer machines she'd heard of as causes of some horrific kitchen and workplace injuries, but not a saw.

'Most don't, unless they process their own meat, which we do,' he said. 'That's the whole foundation of the new restaurant. We use locally sourced meat. It's cut specifically for whatever the chef needs on the night. The super-sized steaks are our signature.'

That was true—she'd never seen steaks as thick or melt in your mouth as the ones at the Coach House. 'Maybe the boss needs to give a refresher course on safety.'

'It's sorted,' Nick said. 'The kid only started his apprenticeship last week. I'm no expert, but those injuries didn't look too promising for him to have much use of his hand.'

'It's bad,' Jenny agreed. 'But with a good enough surgeon, and a lot of rehab, it's surprising how well people can recover.'

'You think he'll be okay?'

'I think the fact he got this far means he's got every chance to make it. They'll put him straight into surgery as soon as he lands. You were able to stem that blood loss and that was my major concern. There was nothing we could do for him here except stabilise and get him to an operating theatre.'

'Do you get much excitement like that here?' he asked, watching her over his coffee cup.

'Thankfully not much. But we get the occasional farm or car accident—sometimes a little too frequently,' she said recalling the last occasion where a local farmer had been trapped under his tractor. She shrugged. 'Mostly, though, we like things nice and calm.'

'Here's to that,' he said, lifting his cup in mock salute.

'Are you doing okay?' she asked after a few moments of silence.

'Me?' He seemed surprised by the question.

'Yeah, you.' She smiled. 'You've been through a pretty harrowing experience. I don't imagine today is something you deal with every shift.'

'Nah, I'm fine.'

'It's just that you didn't look fine at one point, and if you want someone to talk to, or you'd rather talk to someone else, I can arrange some counselling or support.'

'I'm fine,' he said with a lot more emphasis, draining the remaining coffee before placing the empty cup on the table and standing up.

'It's not some kind of weakness, you know,' she said gently.

'Thanks. I'll remember that.'

His unexpected sarcasm caught Jenny by surprise and she took a moment to pull back her initial hurt. This wasn't personal, she reminded herself, slipping back into professional mode. 'Trauma can trigger things. All I'm saying is, if at some point over the next few days you find yourself needing to talk about it, I'm more than happy to help you do that.'

'Like I said, I'm fine. I have to get back to work.'

'I'm sure your boss wouldn't object to you taking the rest of the day off.'

'We're already short-staffed. Thanks again.'

He turned and strode from the room before she could say goodbye, leaving her staring at the doorway. She hadn't imagined the moment he'd looked almost blank or the beads of sweat on his forehead. She made a note to follow it up later, but for now, she had to get back to work—today's excitement meant there'd be a stack of paperwork a mile high she needed to complete.

Twelve

Jenny opened the swinging door of the pub and slid her sunglasses onto the top of her head. The now-familiar scent of beer mixed with new-carpet smell and food cooking hit her as she stepped inside.

There was the merry tinkle of a poker machine playing in the distance, its electronic-sounding whirl and bells ringing indicating someone had just had a win. Jenny noted there were no customers sitting in the bar area, the tables all empty in this time between lunch and dinner service. She'd never been here during the day on a weekday before.

A loud crash behind a set of white doors was followed by a string of foul language that echoed through the quiet pub. Jenny raised her eyebrows in surprise.

'You're useless! Less than useless!' a man practically screamed, with more swearing—some so violent that Jenny felt herself straighten with indignation. Who spoke like that?

Seconds later the doors swung open and a young woman rushed out, covering her face with her hands, just as a tall figure came down the staircase nearby and stepped into her path, holding her by the arms, until she looked up and started crying harder.

'Go out to the staff room and I'll be there in a minute,' Nick instructed, before walking past Jenny to push through the swinging doors of the kitchen with such force they hit the wall behind them and slammed shut. Jenny watched the young woman head out to the rear of the hotel, but her attention was once again drawn to whatever was going on behind the twin doors.

There was a crash and a bang and the sound of something spinning on a hard floor.

'Look what the stupid bitch did! She dropped the whole tray—there's no time to make a new batch before tonight's service—'

'I don't care what happened. You do not speak to staff like that.'

'The kitchen is my domain. Don't tell me how to run it.'

'I'm not telling you anything. I'm promising. If I hear you speak to anyone like that again, you *won't* be able to speak—ever again. Understand?'

'You're just the hired help like me. And don't you forget it. I don't take orders from you.'

'After I put in a report about the Dylan situation, you'll be looking for a new career.'

'It isn't my fault the kid is a bloody halfwit.'

'It was your responsibility to make sure he was trained and supervised. He was an apprentice,' Nick said, his voice low and controlled.

'I'm not takin' the fall for this.'

'If they find out you didn't follow that bloody OHS training you were told to do—'

'I told ya, I did.'

'Yeah, well, they'll be interviewing Dylan when he's up to it, so you wanna hope you did.'

'Like I said—I'm not takin' the fall. I'll take everyone else here down with me.'

'Try it.'

'Get out of my kitchen.'

'If I hear you speaking that way to another employee again, you'll answer to me. You understand?'

Jenny heard the other man mutter something unintelligible seconds before the doors swung open and Nick came out, halting as he spotted her standing at the bar.

'Jenny.'

'Hi. I'm sorry, I didn't mean to overhear . . . I walked in and . . .'

Nick glanced over his shoulder at the closed kitchen door before crossing to her. 'Sorry about that.'

'No, I'm sorry. I don't want to interrupt.'

'What can I get you?' he asked.

'Oh. Nothing,' Jenny said, shaking her head. 'I actually just dropped by to see how you were doing.'

He turned back from reaching for a glass and looked at her blankly.

'I know you said you were fine earlier, but I thought I'd check in case things have had time to sink in.'

'I'm actually busy at the moment,' he said, and although the words weren't blunt, they were final and very clear. He didn't want any help.

'Yeah, okay. It's all good.'

She turned towards the door, hearing his impatient sigh before he called, 'But thanks.'

She didn't bother stopping but lifted a hand in reply. She'd tried. You couldn't push people to take your advice, and who knows, maybe he *was* fine—his training may very well have conditioned him to handle trauma. But it didn't mean that he wouldn't replay what had happened in his head at some point and maybe feel like he needed to talk about it. Or not, she supposed, pushing Nick out of her thoughts. If he wanted help, she'd told him how to get it. The ball was well and truly in his court now.

Nick sat up in bed breathing heavily, disorientated, before the nightmare released its claw-like grip on his brain and his surroundings filtered back in. He wasn't in that dimly lit shed, kneeling in the dirt in a pool of blood, desperately trying to save his mate's life.

He swore—more a groan than anything else. He hadn't had that dream in ages. But it was inevitable after today. The blood and the hospital . . . He'd let his guard down,

He gave a sigh before lowering himself down and closing his eyes. He knew Jenny had been worried about him and he felt bad about the way he'd thrown that concern back in her face when she'd dropped in to check on him earlier, but it'd caught him off guard—the whole thing: the blood, the memories . . . the guilt. He was that kid's boss. He was responsible for his safety. There should never be a concern that a nineteen-year-old could go to work in the morning and not come home. *Fuck. He could have died. Like Richie.*

No, not like Richie—not in the same way. Richie's death hadn't been an accident.

Nick felt despair threaten to engulf him once more. He hadn't picked up on the signs that his mate was struggling after they'd gotten back from their tour—hell, they'd all been struggling in one way or other, but Richie had always been the happy-go-lucky type, always up for a laugh. He was the last one any of them thought would take his own life like that.

Nick should have known—he should have asked—why hadn't he asked if Richie had been doing okay? Maybe that would have made a difference? Maybe Richie would have felt too embarrassed to bring it up first, but if they'd spoken about it . . .

None of them had. None of the mates he'd served with ever talked about the dark stuff. That would have seemed weak. They were trained to be hard, tougher than most. To adapt and overcome. But no one told them how to handle the black moods, the bottomless pit of emptiness—the stuff he didn't even know *how* to describe to someone, even if he had wanted to—that would follow them in the years afterwards. The only good that had come from the whole messed-up thing was that Richie's death *had* eventually got Nick and his mates talking.

It hadn't fixed anything like some miracle on-off switch, but it *had* been a release valve of sorts and he knew that it'd helped him come to terms with a few of his own demons.

Nick glanced over at his phone vibrating on the bedside table and rolled his head back to stare up at the ceiling, ignoring the caller. He swore softly when the phone continued to ring insistently.

'Hello,' he said, hearing the shortness in his tone and not caring. He wasn't in the mood for one of his sister's lectures and he knew he was sure to get one. He'd been dodging her calls for the last forty-eight hours.

'Finally he answers his phone,' Susie's cultured tones came over the line impatiently. He could picture her platinum-blonde hair, meticulously straightened and pulled back in a tight ponytail that flipped over her shoulder like a slinky snake. The fake English accent grated on his nerves more than usual. She'd been born and bred in Penrith, in Western Sydney, just like he had, and he didn't care how long she'd lived overseas, there was no way she'd lost her accent to that extent.

'I've been busy,' Nick said, biting back a weary sigh as he swung his legs to the floor and sat on the edge of his bed.

'So I heard. When were you planning on informing me about what happened in the kitchen?'

'When I finished sorting everything out.'

'I shouldn't have to hear it from the chef. You're the manager, Nicolas. I'm your partner. You need to report to me about these things.'

'Report to you?' he replied, and a hard edge had crept into his voice.

'I am your business partner. It's my money that I'm sinking into this venture. Money that you seem to be happily burning your way through.'

Nick clenched his jaw then made a conscious effort to relax it when his dentist's warning about cracking teeth rang in his head. 'Everything's under control. There's nothing you need to do.'

'Except talk your chef down from leaving,' Susie pointed out. 'You're welcome, by the way—I've convinced him to stay.'

'He's a liability, Susie.'

'He's the *only thing* this business has going for it. If you've got any hope of recouping any kind of investment, you're going to need his name. Which is the other reason I'm calling. I've lined up an interview with *Fine Dining*. As a favour to me, the editor is sending out a photographer to do a photo shoot and there'll be a feature story on the whole "city boy, war veteran, bringing culture to the outback" kind of thing.'

What the hell? 'Don't you think you should have run this past me first?'

'I'm running it past you *now*,' she said, and he could picture her waving a dismissive manicured hand. 'Again, *you're welcome.*'

Nick counted to five under his breath. 'I need to plan for that kind of thing . . . When are they coming?'

'Next week.'

'Next wee—' He let out an incredulous scoff. 'Are you crazy?'

'That's the only spot they had open—an opportunity like this won't come around again. Besides, it's not as though you're rushed off your feet out there,' she said dryly. 'I've seen the books. I'm sure you'll have plenty of time to prepare. Make it happen, Nick.'

He listened to dead air as she disconnected the call then let out a harsh curse. As siblings, they were polar opposites and he both loved and hated her in equal measure.

Hate was a strong word. He didn't hate Susie. He just didn't understand her—or she him. Susie had left home at a young age and fought her way to the top—she was self-made in every sense of the word. Their parents had been strict and held some pretty conformist views on raising children, but they had somehow managed to end up with not one, but two teenage delinquents. After their parents' deaths, Susie had spent most of Nick's adult life trying to mould him into something he'd never be and it drove him nuts. He'd never be the businessman working in her multimillion-dollar business that she wanted.

For all their differences, he and Susie did share a few similarities, but where she was driven to make money and be successful, he was just driven to fulfil his goals—and that was it. He didn't want to make a million dollars or turn his pub and restaurant into a franchise or set up in cities across the world or whatever the hell Susie's grand plan was. All he wanted was his little pub in a country town and a bit of peace and quiet.

Chalk and cheese, he thought again, as he tossed the phone on the end of the bed and rose slowly to take a shower.

Thirteen

Jenny walked out the front door of the vet's, pushing the heavy door with her hip as she struggled with the stupid cat carrier that contained one very disgruntled cat. 'Once again, I'm so sorry, Bruce,' Jenny called to the middle-aged veterinarian who held a swab against his bleeding hand as his receptionist wife fussed about looking for antiseptic. She was going to have to find another vet—even if that meant driving all the way to Hamwell every time Fat Cat needed a check-up. She was pretty sure the two vets who ran the local practice drew straws to see which one got her animal and the time was coming when she'd be asked to take her bad-tempered feline elsewhere.

'Good work, Fat Cat,' Jenny muttered as she shoved the carrier into the back seat and secured it with a seatbelt. 'You're going to get us banned. Would it kill you to, *just once*, not draw blood?'

The cat gave a mournful yowl as Jenny shook her head.

'Hey.'

Jenny swore as her head hit the door frame. She spun to find Nick standing beside the vehicle.

'Are you okay?' he asked, stepping forward.

'I'm fine. You startled me that's all,' she said, rubbing her head.

'Sorry.'

'It's fine,' she said, gingerly examining her fingers, relieved to see there was no blood.

'I, ah . . . I'm glad I bumped into you,' he said, his shoulders hunching as he shoved his hands into the small front pockets of his jeans. 'I wanted to apologise for the other day when you came in to check on me. I probably sounded like a jerk.'

Jenny stepped away from the car and shut the back door, silencing the dramatic protesting still coming from the cat carrier. 'You'd had a rough day,' she said, leaning against the vehicle.

'Yeah. But you'd picked up on something and at the time I wasn't in the right frame of mind to talk about it, I guess.'

Jenny forgot about her throbbing head and the outraged cat noises coming from inside the car as she switched to professional mode.

'I lost a mate, a few years back now. Being in the hospital brought it all back. It was the first time I'd been inside a hospital since, and I don't know . . . it just hit me. Kind of caught me off guard. I didn't mean to brush you off the way I did. I just wanted to say I'm sorry.'

'That's okay. Smells and sounds can often trigger bad memories. I'm sorry about your friend. Was it some kind of workplace accident?'

He shrugged. 'It wasn't an accident. It was a gunshot wound.'

Jenny felt her heart catch. 'Oh, Nick. I'm so sorry,' she said, and lightly touched his arm. She should have suspected. 'Was it during your time overseas? In the army?'

'No. Afterwards—once we came home. It was . . . self-inflicted,' he said. 'He wasn't coping too well after we got back.'

'Oh, Nick.' She stopped, feeling the breath leave her body. At the time, she'd wondered if his reaction had been because of things he'd seen during his time overseas serving in the army. It hadn't crossed her mind that it could have been something like this. She didn't have much experience with returned service men and women, but she had heard enough from other nursing staff to know that suicide numbers in that profession were a concern.

'You probably won't believe me when I say that I'm actually okay with it all now. I mean, not that you can ever be okay with it, but it was a turning point for a lot of us who knew Richie. It was a wake-up call we all needed.'

'That's good, then,' she said and honestly meant it. It wasn't up to her to lecture him about getting appropriate help—clearly he'd dealt with this and probably knew more about counselling and other avenues to turn to than she could ever offer him.

'I'd better let you get back to whatever it was you were doing,' he said, eyeing the car and the source of the noises that came from within it.

'Oh. Yeah. I have to get the cat home. It was good to see you.'

'You too,' Nick said. 'Guess I'll see you around. When's the next big date?'

'When hell freezes over,' she said, reaching for the door handle. She wondered why he looked so nervous.

'Aw, come on. You aren't giving up that easy?'

'I'd rather think of it as a tactical retreat. There's nothing out there in the online dating world for me.'

'Not even some decent conversation?'

A memory of her mystery messenger man briefly appeared before she shook her head with a small smile. 'Nothing online is real.'

She slid in behind the steering wheel and closed the door, giving Nick a small wave as she reversed out of the spot. She endured a feline tongue lashing the entire way home.

Nick watched Jenny drive away and felt a lurch inside, like something had slipped out of place, leaving an empty spot behind.

He enjoyed their evening chats, even though he vowed to tell her the truth each time he opened the chat window, but each time he managed to chicken out of it. Maybe Jenny didn't get as much out of them as he did, though—she'd seemed pretty sure just now that the online world wasn't exactly her favourite thing. He'd been hoping to maybe work in an opening to broach the subject of his identity, but this conversation had changed his mind. He hadn't meant to tell her about Richie—he never spoke about that with anyone—but there was something about Jenny that had him spilling his guts without even meaning to. She was easy to talk to. He trusted her. Was he willing to lose that if he told her he was the guy on the other end of their nightly banter? It was a risk he didn't feel comfortable taking just yet. He was beginning to like that fun side of her way too much to lose it now.

The bell above the door tinkled merrily as Jenny entered the hairdressers. The sound of hair dryers blasting and country music crooning over the speakers greeted her.

'Well, look who the cat dragged in!' a friendly voice boomed from the rear of the salon and Jenny grinned. Laurel had been her hairdresser ever since she had moved here. She'd been part of pretty much every major life event since—from kids going through primary school dramas and the terrible teen years to her marriage break-up. The woman should have a degree in counselling. Jenny had never intended to talk about her marriage break-up in public, except somehow, Laurel had her talking about the whole terrible mess and from then on, she was always a willing ear to vent to. Not that Jenny overshared—at least, she tried not to. The last thing she wanted was for the entire town to be involved in her personal problems.

'I know it's been a while,' Jenny admitted. She'd had to cancel her last appointment when she'd been called in to cover someone's shift.

'*Quite* a while,' Laurel drawled, as she lifted a strand of hair to inspect the split ends critically. 'Never mind, nothing we can't fix,' she said, sending Jenny a confident nod in the mirror before fastening a black cape around her neck with an expert flourish, then disappearing out the back of the salon to mix a batch of her magic potions that would transform Jenny's plain old brown hair into a much more interesting shade of chocolate with caramel and latte highlights.

'So, word around town is you've been busy,' Laurel said, as she began parting Jenny's hair and pinning it up in sections.

'Work's been its usual frantic chaos,' Jenny agreed.

'I'm not talking about work,' the hairdresser said, shaking her long, dark locks. 'I'm talking about the assortment of men you've been spotted dining out with lately.'

Jenny blanched, her eyes widening as she held the amused smirk of her friend's gaze in the mirror, before she shot a look around the salon.

'No one's going to hear,' Laurel said, dismissing Jenny's obvious distress. 'Edna's stuck under the heat lamp and deaf as a post at the best of times and Barb's busy reading about the latest royal scandal. So?' she prompted impatiently. 'Tell me everything.'

'There's nothing to tell,' Jenny mumbled. 'It wasn't my idea. The girls set me up on some dumb dating app and suddenly I had all these dates lined up.'

'And?'

Jenny shrugged. 'And nothing.'

Laurel stopped pinning her hair to hold her gaze pointedly. 'You went out on multiple dates for the first time since your divorce and you're telling me there was nothing? With any of them?'

Jenny tried not to squirm under her friend's disbelieving expression. 'Well, I mean, they were . . . Oh, I don't know.'

She let out a frustrated sigh. 'They were just a little . . . dull. I guess.'

'So, none of them tickled ya fancy?' Laurel asked, wiggling her eyebrows suggestively.

Jenny bit back a smile at the other woman's antics. 'No, not really.'

'Ah, well, there's gotta be plenty more out there to get through. It's a good thing you're not settling for just anything,' Laurel said, nodding her head firmly.

'I'm beginning to think that's all there might be . . . you know, in my age group,' Jenny said, a little despondent at the thought.

'Your age group? What are you talking about?'

'It's just that the men I've seen on there who are within my age parameters, are so . . . I don't know, either sleazy or quite a bit older.'

'Then you need to adjust those age settings.'

'Oh, yeah,' Jenny scoffed. 'Because someone younger would be so interested in a fifty-year-old.'

'A few years isn't going to bother anyone—besides, you're hardly over the hill at fifty, you know.'

'Yeah, I know . . . but I can't imagine dating someone younger. It just seems so . . . cougar-y,' Jenny said, wrinkling her nose.

Laurel let out a loud hoot, drawing the attention of another customer seated further down the salon. 'I think you underestimate the cougar appeal.'

'I don't need another child, thank you very much. I want someone who's my equal, in age as well as mentality.'

'And yet, look what's out there,' Laurel reminded her and instantly Jenny's mood dipped. 'Oh, come on, it's not that bad. You've only started looking. There's bound to be someone out there that'll light your fire again. It'll happen.'

'That's the thing though, I'm not even sure I *am* looking.'

'Honey, we're the same vintage and I'm tellin' you, we have needs. You might have been able to bury them for a long time, but I'm willing to bet they've been stirring. You can't keep denying the fact you are a woman in her prime. You are far too young to let yourself sit around collecting cobwebs.'

'Charming image.'

Laurel shrugged. 'It's the truth. Besides, you don't see men setting their age limits to their own age, do you? No siree. They have no problem dating a woman decades younger, so why the hell can't you? Didn't stop your ex, did it?'

Oh, that was a low blow. A fair point, but still, low.

Laurel changed the topic and they chatted about her kids and grandchildren, but Jenny pondered her advice about the age gap. Maybe there was a stigma of sorts attached to women and younger men and maybe it wasn't exactly fair . . . but could she actually do it herself?

With Jenny's hair washed and towelled off, Laurel pulled her chair over to sit behind her and tilted her head this way and that. 'You've known me a long time now, correct?' she asked, seemingly out of the blue, making Jenny chuckle at the unexpected comment.

'I have.'

Laurel nodded. 'So you trust me, right?'

Jenny eyed her cautiously in the mirror but nodded.

'Okay. So, I'd really like you to trust me now and let me do something a little bit different with the cut today. I promise it won't be anything extreme. Come on, live a little,' Laurel said, playfully pushing her shoulder.

'Oh, fine,' Jenny said, blowing out a long breath.

Laurel gave a little squeal as she bounced up and down on her seat and clapped her hands. 'This is going to be ah-mazing,' she promised, her attention suddenly zeroed in on Jenny's head as she went into some kind of creative trance.

Oh, God, what have I done?

Jenny paused and took a steadying breath before opening the front door and stepping inside. She hung her handbag on the hook and braced herself for the reaction she was about to get from her family.

'Mum, have you seen any long-sleeve T-shirts for Sophie? I swear I washed some the other day but I can't find them anywhere,' Brittany said, walking towards a pile of clothes in a laundry basket on the lounge.

'Ah, no. Can't say I have,' Jenny said, kinking an eyebrow as her daughter walked straight past her.

Chloe came running down the stairs and threw a general 'Bye,' over her shoulder, presumably in a rush and running late for her shift at the supermarket.

'Mum, I can't find my car keys,' Savannah yelled, moments before she came hurtling through the room like a mini cyclone. 'I'm going to be late.'

'Have you looked on the key hook in the kitchen?' *Where they're supposed to be.*

'I looked there,' Savannah muttered, and dropped the cushion she'd been lifting, to about face, and head back to the kitchen. Jenny heard some rummaging about then the clinking of keys. 'Found them!'

'Awesome,' Jenny called.

'Bye, Mum, love you.'

Jenny stood in the centre of the lounge room and listened to the house settle back into calm once again. She could hear the hallway clock ticking loudly. *That went well*, she thought, feeling a little despondent that no one had even noticed her new do, before heading upstairs to take a shower.

Fourteen

Jenny stared at herself in the mirror for a long time as she lightly dusted the powdered foundation across her face. Beth had called and suggested going out for dinner, and considering she'd just had her hair done and it would be completely wasted sitting at home in front of the TV, she'd accepted. It was hard to believe the difference a hairstyle could make. She loved the new blonde highlights and darker base Laurel had talked her into this time and her work as a stylist was second to none. She'd cut Jenny's long, boring hair above her shoulders and it had sprung into its natural curls once the weight of the length had come off. Then she'd reshaped it to create this bouncy, wavy beach style, longer at the front so Jenny could still pull it back or tuck it behind her ears with a slightly off-centre side part. She looked so . . . different. Was this really the mum of three and grandmother who'd been content to live like a hermit for the last two years?

She reached up and touched a curl Laurel had expertly created with her hot wand and that Jenny probably had no hope of ever recreating later and felt a rush of uncertainty come over her. What was happening to her life? Everything felt so different now, yet only a few weeks earlier she'd been blissfully unaware of any of the tribulations that came with entering the dating world. This wasn't her. She wasn't ready to make changes to her life.

Panic began to stir inside her, and she thought about grabbing a tissue and wiping away her make-up, but Brittany calling from downstairs for her to hurry up ended any thought of that. *Just suck it up*, she told herself. *It's only a big deal if you make it into one.*

'Holy cow!' Brittany breathed as Jenny came down the stairs. 'Mum! Your hair!'

Jenny nervously went to touch it, eyeing her daughter's shocked face, before she saw a huge grin spread across it. 'Is it okay?'

'It's amazing! I love it. We need to do new profile photos,' she said, digging in her handbag, presumably for her phone.

'No more profile tampering!' Jenny said firmly. 'I mean it, Britt.'

'Fine,' her daughter mumbled, dropping her phone with a roll of her eyes.

'Can we go out for dinner and forget everything to do with dating? For just one night, please?' Jenny asked, pinning her daughter with a stern glance.

'Okay,' Brittany said, holding her hands up in surrender.

'Although if you ask me, it's a perfectly good waste of a photo opportunity.'

'I didn't ask you,' Jenny said, picking up her handbag and the car keys. 'Let's eat. I'm starving.'

The Coach House was bustling as usual, and Jenny was relieved to discover that Beth was already there and sitting at a table she hadn't sat at yet. She shook off the memories of the dates and reminded herself of the rule she'd just given her daughter: no date talk.

Cassie passed by them on her way out to the kitchen with an order, and Jenny smiled a greeting. 'I think I'm safe tonight. No dates,' Jenny assured her.

'That's a shame. I'm sure there's still some good ones out there somewhere though.'

'I'm sure you're right,' Jenny agreed, but was happy not to be going through the nerve-wracking experience of making small talk with a stranger again.

Cassie exchanged a quick hug with Brittany, promising to catch up in her break a little later.

'It's nice you two have caught up again,' Jenny said after Cassie left.

'Yeah, it's nice to have her back home. I didn't realise how much I missed having an old friend around.'

'So explain to me how you think I need setting up with a man but you apparently don't?'

'Because I'm busy working and raising a baby. I don't need some guy coming in and changing how I do things.'

Jenny realised how hard it had been for her daughter, bringing up a child on her own, juggling work commitments and sleepless nights with teething and temperatures. It'd been hard enough doing it when Jenny had been married. At least Austin had been contributing financially, even if he had rarely been home when things like that happened. She understood her daughter's concern. Brittany and Sophie were a unit—they'd developed a bond. Bringing a partner in now would be life-changing. Fitting another person into the dynamics—someone who might have different opinions on how to raise a child—dividing herself between her child and a new man, would bring Brittany some challenges for sure. 'Just don't forget you have to be happy too.'

'I'm happy. I just don't think it's realistic to believe there's a guy out there willing to take on a mum and a baby that isn't his.' Brittany shrugged, looking down at Sophie, who was busy looking around curiously.

Brittany and her boyfriend had been living life to its fullest potential—drinking, dancing, nightclubbing the weekends away, hungover on Sundays, a part of the whole smashed avocado in a yuppy cafe for breakfast set. Until Brittany found out she was pregnant. Tye didn't want to give up his lifestyle and had given Brittany an ultimatum—him or the baby. She hadn't heard from him since.

'I don't believe that's true. Tye was immature and selfish—that was his nature and, sadly, he showed his true colours when you needed him the most. There's someone out there who'll love everything about you. Including Sophie. Just don't shut your heart off to an opportunity.'

'I won't,' Brittany said and sent her mother a small smile. 'I just want to concentrate on Sophie and me right now.'

'And that's fair enough,' Jenny said, giving her daughter a hug, feeling her heart swell with love and wondering how she'd managed to raise such awesome, strong kids.

'Just us tonight?' Beth asked when they sat down.

'Yeah, Chloe is working and Savannah is . . . out.' Jenny shrugged. Her daughters were at an age where, apparently, they no longer had to inform their mother where they went or when they'd be home.

'And I'm only here for dinner then I'm heading home. This one hasn't had a sleep today,' Brittany said as she sat the squirming two-year-old on a chair and brought out some pencils and a note pad.

'So, Jen,' Beth asked, as she busied herself reading the menu, 'what's good here? You're the one with all the recent experience,' she added with a grin.

'We're not supposed to mention *that*,' Brittany informed her, chuckling at Beth's raised eyebrows.

Jenny eyed her best friend. 'Can we have a nice night out without any of the other stuff, please?'

Beth nodded. 'Okay. Sorry. You're right. You were a good sport about it all. You gave it a shot.'

'Although,' Brittany said slowly, 'I think we need to lower the age parameters a bit . . . widen the gene pool, so to speak.'

'No. Absolutely not.'

'Oh, come on, Mum. We've exhausted all the potential ones in your age bracket. It's time to cast that net out wider.'

'I'm not dating someone younger than me. That's just—'

'It's fine. Literally, nobody cares.'

'Well, *I* care.'

'Just think about it,' Brittany suggested calmly.

'Maybe your mum's right,' Beth put in. 'I mean, why would she want to date some hot younger fella when she could have all those mature men?'

Jenny's eyes narrowed as the other two women swapped glances. 'Your reverse psychology thing isn't going to work this time,' she snapped.

'Seriously,' Beth continued, unfazed, 'it's not your fault none of them were up to scratch.'

Jenny frowned. That made her sound as though she were being extremely judgemental and picky... Well, she supposed she had been, and yet, it was only that none of them had *done* anything for her. 'I'm sure they'll find women they're better suited to eventually. They were all... *nice*.' *Except for Craig, who was a two-timing bastard*, she tacked on silently.

'Nice doesn't cut it in the romance department.'

'That's not what I meant,' Jenny corrected. 'It wasn't because they were *nice*... they just didn't...'

'Ring ya bell?' Beth supplied helpfully.

'Well...'

'There's nothing wrong with that,' Beth said. 'I mean, there has to be sparks or what's the point, right?'

Jenny glanced over to the bar and spotted Nick before she swiftly pulled her gaze away and cleared her throat. 'Right.'

'What?' Beth asked abruptly.

'What?' Jenny replied, confused.

'You're blushing.'

'No, I'm not. It's just warm in here.'

'No, it's not,' Brittany said, watching her mother and Beth closely.

'Who's got you all hot and bothered?' Beth demanded curiously, suspiciously scanning the room like a seasoned detective looking for a likely suspect. 'I don't see anyone under seventy,' she said, almost disappointedly, 'only . . .' She stopped, her laser gaze zeroing in on to Jenny, '*the bartender.*'

'The bartender!' Brittany gasped, and Jenny shot her daughter a frantic look before shushing her quickly.

'Oh, wow.' Beth chortled, delightedly. 'Jen, you have exceeded my expectations. That's some mighty fine-lookin' male, right there.'

'Would you keep your voice down?' Jenny practically growled across the table. She could feel her face heating up further. 'I *do not* like the bartender.'

Beth continued to laugh. '*Sure* you don't.'

'Oh, for goodness' sake,' Jenny huffed, sitting back in her chair and crossing her arms.

'Oh, don't pout. We're not making fun of you—we're proud of you!'

'Mum, he's really hot,' Brittany said in a stage whisper, as she snuck a glance across the room. 'I mean, for an old guy.'

'He's hardly an old guy . . . he's probably barely out of his thirties,' Jenny said.

'Nah . . . he's way older than that,' Brittany said, shaking her head. 'I reckon mid-forties.'

'Definitely,' Beth said, 'maybe even *late* forties. He's got some miles on the speedo. Not that it's done him any harm, mind you.'

'He's not a used car, for goodness' sake,' Jenny snapped.

'Well, he's not a new one . . . Is that what's bothering you? You think he's too young?'

'Yes!' Jenny said, exasperated by the turn of events.

'That's so not even an issue. Look at you . . . What guy in his right mind is going to turn down all this?' Beth asked, waving her hands at Jenny like a game show hostess.

'I'm fifty,' Jenny hissed.

'So? Fifty is the new forty.'

'Says who?'

'Says every fifty-year-old woman who isn't ready for the scrap heap yet.'

'Go and talk to him,' Brittany said, leaning across the table to grab her mother's hand. 'He's just finished serving.'

'I'm not going over there.'

'Go and order our drinks,' Beth said, making to stand up.

Jenny wasn't sure what Beth intended doing, but it made her scramble to her own feet in case her friend planned on making a scene and dragging her out of the chair.

'This is ridiculous,' she muttered irritably.

'What? You're ordering a drink.'

'You two will be sitting here leering at me.'

'We would *not* leer,' Beth said, sounding almost indignant.

Jenny rolled her eyes at them before turning away. *Just ignore them. You're simply ordering a drink. The same way you've done before. He's just a bartender.*

A really, really good-looking bartender, a little voice pointed out inside her head.

'Hi. Wow. I like the new hair,' Nick said, bracing his hands on the bar as he ran his gaze over her face.

Jenny swallowed hard. *Get. A. Grip.* 'Thanks. It's new,' she said, then winced. Of course it was new, he'd just said that. 'I mean, today. I had it done . . . today.'

She followed the curve of his smile and felt her pulse go all fluttery. This was insane. She'd spoken to this guy before, only now it was different. There was no date or life-threatening event to distract her, and she couldn't deny that he'd been popping into her mind at strange times lately. What was that even about?

'What can I get you?' he asked when the silence threatened to stretch a little too long between them.

'I think I'll try a grown-up cocktail tonight,' she said, feeling a little braver.

Nick nodded encouragingly. 'Okay, I like it. Which one?'

'I don't know, surprise me.' Was that really her voice? Had it actually taken on a sultry tone? She wasn't even aware she knew how to *do* a sultry tone. It had to be the hair. Oh no! Laurel had gone too far in her transformation and it was spreading!

'And for the other two ladies?'

'They'll have cocktails too,' Jenny said. Why not? They never lashed out on pretty drinks and now that the pub was offering a more sophisticated menu, they should support it.

'Oi! People are dying of thirst down here,' a loud voice called from the other end of the bar, but Jenny didn't know the owner. It did, however, interrupt whatever moment she'd been having with Nick and brought her back to her senses faster than a bucket of cold water over her head ever would.

'Righto. Hold your horses, Frank,' Nick called back. 'Sorry.'

'It's okay, I shouldn't have been holding you up when you're so busy,' she said, scrambling for her purse to take out her card.

'Never too busy for you,' he said, looking up as he began selecting bottles from the shelf behind him, making her smile falter a little.

Okay, so maybe he *was* flirting with her. He didn't seem to talk like that to anyone else, that she could tell.

'I'll bring them over to the table,' he said after she had paid for the drinks.

She managed a nod before heading back to the others, trying to get her flustered nerves under control before she sat down again.

'Well?' Beth prompted when Jenny fiddled with her coaster. 'What happened? Where are the drinks?'

'Nothing happened. Calm down, I ordered the drinks and they'll be brought over.'

'You were gone a long time just to order drinks.'

'Did you ask him how old he is?' Brittany asked, looking up from where she was helping Sophie colour in, or rather scribble, across the paper before them.

'No,' Jenny said, giving a surprised laugh. 'There's literally no way you can bring that question up in general conversation that doesn't sound weird.'

'Sure there is. "Hey, you're cute. How old are you?"' Brittany said and shrugged without glancing up from her artwork.

Jenny snorted rudely and leaned back in her chair.

'Thirty-eight, in case you were wondering,' a deep voice said from behind her, causing her to shoot upright, knocking her knee under the table. She bit back an expletive as she rubbed her injury.

'Sorry, couldn't help but overhear.' Nick didn't look sorry at all as he held a round tray with brightly coloured drinks on it.

'We were just . . .' Jenny tried to think of a logical reason three women would be sitting around gossiping about his age.

'Hi, I'm Beth, and this is Brittany, and you already know Jenny,' Beth said, then lowered her voice a little. 'Maybe you can settle an argument we're having. Jenny here thinks younger men won't date older women. You're a younger guy—what do you say?'

'I reckon it's less about the numbers and more about the things you have in common,' he said easily.

'See!' Beth crowed. 'Told you.'

Jenny shook her head tiredly.

'You don't agree?' he asked her.

'I think an age gap can cause . . . issues.'

'Depends on the people, I guess. I've known twenty-year-old kids in the army who've seen and done more things in their life than the mates they grew up with back home,' he said. 'It's all about experience.'

Jenny grudgingly conceded he might have a point, but it didn't change the fact that at some point, an age gap was going to be an issue in a relationship.

'Your drinks,' he continued smoothly. 'I made a selection, I hope you like them.'

'What are they?' Brittany asked, selecting a pretty purple one.

'That one's called Unicorn Kisses,' he told her and received a gasp of awe from Sophie as she looked up, intrigued by the name. 'And this one's a baby Unicorn Kisses—without the vodka,' he said, placing a small glass in front of the wide-eyed little girl.

'For you, a Pink Bikini,' he said, placing the next glass in front of Beth, before turning his attention to Jenny and holding her flustered look calmly.

'What's that one?' Beth asked curiously, as she eyed the glass he placed in front of Jenny.

'This,' he said lowering his voice as he looked down at Jenny, 'is a Screaming Orgasm.'

Beth spat her drink, almost drowning out Brittany's strangled sound of surprise. They both gaped.

Jenny felt her mouth drop open too, before closing it quickly to clear her throat. *Dear God.*

'You ladies have a nice night,' Nick said, giving them a nod before turning away.

'Wow,' Beth mouthed as she dragged her eyes away from watching his denim butt retreat, dabbing at her blouse to clean up the drink she'd spilled. 'You so have to get onto that.'

'Get onto it?' Jenny scoffed.

'He's into you, Mum,' Brittany said.

'Oh, please.' Jenny shook her head. 'Can we just order some food?'

Jenny wasn't sure she'd be able to stop these two from harping relentlessly on about the whole situation but was pleasantly surprised when they took the hint and wisely dropped the subject.

For the remainder of the evening, she refused to let her gaze wander near the bar and was very proud of herself for resisting. She had self-control. She was sensible. Someone around here had to be, after all.

Fifteen

A bleep came from her phone and Jenny frowned at the coffee table where it sat. She paused *Yellowstone* and reluctantly dragged her eyes away from Rip Wheeler to pick up her phone.

Caffeine_Addict
How was your day?

Jenny couldn't deny the leap of excitement when she saw the name.

She hesitated only briefly before replying, *Fine, thanks. Yours?*

Well, that was riveting. She wondered if he was settling in for another long conversation or if this was just a random hello.

Caffeine_Addict
Long. But better now.

She glanced at the clock and saw that it was almost eleven.

> **Florence_71**
> You're working late tonight.

Caffeine_Addict
Paperwork waits for no man . . . or woman. Had any more luck on here since we last spoke?

> **Florence_71**
> I haven't actually been on here for a while. I was watching TV.

Caffeine_Addict
What were you watching?

> **Florence_71**
> *Yellowstone*. Have you seen it?

Caffeine_Addict
Of course. So I'm guessing you watch it for the horses . . . not Kevin Costner?

> **Florence_71**
> Well, Kevin Costner is pretty amazing, but I have to be honest . . . Rip isn't hard on the eyes either. A girl's spoiled for choice in this show.

Caffeine_Addict
Will you lose all respect for my manliness if I admit that even I have a slight man-crush on Rip?

Jenny chuckled.

> **Florence_71**
> It's okay. You really didn't have that much of my respect to start with.

Caffeine_Addict
Ouch.

Florence_71
Your secret man-crush is safe with me.

Caffeine_Addict
Thanks. I think. So, you're partial to cowboys?

Florence_71
I wouldn't have said so before I started watching this show. My daughter got me watching it. I blame her.

Caffeine_Addict
Help me out here, do I put the chaps in my shopping cart or not?

Jenny grinned and eased back against the cushions on her lounge.

Florence_71
Actually, to be honest, I fell in love with *The Man from Snowy River* when I was a kid, so maybe it's the horses I like after all.

Caffeine_Addict
Okay, so take the chaps out then.

Jenny restarted the show when there was a break in conversation, thinking maybe that was it. After a few moments though, curiosity got the better of her.

Florence_71
What's your favourite show?

Immediately the little curser began doing its bump thing as he typed out a reply.

Caffeine_Addict
You'll laugh.

Florence_71
No, I won't. Anyway, if I did, you wouldn't know, so what do you have to lose?

Caffeine_Addict
My dignity.

Florence_71
I promise I won't laugh.

Caffeine_Addict
McLeod's Daughters. There. I said it.

Jenny did laugh at that. A lot. But when she finished, she typed back.

Florence_71
There's nothing wrong with that. Everyone loves *McLeod's Daughters*.

Caffeine_Addict
You laughed.

Florence_71
No way. I wouldn't.

Caffeine_Addict
That's okay. I'm man enough to take it.

> Florence_71
> I never doubted it for a minute. I should get to bed. I'm already up way later than I should be.

> Caffeine_Addict
> Goodnight, Florence.

> Florence_71
> 'Night.

She switched her phone off to stop herself doing something dumb like talking to this guy for the rest of the night like some teenager, then switched off the TV and went up to bed.

That night she dreamed of a faceless cowboy riding off into the sunset to the theme song from *McLeod's Daughters*.

❖

Jenny walked past the bathroom and banged on the door. 'Three minutes!' she called over the loud music blaring from inside, before continuing downstairs with a load of laundry.

'Nanna,' Sophie cried excitedly as Jenny walked into the kitchen from the laundry. She'd never get tired of hearing that gorgeous little voice calling out her name.

'I swear, every morning, it's like she hasn't seen you in a year,' Brittany said from beside the highchair in which her daughter sat eating toast.

'Good morning, my angel,' Jenny said, holding the sweet cherub face between her hands and kissing the plump little cheeks. 'Did you have a good sleep?'

'Yeah!' the toddler called out, as she always did.

Jenny flicked the jug on, leaning against the bench as she waited for the water to re-boil, her half-made cup of coffee with the granules and sugar already added sitting where Brittany had left it for her. She smiled at how their little world had fallen into this new, grown-up version of a routine. It was different from only a few years earlier when Jenny was running from the moment her feet hit the floor in the morning till she fell into bed at night: getting kids dressed; making lunches; organising pick-up times and sports practice, play dates and homework—always looking at the clock and wondering where the time went.

She glanced at the clock now, more out of habit, and swore under her breath as she called out, 'Chloe! Get out of the shower!'

Some things never changed, she guessed.

'Morning,' Savannah said with a yawn as she shuffled into the kitchen with bed-hair and bleary eyes.

'What time did you get in last night?' Brittany asked, eyeing her younger sister doubtfully.

'Late,' Savannah snapped.

'Geez, have some coffee or something. I was just asking.'

Wordlessly, Jenny passed a cup to her daughter and watched her sink into the chair across from Sophie.

After a few sips of coffee and a bite of Sophie's soggy Vegemite toast, Savannah was ready for conversation. 'So, Mum, I wanted to run something by you.'

'Okay,' Jenny said, buttering her toast.

'It's my birthday next week,' Savannah said.

'I am aware. I was present on the day.'

'Yes. Well. I'd like to have a party and I thought we could have it at the Coach House.'

'Why?' Jenny asked, as blandly as she could manage.

'Because I don't want two separate birthday dinners with Dad and you this year. I want to hang out with my friends as well as my family, and I can't do that if I have to spend this day here, and that day there, and then try and find time to go out with my friends. Everyone in the one location would be easier. And I assume you don't want to host it here with Dad and Christy . . . So, I thought, the pub,' she finished brightly.

'You just don't want to get stuck at Dad's with Christy,' Brittany commented, passing her daughter another piece of toast.

'Well, that too.'

Jenny thought about reminding them they should try and get on with their father's girlfriend for his sake, but then realised Austin was a dick and she didn't really care if they liked his girlfriend or not.

'Well, okay. If that's what you want.'

'Great. I booked a table for next Saturday.'

Too bad if she'd had any misgivings then, Jenny thought sarcastically.

The rest of breakfast passed in a blur with Savannah issuing jobs and making lists, and Jenny was relieved to head off to work for a break. Somehow, she'd raised a mini dictator—when it came to social events, Savannah was like her father.

Sixteen

Nick had to remind himself he was a grown-arse man who owned a business and not a fourteen-year-old waiting at the Blue Light Disco for the girl he liked to turn up. Ever since he'd noticed the booking they'd taken for the Hayward private party, he'd been catching himself being ridiculously happy. His adult brain was sick of reminding him to *be cool, man!*

Sadly, it hadn't been Jenny who'd come in to discuss the menu with the functions coordinator, but her daughter. Nick had left them to it.

Thankfully, the day of the party was hectic, which stopped him becoming too jumpy and looking like an idiot. But when Jenny walked in, he found his eyes following her around the room as she greeted people with a bright smile. He caught himself wishing he was on the receiving end of one of them. In the few times he'd been around Jenny, her default modes had been stressed or—in the case of the hospital—super professional. He'd never really seen her shine like she did tonight. Her whole face lit up. She was . . . beautiful. He felt something akin to being kicked in the chest.

With customers waiting patiently, Nick dragged his gaze from Jenny, and for a few minutes he was kept too busy to continue watching her. But when he did have time to catch his breath, he saw her smile slip. He followed her gaze towards a couple who'd just walked inside and begun greeting people. The older guy had an arm resting around the younger woman's waist. Nick wondered who they were.

'I still can't believe he has the nerve to bring her to stuff like this,' Cassie said as she came up beside him.

'Who are they?' Nick asked, hoping he sounded only mildly curious.

'Savannah's father and his girlfriend,' Cassie said in a disgusted tone. She shook her head. 'Poor Jenny. Everyone was talking about it when it happened. It was horrible.'

Nick felt a rush of protectiveness flow through him for the woman who seemed to be bracing herself as the pair headed over to her. What man in his right mind would trade Jenny for the swollen-lipped Barbie doll beside him? Maybe that look was the current hot trend, but it did nothing for Nick. Of course, that could be because he felt ancient nowadays, but still, as a normal, red-blooded male, all that fake eyelash, lip filler and butt implants crap turned a perfectly good-looking woman into someone who looked like she was made out of plastic. It wasn't for him.

His forearms flexed automatically as he saw the woman lean in and whisper something to the man before they shared an eyeroll. Maybe he was just super sensitive, having just found out who these people were—they could have been discussing the weather for all he knew—but he had a sudden urge to shield Jenny. He watched her straighten her shoulders as though preparing to take on the entire front line of an enemy division.

'Jen,' Austin said with a curt nod, barely glancing at her, until he did a double take.

'Hello, Austin. Kirsty,' Jenny forced out politely. Austin's girlfriend was dressed in a short, clinging dress with a plunging neckline that ended just above her belly button.

'It's Christy,' the younger woman said, barely managing to cover her snarkiness.

I know, you bimbo-faced whor— 'Oh, sorry,' Jenny amended with so much saccharine in her tone that her teeth began to ache.

'New haircut? Cute,' Christy said in a bored voice before turning away, dismissing Jenny.

'I thought this was going to be a small gathering,' Austin said, looking at the crowd.

Jenny shrugged. 'You know Savannah. Miss Socialite. Hard to believe we have a twenty-six-year-old daughter, and a nearly twenty-eight-year old,' she said, letting her gaze settle on Christy, who had only just turned twenty-seven a few months ago.

'There you are,' a voice said from behind her as an arm slipped around her waist. Jenny straightened in surprise. She stared up at Nick's smiling face and felt her mouth drop open.

'Hey. I'm Nick,' he said, ignoring her shocked expression as he extended a hand towards her ex-husband.

Austin seemed equally as surprised and hesitated a moment before reaching for the offered hand. 'Austin.'

Nick nodded. 'Ah, okay, the birthday girl's dad.'

'Yes,' Austin said, and Jenny was quietly impressed at how well he was able to cover his obvious confusion.

Unlike herself. What was going on?

'If you don't mind, I need to borrow this sexy woman for a minute,' Nick went on, drawing a startled snort from Jenny, as he took her hand and led her away.

She finally regained her wits as they reached the corner of the room. Jenny tugged her hand out of his and took a step away. 'What on earth are you doing?'

Nick folded his arms across his chest and gave an offhand shrug. 'I figured you could use some help.'

'Help?'

'I overheard that was your ex.'

'So you decided to create some gossip to add fuel to the fire?' she snapped.

'I thought it'd wipe that smug look off his face.'

'That's his usual look!' she said. 'I don't know why you thought I needed rescuing, but I was fine.'

'I thought you could use a hand.'

'What I *don't* need is gossip,' she said, lowering her voice. 'You have no idea how little it takes to start people talking around here. The last thing I want is everyone thinking you and I are having some kind of sordid . . . fling.'

'Sordid?' he repeated, and she caught a flash of amusement cross his face.

'You know what I mean.'

'No, actually. I have no idea why you'd think our relationship would be sordid . . . or a fling, for that matter.'

'We don't have a relationship!'

'Well, apparently that's what everyone is going to think.'

'I don't have time for this,' she said, glaring at him.

'Sorry. Was just trying to help.'

'Well, next time. Don't.'

'You look beautiful tonight, by the way,' he said as she went to move around him.

She lifted her eyes to meet his. Instead of the teasing glint she'd half-expected to find there, she saw instead a look that made her breath catch. For the life of her, she couldn't drag her eyes away. It was easy to forget they were in the middle of a busy pub surrounded by her family and half the town.

She wasn't sure how long they stood there, his intense look holding her prisoner, but the loud squeal of excited twenty-somethings greeting each other cut through the weird moment, bringing Jenny back to reality without warning. She backed away, finally feeling common sense returning.

That had been . . . unsettling, she decided, as she smiled at familiar faces and waved at newcomers across the room. She was not going to analyse any of it right now. She had no idea how she'd even begin to.

'What. Was. That?' Beth asked, in a low voice as she joined Jenny in the bathroom, where she'd scampered to in order to get her head together.

'What was what?' Jenny asked, opening a stall door.

'You know *what*. Mr Hottie, whisking you off like that.'

'He just wanted to go over the drinks menu,' Jenny said, hoping her friend would drop the subject.

Jenny heard the tap go on at the sink. 'Sure didn't look like that's all he was going over.'

Jenny blew out a cross breath. 'It was nothing. For some ridiculous reason, he thought I needed saving from Austin.'

Beth chuckled. 'Well, it worked. You should have seen his face when Nick came up behind you like that. His eyes almost fell out of his head.'

His weren't the only ones, Jenny thought, recalling her own shock. What on earth had Nick been thinking?

'So we can add knight in shining armour to his list of attributes,' Beth said in a wistful tone.

'I didn't need saving,' Jenny pointed out dryly.

'He obviously thought you did.'

'Yeah, well, he's probably just gone and stirred up a whole heap of gossip that I don't need right now.'

'Oh, come on, Jen. Who cares? Let people talk. They will anyway—at least this way you get a say in what they're fed. Go play it up, I reckon.'

'Are you insane? I'm not *encouraging* it.'

'It's about time someone turned the tables on the gossip mill. Why not enjoy yourself in the process? I'll see you back out there,' Beth said, and Jenny heard the door swish shut.

Jenny closed her eyes for a moment to gather herself before reaching for the cubicle's door latch. That was the craziest idea she'd ever—

'Poor Jenny,' a woman's hushed voice was saying as the door opened again and someone came in. 'Can you imagine how embarrassing it would be with your ex-husband strutting about with a child on his arm? I'd be humiliated.'

'Just horrible. I mean, she's trying to move on from the whole thing,' a second woman said, dropping her voice. 'I heard from Vince the other day she's been spotted in here with at least five different men.'

What? Oh, for goodness' sake.

'Mind you, they all looked much older, poor dear, and here's her husband running around with a woman the same age as his own children. It's disgusting. Can you imagine having to stand by while your husband flaunts his affair in front of the whole town like that?'

The women tsked and made a variety of other suitably pitying sounds, each one slicing through Jenny's pride like a scalpel.

She wondered why she was hiding in the cubicle, listening to these silly women. She didn't want their pity.

As the doors either side of her closed, she opened hers, washed her hands and went back out to the party.

She'd worked hard to move on with her life. It hadn't been easy to accept that, at forty-eight, she'd effectively been traded in for something newer. And yes, her confidence had taken a beating over that, but it had been two years ago. She'd since rebuilt her life and she was happy with what she'd achieved.

The conversation repeated inside her head once more. They thought she could only attract older men? She could still pull a younger man in if she really wanted.

Jenny straightened her shoulders, her cheeks still sporting spots of indignation, and marched across the room.

Nick had just placed a fresh platter of chicken wings on the table and was turning to leave with an empty tray when Jenny stopped in front of him. She didn't give him time to react—or herself to change her mind—before reaching up and kissing him, right there in the middle of the pub.

She pulled away, instantly regretting her rash behaviour. He looked down at her, seeming to search her eyes for something—most likely checking to see if she was intoxicated or just plain crazy. Shame filled the void that the anger that had driven her earlier had left.

'I'm sorry,' she said, before stepping back.

He put an arm around her waist to stop her retreat. 'Can't say I am.'

'I shouldn't have done that.'

'Well, it's too late to take it back now. May as well make the most of it.' He grinned, leaning down to kiss her again.

Okay, this is getting a tad out of hand. She hadn't thought her actions through past planting a kiss on him to make a point—a point she wasn't even sure she was making to the relevant people. She'd allowed herself to be riled up by stupid pride. But this kiss was . . .

'I think we've made the most of it now,' she said, her voice not quite as steady as she would have liked when he lifted his head and allowed her to move out of his reach.

'Happy to help.'

'Right,' she said with a quick nod. 'I'll let you get back to work.'

He gave a small chuckle before making his way towards the kitchen with his empty tray, leaving Jenny to navigate her way to where Beth was sitting at a table, grinning at her like the Cheshire bloody cat.

'Do *not* say a *word*,' Jenny warned her, pulling out a seat across from her.

'I don't think I've ever been more proud,' Beth said, before taking a sip of her cocktail. 'And that's all I'm going to say.'

Jenny had no doubt there would be more said—lots more—but she also knew her friend would wait until they were alone before she made her tell her all the nitty-gritty details. Maybe between now and then a major natural disaster would occur and Beth would forget all about it.

Seventeen

Jenny steadfastly refused to look in Nick's direction for the rest of the night, which was no mean feat when she could practically feel his magnetism drawing her across the room. She'd acted like a complete moron, allowing gossip to make her do something so out of character. She used to lecture the girls about peer pressure and here she was doing the exact thing she'd always despised. *Idiot.*

Thankfully, none of the girls seemed to have witnessed her moment of insanity; they were happy socialising, oblivious to anything going on outside their own social groups.

As the evening progressed, Jenny thought maybe, just maybe, she'd gotten away with it, then Austin sat in the chair across from her when Beth had gotten up to dance.

'I think it's been a success,' he said after a while, leaning forward in his chair to be heard.

'Seems so. Where's Christy?'

He nodded towards the dance floor and she spotted his scantily-clad girlfriend dancing with a group of Savannah's friends.

'I thought you'd be out there, too,' Jenny said, trying to keep a straight face. Austin had never set foot on a dance floor in his entire life.

'You look . . . different,' he said after another silence had stretched between them.

'I *am* different.' Jenny shrugged. 'I'm happier.'

'Yeah. I suppose it's got something to do with the new boyfriend?'

It felt strange to have him looking at her. They rarely ever held each other's gaze anymore. They didn't talk, other than about kid-related stuff. In fact, Jenny could count on one hand the number of times she'd actually seen him in the last two years. She didn't have to. Didn't have to talk to him about custody requirements as they would have done if the girls had been younger, and the girls were all old enough to drive themselves to see him. They'd simply stopped talking to each other once the marriage ended. Now, though, as he sat there across the table, it felt like a stranger looking at her for the first time.

'No, actually. I'm just finally in a good place in life. My career is going great. The kids are all happy. Life is good.'

'So this guy is only new, then?'

'Nick has nothing to do with anything.'

'You've just never been the impulsive type before and he seems . . . impulsive,' Austin finished somewhat lamely.

'That's really none of your business.' She turned to the dance floor.

'He doesn't seem much older than the girls.'

Jenny's head immediately snapped back. 'Are you *seriously* going there?'

'It's different with Christy and me,' he started, and Jenny felt her eyebrows disappear into her hairline. 'This is a male. In a house with young women. You need to think about the girls.'

Was he out of his ever-lovin' mind?

'All I'm saying is, what if he looks at the girls, decides he'd rather be with someone more his own age? What are you going to do? I'm trying to warn you before something like that happens.'

'Oh, right, so a younger, attractive male can't possibly stay attracted to an older female, yet a bimbo in a dress that barely covers her backside is supposed to find a fifty-year-old balding man completely irresistible? Maybe you should take your own advice.'

'I knew you'd take it as an attack. You never could handle criticism.'

Jenny let out a small laugh. 'And yet, I really should be an expert at it, since all you ever *do* is criticise.'

'Sorry I said anything,' he snapped, scowling and slumping back in his chair.

Jenny fought the urge to bring up a few more, 'and another thing's, that were desperate to get out, wanting instead to take the higher road and not give anyone more ammunition for gossip, so she sat there and fumed until the music stopped and the dancers broke up and came looking for drinks.

❖

Nick was still grinning as he walked around the corner, heading to the storeroom, when he noticed someone sitting across the hall in the armchair he'd placed in the empty nook during the renovations.

'Jenny?' Instantly his smile was replaced by a concerned frown. 'Everything okay? What are you doing out here, all alone?'

'I just needed to get away from the noise for a while.'

'I can show you upstairs to a quiet room if you like?'

She sent him a dry look.

'Not like that,' he said quickly. 'I just meant there's a common room with a TV and a verandah that's quiet.'

She seemed to be weighing up his sincerity and he must have passed, because she lost the sceptical side-eye she'd been giving him and shook her head. 'Thanks, but I'm fine. I just needed a minute.'

'The ex?' he asked, leaning against the wall across from her. What he really wanted to do was tug her out of that chair and wrap his arms around her like he had earlier in the night. His chest still tingled with warmth, like he could feel her pressed up against him.

She gave a small grunt, which he took for a yes.

He fought to contain his irritation and lost. 'What the hell did you ever see in that jerk to marry him in the first place?' he heard himself asking. The guy was an arrogant prick. He'd ordered a drink earlier and Nick had had the urge to punch him in the face just for the way he spoke to the staff. He couldn't even comprehend what someone like Jenny had been doing married to a guy like that.

'He wasn't always like that,' she said with a long sigh.

'I take it he's part of the reason you're hiding out here, though?'

'I'm not hiding,' she started to protest, then stopped. 'Okay, maybe I am, but only because it would upset Savannah if I left the party this early. I'm just waiting until she cuts the birthday cake, then I can go home.'

'It seems a bit unfair that he's out there enjoying himself while you're missing out. You want me to come and keep you company?'

'No thanks. I think you've helped out enough for one night.'

'Well, to be fair, you were the one who actually took it further with the whole kiss thing. Not that I'm complaining.'

He saw her eyes close briefly and her jaw clench as she gave a small chuckle.

'It's okay. Really. I was just stirrin' you.'

'It's not okay. I shouldn't have done that.'

'No harm done.' He shrugged, striving for an offhand tone if only to put her mind at ease. Clearly she was still stressed about the whole thing, which he had to admit hurt a little bit.

'Let's just forget it ever happened, okay? Put it down to a stress reaction on my part.'

'Okay. If it makes you feel better.'

'That's exactly what it was,' she countered, firmly.

'Okay,' he agreed, but couldn't help the small grin that appeared. She was even sexier when her feathers were getting all ruffled.

'I better get back out there and see what's happening with the cake,' she murmured, avoiding his eyes as she stood up.

He pushed off from the wall, bringing them closer, and caught the slight widening of her eyes as she looked up at him. For the briefest of moments he imagined kissing her again, but a loud laugh nearby cut through the tension, ending the moment. He stepped back slightly and she all but scampered away, leaving him to watch her disappear into the party crowd, feeling more than a little disappointed.

Eighteen

'How was your weekend?' asked Donna, as they sat at the nurses' station a few days later.

'Fine. Busy, actually,' Jenny said, pulling up her patients' blood results on the computer. 'My daughter had a birthday party that somehow seemed even more exhausting at twenty-six than her parties at six ever were.' She smiled tiredly.

'Oh, to be young and fun again,' Donna sighed.

'Come on, we can still be fun,' Jenny chided lightly.

'Not me. Nowadays, fun to me is going home from work and getting straight into my PJs, eating chocolate while I watch TV and not having to cook dinner for anyone. Divorce was the best thing that ever happened to me.'

'How long have you been single?'

'Five years now. Just me and the cat.'

Jenny had a cat. And she did tend to find herself checking the time until it was acceptable to get into her comfy pyjamas and climb into bed... Oh, wow, she really *wasn't* fun anymore.

Nick popped up in her thoughts and she felt a tiny flutter in her chest as their kiss played in her mind. That hadn't been boring—at all. But it was just a one-off, a moment of insanity fuelled by an immature urge to rebel against her ex and his ridiculous double standards. She returned her attention to Mr McCauley and his raised creatinine levels.

During her break, Jenny headed down to the hospital cafe, the aroma of fresh coffee drawing her like a magnet.

'Good morning, Nola.'

The familiar face popped out from the kitchen area. 'Jenny! How are you this morning, pet?'

'I'll be a lot better once I get a coffee.' She grinned.

'Coming right up. How about a nice raspberry slice to go with it? Freshly made today,' Nola added, and Jenny groaned. These women would be the absolute death of her will power. She could never resist and knew those few stubborn kilos she'd been trying to budge for the last eighteen months were all there because of these women's baking skills.

'Sure, why not?' she said, giving in with barely even a fight today. What was the point? She was never going to say no anyway.

'Hello, Jenny,' Betty said, carrying a tray of individually wrapped cake, slices and sandwiches from the kitchen.

'Hi Betty. That all looks so good,' she said, contemplating changing her order to cake.

'I hear Savannah's party was a huge success,' Nola said as she prepared the coffee.

'Yes, everyone seemed to enjoy themselves.'

'And a little birdy told us that you had a lovely time too,' Betty said, wiggling her bushy grey eyebrows at Jenny.

'Me? Well . . .' Oh, crap! The kiss. Of course. She knew she'd let her defences down too soon. Just because none of her family had witnessed it, didn't mean it had escaped the sharp eye of someone else. It only took one person to see and tell someone else. *Just play dumb.* 'Yes, it was a great night. Savannah really enjoyed it.'

'We heard mention that a certain young man and a certain young lady we know seemed rather close,' Nola said. 'I think it's all very romantic—handsome younger man falling for our lovely Jenny.'

'It's just like the Harlequin medical romance I'm reading right now. Dr Lawrence, the tall, brooding new doctor in town, falls in love with his nurse.' Betty clutched a hand to her chest. 'It's just so perfect.'

'It's not like that,' Jenny hurried to explain.

'Well, I know he's not a doctor—and let's face it, the pickings are mighty slim around this place for those,' Nola said in a loud whisper that still seemed to carry across the front lobby. 'But this is the next best thing.'

Jenny had no idea *how* this was the next best thing, but she really didn't want to encourage the conversation any further either, so she let it pass. *This is your punishment for letting your pride talk you into doing something stupid.* 'Yes, well, anyway, it was a bit of a storm in a teacup, that whole thing, and nothing really came of it,' Jenny said, willing the coffee to hurry up.

'What? It's all over? So soon?' Betty asked, her face dropping in dismay.

'Ah, well . . . yes, it's a bit embarrassing. It was all a big misunderstanding.'

'What kind of misunderstanding? Oh, no . . . what did he do?' Nola demanded, plonking her hands firmly on her hips.

'He didn't really *do* anything—'

'I bet he had a bit on the side—stashed away somewhere. I mean, no one really knows much about him, do they?' Betty continued in a rather snippy tone that was a complete turnaround from her love-silly mood of moments before.

'That's true. A few of us have tried. I mean, *where* did he get all his money from to buy the hotel? He's not very old, is he?'

'Buy the hotel?' Jenny cut in. 'He's just the bartender, isn't he?'

The women's fierce expressions began to slip.

'Oh, dear. You didn't know?' Nola asked.

'I just thought he—'

'No, dear. He's the new owner.'

How on earth had she not known this? She groaned silently; he must have thought her dismissive comments about doing his job were hilarious . . . not. Jenny shrivelled up inside at the memory.

'I suppose that was never going to end well, was it,' Betty said, shaking her head sadly. 'Lies are never a good foundation to build love on.'

'He didn't lie—' Jenny started, but the women had already decided that she'd been spurned and were now fuelled by indignation on her behalf. She couldn't be bothered arguing—she was still trying to get her head around the assumption she'd made and what Nick must be thinking of her for doing so.

She paid for the coffee and the slice and retraced her footsteps back to the staff room. Just when she thought she'd been as dumb as she could possibly be . . .

The Gift of the Gab was a Barkley institution: a newsagent and a clothing store as well as a newly revamped gift and homewares shop. It had been owned by Shelly Mitchem for the last fifteen or so years and by her mother, Sandy, before her. It was aptly named, since the Mitchems seemed to be the first to know pretty much everything going on around town.

Jenny had had her eye on a new table lamp for the last few months and had finally decided to give in and buy it.

'Apparently, Barkley is on the map,' Shelly announced, nodding at the magazine on the front counter.

Jenny craned her neck to read the headline. 'Wow.' She picked up a copy of the magazine.

The two-page spread had a photo of the pub in all its renovated glory, along with two men, one of whom Jenny recognised as the chef. But it was the other man, leaning against the wall of the pub with a decided aura of rugged masculinity, who caught her attention. *Entrepreneur Nicolas Mason, younger brother of prestigious businesswoman of the year, Sussanne Angelopoulos, is the brains and the brawn behind a new dining revolution—bringing fine dining and culture to the outback*, the article read.

'"Culture to the outback"?' Jenny read out loud. They were hardly the outback. Reasonably remote because they were off the main highway now, but hardly the red, arid desert image Jenny would expect when outback was mentioned.

Shelly chuckled. 'You know how it is—to anyone from a big city, anything more than five minutes west of them is considered the outback.'

'How stupid do these magazine editors think people are?' Jenny muttered.

'Must be working, though.' Shelly shrugged. 'The motel in town's booked out for the next few weeks and a heap of places over in Hamwell have been making group bookings at the pub. The phone's been ringing off the hook, Marissa Woods was saying this morning. Seems like that young bloke might have been on to something after all, sinking all that money into his renovations,' she mused, before tilting her head curiously as she looked at Jenny.

Jenny glanced down at the photo and cleared her throat, remembering Shelly was still watching her, waiting for her to pay. She hadn't seen Nick since the kiss, and the memory sent an unexpected tingle through her. *Oh, don't be an idiot.* This was not the place to be caught daydreaming about the hunky bartender . . . or rather, owner, Jenny corrected herself. She hadn't even known who he was and there she was kissing the man in front of everyone, making a complete fool of herself.

She didn't waste any more time chit-chatting with Shelly, positive the woman knew all the gossip and was hoping to get an inside scoop on something juicy and new. She was at least restrained enough not to come out and ask about it, which saved Jenny from further humiliation.

On the way out to her car, Jenny found herself thinking about the article. Sussanne Angelopoulos was Nick's sister? She didn't know a great deal about the woman but she had heard of her—mainly from glimpses of the name splashed across tabloids while she waited in line at the supermarket. She supposed that answered the question about where Nick got the money to buy the pub—then she silently reprimanded herself for making assumptions. For all she knew, he may have his own money. Just because Nick had a sister who'd once been married to some Greek business tycoon, it didn't necessarily mean she funded his lifestyle. It certainly gave him a very interesting background story, though. She gave a small grunt; the gossip mill around town was going to have a field day with all this. By the end of the day the poor guy would surely have connections with the Mafia and own a private island somewhere in the Mediterranean.

'FML,' Savannah muttered.

'What?' Jenny's brow furrowed as she looked at her daughter.

'Fuck my life,' Savannah elaborated with a surly growl.

'Savannah!' Jenny snapped, sending a meaningful glare as she nodded towards the toddler swinging her chubby little legs happily as she ate her Icy Pole at the table.

'She isn't even listening,' Savannah said, rolling her eyes.

'They take in *everything*,' Jenny hissed. Only the previous day, Jenny had heard her sweet little cherub of a granddaughter tell the cat to 'get out of the bloody way', when it walked out from the laundry as Sophie walked down the hallway. She'd winced later as she realised *she* may have been the one responsible for the toddler's outburst, since she had said the same thing as she'd carried a full basket of laundry towards the back door and almost tripped over said cat.

'What's wrong?' Jenny asked, getting back to her child's pouty expression. The sight brought to mind a time when Savannah was a toddler herself. *Where have the years gone?* Jenny wondered with a silent sigh.

'The job in Bali fell through.'

'In Bali?' Jenny's eyebrows shot up. 'What job? I didn't even know you were applying for anything.'

'Well, I can't stay here forever, can I?'

'You can stay as long as you want to,' Jenny said, searching Savannah's eyes carefully. 'I didn't know you were thinking about heading back overseas.' It wasn't that Jenny didn't want her daughters to follow their dreams and go out and experience life and travel and excitement while they were young, but part of her had been relieved when her middle child had finally returned home and she no longer had to worry about where she was until she got a call or saw a post or Instagram story from some exotic location showing Savannah safe, happy and, most of all . . . alive!

'That was always the plan, Mum,' Savannah said. 'I just had to save up and find another job first, which we had, but Nael and Juliette have changed their minds and they're not going to Bali now. Which means the caretaker and cleaner job at the resort *and* the accommodation that went with it has fallen through because Nael was going to do the maintenance.'

'Oh. That's a shame,' Jenny commiserated.

'Now I don't know where that leaves me.'

'Maybe it's a chance to go in a different direction. You could always go back to study and get your degree.'

'How can I go back to that when I've been *living*,' Savannah said dramatically. 'University will be so . . . boring.'

'Most people don't get to have the experiences you've had, but at some point you need to start thinking about a future and a career. It's all well and good to backpack around the world and work at odd jobs so you can eat,' Jenny said, 'but your work visa won't last forever and by the time you decide to settle down back here, you won't have any qualifications behind you to get a job.'

'I'll have life experience,' Savannah countered breezily.

'Life experience is good to have—but unless you're going to apply it to something, you'll only be working hospitality and supermarkets for the rest of your life.'

'Are you saying there's something wrong with that kind of work?' Savannah planted a hand on her hip in a way that told Jenny she was settling in for an argument.

'As you well know,' Jenny started, refusing to back down, 'I worked for a long time in a supermarket. There is absolutely nothing wrong with that kind of work. However, if you want to keep living the kind of life you do, then you're probably not going to be able to do it on a check-out cashier's wage.'

'I'm not cut out to study for years on end, stuck in a stifling lecture hall!'

'Then opt for doing a degree online. Work part time and study at home. But if you don't do it now, it's not going to get any easier later. The sooner you start, the sooner you'll finish.'

Savannah gave a frustrated growl and muttered under her breath as she left the room. The subject wasn't a new one and it never seemed to get any less frustrating. One of the most annoying things to have to deal with as a parent was being able to see the problem in a situation but unable to make your child take your warnings seriously, until it was too late. Ever since Savannah had deferred her business degree after the first semester to go backpacking, Jenny had been trying unsuccessfully to get her to return to it. She didn't want any of her daughters to get to where they wanted to go the hard way, like she had—juggling study with small children, a husband and a mortgage. Since Savannah had come back, Jenny knew she'd noticed how many of the kids she'd gone to school with were qualified and working in their chosen fields, some getting married and settling down while others were well on the path to career success. She worried about Savannah; even as a child she'd had a carefree nature that often made getting her to school or getting her to do anything that involved any kind of self-discipline a constant battle. Jenny had hated doing anything that dulled that free spirit, but there were times when even the freest ones had to follow a routine. Over the last few years, it had become increasingly difficult to step back and let her run her own race, knowing full well that if she didn't commit to something soon, life would only get harder.

'Grant me the serenity to accept the things I cannot change,' she murmured with a long-suffering sigh. Those words had come in handy more times than she cared to admit over the years. Still didn't make the situation any less frustrating, but it was her way of counting to ten and letting go of some of the exasperation her daughter had left behind.

Nineteen

Jenny walked out of the post office after spending fifteen minutes talking to the owner, Mavis Bennet. Mavis had a barrage of questions about her elderly husband Frank's recent diabetes diagnosis. This kind of thing happened all the time. Jenny would usually end up in a lengthy discussion with someone about a medical condition or be asked if she could take a quick look at something—always an interesting request that could sometimes raise a few eyebrows from people passing by. She didn't usually mind the odd question out of the office, so to speak, but it could be annoying when she just wanted to duck into a shop quickly and get home after a long shift at work. Sometimes it was easier to get the girls to pick up parcels or shopping. In this case, she'd organised for Frank to get an appointment with the visiting diabetes education nurse who would be seeing patients later the following week and felt better that she'd at least put some of the older couple's uncertainty at ease.

She bit back a yelp when she rounded the corner of the post office and almost collided with someone.

'Sorry!' she said, as she looked up, then felt her breath catch suddenly. 'Oh. It's . . . you.'

Nick's grin widened as Jenny tried to apologise but ended up sounding even more flustered. 'All good. Nice to bump into you,' he said. 'Literally,' he added, still holding her arms from where he'd reached out to steady her. 'Are you all right?'

'I'm fine,' Jenny said, clearing her throat and stepping back, causing him to finally release his hold. Damned if she didn't miss the warmth as soon as it was gone.

'Where are you off to in such a hurry?'

'Oh. Nowhere, just home. I was a bit distracted and didn't see you. I should have looked where I was going.'

'No harm done. Everything okay, though?'

The genuine concern on his face momentarily threw her. 'Yes, of course,' she said, managing a smile. 'How have you been?' *That's good*, she congratulated herself calmly. *He's just a fellow Barkley resident. Nothing special.* Except he was looking really nice in those jeans and that tight T-shirt that seemed to barely contain his biceps, and he smelled so good. What *was* that he was wearing? It smelled like a luxurious leather lounge with a touch of sandalwood and citrus. Divine.

'Sorry?' she asked in alarm as she realised he was looking at her a little oddly.

'I was just wondering if you had any idea why the whole town seems to suddenly have it in for me.'

Maybe she blacked out or something. What the heck was he on about?

'Apparently, I'm some bastard who's broken your heart and should be run out of town,' he went on, when her confusion became apparent.

'*What?*'

'That's the gist of what some old bloke buying a beer told me earlier. He reckons he was risking being skinned alive if his missus found out he'd been in the pub because of what I did to you. Whatever I did, I'm being given a rap over the knuckles for it now.'

'I have no idea what—' she started before recalling the conversation she'd had the day before with Nola and Betty. 'Oh, no . . .' She filled him in on what had happened. 'I'm sure it's not the whole town who has it out for you, though.'

'Hmm,' he said, scratching his chin, which had a shadow of stubble. 'I had a lunch booked for some ladies' social day and they cancelled late yesterday afternoon. I thought it strange at the time, but now it kind of makes more sense.'

Jenny was horrified. 'Are you serious?'

He shrugged. 'I guess that's what you get for poking the rumour-mill bear.'

'This is my fault. I shouldn't have kissed you.' She saw him grin and shook her head adamantly. 'No, I mean it. This is my fault. People had us down as the modern-day version of *The Graduate*, with me as Mrs Robinson and you as that guy Dustin Hoffman played.'

'The what?' he asked, eyeing her oddly.

'It's an old movie,' she said. 'Out even before my time,' she added dryly.

'I was kidding, I've heard about it. Good movie. But you're way hotter than Mrs Robinson.' He grinned.

'Excuse me if I don't find the potential ruin of your business a laughing matter.'

'Don't stress. It's not your fault. It'll all blow over.'

'But it is. Everyone's jumped to the wrong conclusion about you . . . which is also my fault because I panicked. I feel really bad,' Jenny said, biting the inside of her lip as she risked a glance up at him. 'I promise, I'll get this all sorted. I'll have a word with Nola and Betty. They'll be able to put a stop to the backlash.'

'The benefit of being the only pub in town with a qualified chef is that, eventually, everyone will feel that I've been suitably punished and they'll come back. I'm not that worried about a cancellation or two.'

'You should be. Once the folk in this town get a bee in their bonnets about something, they can hold a grudge like nobody's business,' she warned.

He still didn't look too fazed. 'You know, there is a way to turn it around even quicker than squashing all the rumours.'

'How?' Jenny asked warily.

'We could make it official. Go out on a date with me.'

'That's how all this crazy business started,' she told him, throwing her hands in the air. 'No more messing about with the gossips. I'm done.'

'I wasn't talking about messing with them. I mean it. For real. Let me take you out on a date.'

'Why?'

'Why does anyone take someone out on a date?'

'It was just to show off to Austin.'

'Was it?' he asked lightly, although the seriousness she could read in his eyes belied the offhand tone.

'I don't think so. I mean, there's the whole age thing. It wouldn't work.'

'There's not that much of an age difference.'

'Twelve years,' she shot back. 'That's over a decade.'

'It's only four thousand, three hundred and eighty-three days, though. If you say it like that, it doesn't sound as big.'

'You did *not* just work that out in your head.'

'Maybe I've been giving it some thought,' he said, with a slow smile that began melting some of her resistance.

'When were you going to tell me you were the owner of the pub and not just the barman?' she asked.

'I was wondering when you'd figure it out.'

'I didn't. I was told. Why didn't you say anything?' she asked. 'I'm sorry. I certainly never meant to come across as though I thought a barman was anything . . . well . . . lesser.'

His grin tilted, setting off yet another avalanche of unexpected tingles inside her. 'I didn't take any offence.'

'But you probably should have. Anyway, I'll fix things,' she said, beginning to back away.

'Dinner, Tuesday night,' he said, leaning against the post office wall and crossing his arms, which drew her attention to his chest and made her swallow hard before she dragged her eyes away.

'No,' she said.

'I'll pick you up at seven,' he continued, unfazed.

Jenny shook her head and stared at him, exasperated. 'No.'

'See you then, Jenny.'

'I'm not going out with you.'

'Seven,' he repeated, sending her a wink.

'I won't be waiting,' she called as she swung around to leave, then clamped her mouth shut impatiently as two men walking past turned to look at her. *I won't*, she added silently as she reached her car.

Jenny paced her bedroom and swore under her breath. It was six o'clock and she wasn't sure if she was angry or nauseous—maybe both. A ding distracted her and she crossed the room to pick up her phone from the desk.

Caffeine_Addict
How's your day been?

Her nerves dissolved and something close to happiness seeped in.

Florence_71
Not too bad. How about you?

Caffeine_Addict
Same. You've been quiet on here lately.

Florence_71
Work . . . kids . . . life . . . you know how it is.

Caffeine_Addict
Got time to chat now?

Florence_71
I wish, but no. I think I'm heading out soon.

Caffeine_Addict
You think?

Florence_71
I'm meeting someone for dinner. At least, I think so. I don't know.

A wave of uncertainty and nerves washed across her once more and she let out a small groan. Why couldn't she just be left alone to get into her pyjamas and climb into bed?

Caffeine_Addict
A date? You don't sound too keen. Is he that bad?

Florence_71
It's not that. It's just that . . . he's . . . it's just . . .

She stared at the words on the screen and kept deleting and retyping, trying to work out what she was feeling.

Caffeine_Addict
Maybe you're putting too much pressure on yourself?

Jenny chewed the inside of her lip as she considered that. It was possible. Perhaps if she stopped thinking of it as something monumental and treated it like any of those other dates she'd been on—just a temporary thing. Though, deep down, she knew Nick wasn't going to be as easy to discount. He certainly didn't seem boring or arrogant, and she suspected he'd be able to hold a conversation and even make her laugh if she allowed herself to drop her guard long enough.

Florence_71
I haven't had the best track record with dates lately.

Caffeine_Addict
Maybe this one will be different.

Florence_71
That's what I'm afraid of.

Caffeine_Addict
Get out there and have some fun for a change.

Florence_71
And do you have any plans for a date?

Caffeine_Addict
I wish. Sadly, work's getting in the way at the moment, so I'm living vicariously through you. Go on. Take one for the team.

Jenny sent a lopsided frown at her screen.

Florence_71
Fine.

Caffeine_Addict
Your excitement is palpable. Maybe practise making it a little more believable for the poor bastard's sake.

Florence_71
I'm sure he'll cope.

She closed the chat window and let out a long breath as she stared at her reflection in the mirror. *Just go and get it over with. He'll realise you're boring and work out this whole older-woman thing isn't as exciting as he somehow thinks it is.*

Suitably pep-talked, Jenny checked her make-up and tugged at her caramel denim jacket, then smoothed her new jeans and eyed her short suede boots. *You got this*, she told herself, grateful that no one else was home tonight.

The nerves came back tenfold as she sat on the edge of the lounge and waited. Why was she ready so early? Her hands felt a little clammy and she wiped them on her thighs. This was so dumb. She needed something to take her mind off the impending doom of the doorbell ringing. She noticed there was a streak of dust on her boot and leaned down to brush it off, but as she went to sit up, a sharp pain shot through her earlobe—she'd managed to get her earring snagged in the lace of her top. She tried to turn her head but it seemed to be twisting, and each time she moved, it tugged at the hole in her ear.

Getting to her feet with a frustrated growl, still bent over, she turned in a half-circle in front of the wall mirror to work out how she was caught up but couldn't quite see. 'Oh, for goodness' sake,' she muttered as she turned the other way, trying to find a better view.

The knock on the door made her freeze and her eyes widen in panic. Crap. He was here. Jenny didn't move. Maybe she could just stay quiet and he'd think she wasn't home . . . Then again, she'd be stuck looking like the Hunchback of Notre Dame with her head tucked into her armpit.

'FML,' she whispered mournfully.

With a resigned sigh, she hobbled to the front door and opened it, bracing herself for his reaction.

The silence was deafening and she gritted her teeth. 'My earring is caught in my shirt.'

'Oh. Right,' he said slowly, before he stepped inside and placed a pink-wrapped bunch of flowers on the hall table. 'Let me have a look.'

To his credit, he didn't sound as though he was laughing at her, but she couldn't see his face properly so she couldn't be sure. 'Ouch!'

'Sorry. Wow, it's really stuck. What the hell were you doing?'

'Cleaning my boot,' she snapped.

'Of course . . .'

'I was sitting down— It doesn't matter how I did it, would you just hurry up and untangle it.' *Oh God.* She clamped her eyes shut tightly, as she realised their positions put her at face level with his crotch. *Kill. Me. Now.*

'I'm trying, just hang on a minute.'

'Ouch!'

'Sorry.'

'It's really in there tight,' he grunted, and she could feel his fingers trying to work the earring free.

'Just get it out.'

The sound of a throat clearing made them freeze. Jenny tried to turn her head to see who had appeared without them hearing.

'I'm not sure what I'm interrupting here, but I, um . . . Mum? Are you okay?' Brittany asked.

Jenny smothered another curse. 'I'm fine. My earring is stuck in my shirt.'

'Oh. Okay.'

She heard the awkwardness in her daughter's voice and muttered some more choice words. 'I was bending down to—'

'No. Stop. I don't want to know,' Brittany cut in quickly.

Jenny swayed between feeling mortified and indignant. 'It wasn't what you're thinking,' she said, letting out another gasp as the earring pulled on her ear.

'I'm trying not to think of anything. I'm going to head upstairs. Come on, Sophie, time for your bath.'

'Brittany!'

'She's already gone. I think she's traumatised.'

'She's not the only one,' Jenny said through tightly clenched teeth, then gave a sigh of relief as her ear came free and she could straighten up. This was so bloody embarrassing.

'There you go,' he said, stepping back. 'You okay?'

'Nothing disappearing into a hole right now wouldn't cure.'

He grinned but schooled his face into a concerned glance. 'Your ear okay?'

'It's fine,' she said touching it tentatively and wincing. 'Thank you.'

'You ready to go?'

Oh God, they still had to get through an actual date. 'Sure.'

'The good news is the night's got to get better from here, right?' he quipped, following her to the door.

She really hoped it didn't get worse.

The black four-wheel drive in the driveway didn't surprise her; it looked much like the man himself: big, a little rough around the edges, but kinda sexy.

'Where are we going?'

'I thought maybe you'd have had enough of the gossip for a bit, so I booked a table over in Hamwell. I've been wanting to check out some of the competition anyway.'

She found herself able to relax a little into the leather seat. At least they could eat their meal without the whole damn town watching on like it was some live show for their entertainment.

'Is this okay?' he asked as crooning country music softly filled the cabin of the ute.

'It's fine.'

'I wasn't sure you'd actually answer the door tonight,' he said once they were out on the dark road heading out of Barkley. Tonight the moon was almost full, throwing a blue-silver light across the mostly flat paddocks either side of the road, the trees creating dark silhouettes and standing out like soldiers along the ridges of the hills in the distance.

'I almost didn't,' she said in a deadpan tone, recalling her recent humiliation.

'No, I mean, I didn't think you'd agree to come out.'

'I figured you'd probably just stay out there all night until I agreed.'

His chuckle spread a warm glow across her skin. 'I'm not some weird stalker.'

'No, but you're persistent.'

'It's the only way to get anything you really want out of life.'

She wasn't sure how to respond to that so she decided to change the topic. 'Have you had any further updates on Dylan?'

'Yeah, I called him the other day and he sounded a bit more positive than the last time I spoke with him. He's started his physio. I think they have another operation to do soon and then they'll have a better idea of how much use he'll have of his hand.'

'It'll be a long process—poor kid. That chef of yours certainly seems to have a temper. I hope he's settled down after the other week.'

Nick sent her a quick glance.

'He didn't seem particularly worried about Dylan, only covering his own backside,' she explained.

'He's not the easiest person in the world to get along with.'

'He sounds like a jerk.'

Nick gave a small grunt in agreement. 'My sister keeps reminding me he's a creative,' he said, rolling his eyes. 'I can't argue with his talent and experience where cooking's concerned, but as a person, he's an arsehole.'

'So in the interview you were happy to overlook his personality for his cooking ability?' she asked doubtfully and saw Nick shrug.

'All chefs have a bit of a temper—kinda goes with the territory. The more qualified they are, the bigger the ego, I think.'

'How did you get someone like him to accept a position in a place like Barkley? I mean, if he's worked all over the world and has such a huge reputation.'

'He's a friend of the family. When his career took a nosedive a while back, he pretty much lost everything. He was in a bad way. My sister gave him the job . . . she's my not so silent partner,' he said. 'It wasn't the worst idea she's ever had. I was looking for a chef. He was a recovering alcoholic who needed something to focus on. He'd burned all his bridges with everyone he'd ever worked with and was sitting at rock bottom.'

'Well, that was nice of you.'

'Not really,' he said, grinning. 'I picked up a world-class chef for my restaurant for next to nothing.'

'I think you took a risk that you didn't have to in order to help him out.'

'Yeah, maybe. I'm not sure if I did the right thing or not. He's hard work.'

'Do you still think he had something to do with Dylan's accident?'

When he looked across at her, she hurried to explain, 'That day I dropped in and he was yelling at the other kitchen hand . . . you two were having an argument.'

'Dylan confirmed he'd been run through the safety checks and his hand just slipped. But Saville's been warned—if I catch him drinking, he'll be out. I haven't been able to prove anything, but I've been keeping an eye on him. It'd suck for my business plan if he had to go, but I wouldn't be entirely cut up about it. He's a pain in my arse—in everyone's arses. I'm about this close,' he said, lifting one hand off the steering wheel, 'to having a mutiny on my hands with the rest of the staff over the way he carries on sometimes.'

She could imagine it had to be difficult for someone with an international career such as Jeremy Saville to suddenly find himself at rock bottom in a little place like Barkley—yet, celebrity or not, the guy was a recovering alcoholic and that in itself would be an ongoing issue. She made a note to try and catch Saville alone some time and see if he wanted any referrals to programs and support groups run through the hospital.

When they parked out the back of the restaurant, Nick told her to wait while he ran around the front of the vehicle and opened her door for her.

'Don't want you thinking I can't be a gentleman or anything.' He winked.

'I've never thought that.'

'Somehow I get the feeling I have a lot to prove to you, Jenny Hayward.'

The seriousness of his tone caught her a little off guard, and neither of them moved from the close proximity they found themselves in. Another car pulling into the carpark ended the moment and Nick stepped back, closing the door behind her.

Twenty

'Wow, this is kinda fancy,' Jenny breathed as they walked into the low-lit restaurant. The décor made her feel as though she'd somehow been transported to France. A huge chandelier dominated the centre of the room, its raindrop crystals capturing the light and sparkling like diamonds. She'd been impressed by the chandelier in the ladies at the Coach House, but this one was elegant and on a whole different scale.

'"Wow" is right.'

They were settled by an expressionless waiter and Jenny bit her lip a little as she cast her eyes over the menu. It was certainly not the same type of cuisine the Coach House served.

'This is the kind of restaurant my sister would have created if I'd given her free rein,' Nick said.

'It's very nice.'

'It is. Just not what I was trying to do.'

'Well, you succeeded. This isn't the Coach House. I'm not sure a place like this would have suited Barkley.'

'Me either.'

'It's certainly a big step up for Hamwell as well—at least the old Hamwell, when I used to live here,' she said. 'I don't even recognise the town now. Everything's changed—the whole vibe is different.'

'How long did you live here for?'

'Around ten years or so. I came here after I was married, then we moved out to Barkley after the kids came along.'

'Do you still have family here?'

'Just on Austin's side. My parents relocated to the coast years ago. What made you choose Barkley to move to?'

'Initially it was the hotel itself. I'd seen it online when I was in planning mode. It kept coming up on different sites and something always made me take a second look at it. I didn't think it would still be around by the time I was ready to make an offer, but there it was . . . again,' he said. 'It had been bought a couple of times and the deal had fallen through at the last minute on both occasions, so the owner had pulled it from the market.'

Jenny nodded. 'Lionel Gosson.'

'You knew him?'

'Of him. I'd met his wife a few times. She always seemed so sad. I think they'd lost a son early on and she never really got over it, was how I remembered her. I didn't know her well though. Lionel was a bit of a drinker, from all accounts. I remember the car accident some years back—quite a while now, actually, his wife and their only surviving son were killed in it. I think that's when he put the pub on the market, then sadly passed away himself. I did hear it was tied up in legal issues and whatnot with extended family for a number of years. The whole town was talking about it—closing the town's only decent pub was a big thing.'

'Yeah—so I've been told.'

Their food arrived and Jenny picked up her cutlery then looked over at Nick. 'So what were the other deciding factors for making the move to Barkley? You said initially it was the pub?'

'I had to look up where it was,' he said, cutting his steak. 'I'd never been out this way before. That's when I came across an article about Hamwell and the revival with the arts community. The numbers they were talking about the town's growth and the housing prices thanks to the relocation of some pretty major companies setting up regionalised offices told me this was an area that was starting to show its full potential. Once you get a town that explodes like that, after a while, people are going to want to start exploring the local district. Barkley is the perfect distance from Hamwell for a weekend drive. It has the heritage factor and charm of another time—all the things city people moving up here would be looking for.' He shrugged. 'I figured if I bought the pub before this whole area realised the potential of the place and jacked up the prices like they have in Hamwell, then I'd be in on the ground floor and make a killing.'

'So it was a purely business-based decision?' she asked, studying him carefully. It sounded all very . . . clinical.

When he hesitated, she tilted her head slightly. A flutter of something strange crossed his face.

'Mostly, although—' He stopped, glancing up at her with an almost embarrassed expression. 'It's weird to admit out loud,' he said slowly, 'but it wasn't just that. The whole thing with the pub appearing. It was probably just the fact I'd looked at it once and from then on the analytics automatically threw it into my search engine, but I don't know.' He shook his head irritably. 'There was just something about it that I couldn't shake.' He dragged his gaze from hers to study his food.

'Well, that's kinda normal . . . I mean, sometimes you just *know* when something's meant to be.'

'It was weird.'

Jenny smiled at his confusion. 'It was obviously fate or something.'

'I don't believe in fate.'

'Really?'

'Nope. I believe in hard work and planning.'

'Well, you have to do that too,' she said amicably.

'I reckon our steak still beats what they're using here,' Nick mused as he studied the piece of meat on his fork. 'The marbling in this is nothing compared to our cuts. What do you think?'

'I agree. I think you win in the steak department.'

He flashed her a brief grin.

'So how does that all work? I know you mentioned you do all your processing in house—hence the bandsaw incident,' she reminded him.

'We're in partnership with a local farmer—we sourced the breed of beef we prefer and he raises them. We get control of the whole process from breeding to feed and everything in between. The complete paddock-to-plate experience.'

'So that's a big deal? How the beef's raised?' she asked curiously.

'Absolutely. Choosing the right breed is vital for the marbling effect and the quality of feed—pasture versus feed lot and what they're fed—and the environment they're raised in all plays a role as well. Our cattle are kept quiet and happy and the lack of stress is really important. Especially compared to large feed lot–bred cattle, where they're under more pressure with greater numbers of cattle kept in smaller areas. Even the abattoir experience can affect the meat quality—since we have smaller numbers, don't need to transport them as far and keep the whole process as calm as possible, our quality is unsurpassed.' He said it without any hint of ego and Jenny smiled at the passion she heard in his voice.

'Have you always been interested in cattle breeding?' He certainly didn't give off a farmer vibe.

'Nope. Didn't know a thing about it until I began researching for the restaurant. If you want to make a business stand out, you need an edge,' he told her. 'Something that makes your place different from anything else around. People want to support food that's been sourced responsibly. They also want to know where their food's coming from. What better way is there to support the town than to grow your food locally?'

'I think it's amazing,' she said honestly.

'It started out as a purely business-based choice,' he admitted, 'but once I got involved, met the people I work with and saw what went into raising these cattle, it was hard not to get inspired. Best decision I ever made . . . other than buying the pub,' he said with a smile.

As beautiful as this place was, it really didn't hold a candle to the Coach House. It had class and sophistication, but it lacked the warmth and hospitality of the pub. The staff here were more aloof, elegant, the waitresses dressed in slim black dresses and the waiters in white shirts and black trousers, completely at odds with the jeans and coloured work shirts the servers wore in Nick's place. The music was classical and delicate—but only background atmosphere. Exactly the kind of place Derrick would frequent, unlike the Coach House, where the music was often live and the patrons interacted with it.

She knew which one she preferred.

Jenny eyed the dessert menu the waiter brought over and shook her head. 'I don't think I can fit dessert in,' she said, a little regretfully.

'Can I tempt you with dessert from the Coach House? Give dinner time to settle so you can make some room?' Nick suggested.

She really did feel like something sweet, and she knew what was on the menu back there. 'Depends,' she said slowly. 'Is the lemon meringue going to be on tonight?'

He grinned. 'I believe it is.'

'Deal,' Jenny said, closing the menu and placing it on the table.

'Right.' He nodded. 'The way to Jenny's heart is through lemon meringue. Noted.'

'I'm not that complicated, really.'

'I wouldn't say that. There's plenty about you I've been trying to figure out.'

The conversation had somehow gone from light-hearted to something else in a matter of seconds and she wasn't sure what to do with it. Luckily, Nick stood up to go and pay.

The air smelled fresh and cool as they crossed the carpark and the moon cast a silvery shine through the darkness. They came to a stop beside the car and Nick stepped closer, placing Jenny between him and the vehicle.

'Thank you for dinner,' she said nervously, and a shot of desire raced through him as she caught her bottom lip with her teeth.

All night he'd been battling the urge to kiss her. Watching her lips close around the end of the fork as she ate had almost been his undoing. He liked to think he was mature enough to control his urges—he wasn't some volatile hormone-induced teenager after all—but everything Jenny did seemed to send him flying backwards to that era when all it took to make him hard was a smile from a cute girl.

Ever since spontaneously making the date with her the other day, he'd been giving himself a lecture about taking things slow and not spooking her but, hell, everything the woman did turned him on. He was going to blow it if he didn't calm the hell down. She was already skittish about the whole age thing, not to mention the fact she was slightly paranoid about gossip . . . If he didn't take things slow, he was going to scare her off and he'd never get a second chance.

But right now, his gaze locked on that bottom lip as she stared up at him with those wide eyes, he realised he was fighting a losing battle.

He let out a harsh breath and stepped back a little. He didn't want to ruin this. She'd agreed to come out on a date and that was momentous enough—he couldn't risk moving too fast now.

'Jenny, I know you have your reservations about all this,' Nick said, forcing himself to take the mature higher ground. He had to prove to her he could be trusted—show her that he wasn't just thinking of her as some casual one-night stand. He wanted more than that.

The thought momentarily distracted him. When had he decided that? Not that he'd intended to be something casual, but the wrongness of the idea made him realise that, at some point, Jenny had become important to him. A relationship had not been on the cards for him, not until he knew his business was up and running. He'd always been so focused and driven, making certain nothing distracted him from what he wanted to do, but that had changed and he wasn't sure why.

He forced himself to get back on topic. 'I know you think this is a bad idea. I get that you've had a good reason to steer clear of men and you've been focusing on your kids and your job, but I can't help but think it's such a bloody waste for someone as amazing as you to be sitting out life just because you're worried about what everyone else might think. You deserve more than that.'

He saw the surprise in her eyes and pressed on quickly. 'I don't want to pressure you into something you're not ready for. I just want you to give this thing between us a go. See if it is—or could be—anything. You've got too much to offer to bury yourself at home.'

The way he looked at her—so honest and intently, made Jenny's breath catch.

'I just don't see how this could wor—' Her protest was cut short as he leaned in and kissed her. It was nothing more than his lips gently probing hers, but the action sent a lightning bolt throughout her body. Her hands went to his shirt, bunching it up in her fingers as she fought to find some kind of hold against the rush of emotions racing through her. She tried to think of all the logical arguments she'd been prepared to make moments before, but she couldn't recall a single one. Instead, she found herself kissing him back.

For the longest time, she forgot where and who they were and simply allowed herself to be swept away in the moment. How long had it been since she'd been kissed like this? *Like this?* a little voice queried doubtfully. *Never.*

Maybe when she'd been young and blissfully in love, kissing Austin had felt like this, but that had been a long time ago . . . a very long time ago. They'd stopped doing a lot of things over the years and kissing had been one of the first, other than a quick peck goodbye. She wasn't even sure *when* they'd stopped kissing.

As they parted, Jenny found herself staring up into two lazily satisfied eyes.

'It seems to *work* just fine,' Nick said, gently smiling down at her.

She couldn't very well disagree, not when her heart was still beating against her chest like some frantic trapped animal. Maybe that's what had just happened—she'd realised too late that she was trapped. He'd proven her body, at least, knew what it wanted, despite what her common sense was saying.

'Come back to my place tonight,' he said, his voice husky.

She opened her mouth to say no but found only silence.

Nick clearly decided that wasn't an outright no and helped her into the car.

The music played softly as he drove. Neither of them really spoke. There was a definite tension in the air—not an awkward one; this one crackled with electricity. Was she seriously considering this?

As they arrived in town, Nick looked across at her. 'My place?'

For the life of her she couldn't say no, she simply gave him a small nod and let out a shaky breath.

Twenty-one

The hotel was quiet when they made their way through the carpark towards a side door at the rear of the building. Nick inserted a key into the lock and pushed the old timber door open then held it for her to walk in ahead of him.

A dim glow from the night lights lit the lower floor, reminding Jenny of the restaurant they'd eaten in earlier and its dark interior. Such a stark difference from the busy hotel the Coach House usually was when she'd been here before. Now, late at night with everything locked away and no customers, there was a kind of peace she hadn't expected.

'It's a beautiful building,' she said as they approached the big staircase leading to the second floor.

'She's pretty special,' Nick agreed. 'Wanna see something really cool?'

Jenny smiled at the mischievous grin that reminded her of an excited little kid. 'Sure.'

She followed him away from the bottom step and walked under the staircase, watching as he pushed on a section of the white timber wall panelling. Her eyebrows raised as the panel swung open to reveal a dark void behind.

'Is that a secret door?' she asked, feeling a tingle of excitement.

'Yep. We found it when we pulled off the old water-damaged plasterboard.'

'Why would they have boarded it up?' she asked, eyeing the doorway.

'No idea.'

'What's in there?'

'I'll show you.' He switched on the torch on his phone then ducked under the low entrance and disappeared inside. Jenny hurried to follow, barely having to lower her head, stepping into the surprisingly cool, rough stone-walled tunnel. A damp, old smell hit her senses almost immediately and she shivered as she followed Nick closely until he came to a stop. She heard the squeak of a door opening and stepped into a wide open space that instantly filled with light as he flicked a switch. They were in the centre of a square spacious room.

'What is this place?' she asked, confused by the discovery.

Nick shrugged. 'I have no idea. I'm assuming it was some kind of cellar at one time, maybe from the original, much smaller, building the pub started off as just after the gold rush.'

It was definitely *not* an inviting room by any account. It was cold and dark and had no window. Another shiver ran through her body and Nick quickly ushered her out.

'Come on, let's get out of here. You're freezing.'

'You could do ghost tours,' Jenny said, once they were back in familiar surroundings.

She heard him give a small grunt and eyed him warily. 'What?'

'Well, not to freak you out or anything, but a few of the old regulars have been telling me the odd story or two of strange things that have happened around the place over the years.'

'Ghosts? Here?' she replied, smiling. Recalling the creepy cellar, though, she soon decided she'd rather not know.

'Nah, I reckon all the banging and building lately would have chased off any hanging about,' he told her cheerfully. 'I promised you dessert,' he said, leading her towards the kitchen. He switched on the bright overhead lights and crossed to a large cool-room door, which he pulled open, disappearing inside before re-emerging with two slices of lemon meringue.

'Can you grab a pair of forks from under that cupboard over there?' he asked, pointing his chin.

When Jenny held the cutlery up triumphantly, they headed upstairs.

At the top of the staircase was a hallway with several timber doors. They passed the doors and reached a set of French doors that opened onto a wraparound verandah. Jenny took in the view of the town below.

'This is really lovely,' she said, taking a seat at a small table and shrugging out of her jacket to hang it on the back of the chair.

'Yeah, I like to wind down out here at night.'

'Are you the only one who lives onsite?' Jenny asked, digging into her dessert, savouring the flavour as the fluffy meringue melted and the sweetness mixed with the tangy lemon.

'Yeah. I have the whole place to myself at the moment. Eventually I'll get all nine bedrooms redecorated and ready as boutique accommodation.'

'So, not your basic pub room then?' she asked, kinking an eyebrow.

'Nope. Pub accommodation has taken a big step up over the last few years. Nowadays, it's luxury all the way.'

'Sounds exciting.'

'Sounds expensive,' he said dryly and she watched as the fork disappeared into his mouth, realising too late that she was still staring when she shifted her gaze and met his eyes, which were watching her curiously.

Jenny cleared her throat and lowered her eyes. 'I can see how it would fit in with the refurbishment though. People would expect the accommodation to be as sophisticated as the rest of the place.'

'Exactly. Although that's phase two. The first priority was always to get the bar and restaurant up and running.'

'Phase one seems to be going well, then.'

'It's getting there,' he said with a lightness Jenny suspected hid a note of concern. Running any business in this climate, she imagined, would be a worry for anyone, let alone starting up a new venture with as large a renovation as this one had had.

Putting her plate on the table, Jenny stood up and walked to the railing, taking in the clear night sky above. A few moments later, without hearing him move, she felt Nick standing behind her. It shouldn't be a thing, but she swore she could feel the heat radiating like a damn furnace between their bodies, even though he hadn't touched her. Her eyes fluttered shut at the first touch of his fingers against her skin as he softly traced them up and down her arms. Her body swayed backwards until she came into contact with his solid chest. Before she could stop herself, she turned.

His lips found hers and, just like the first few times, her body instantly reacted, drawn to him like an unspoken calling, as she returned his hungry kisses that suddenly grew deeper and more demanding, leaving them both breathing hard when Nick eventually broke away to look down at her with a smouldering gaze that sent a quiver of longing from her scalp to her toes.

'We should take this inside,' he murmured, and she simply nodded, unable to do anything more.

They stepped through the doors and walked down the hallway to a door with a brass doorknob that she suspected was as old as the building itself. Jenny took a moment to soak in her surroundings. The room was draped in a rosy warmth thrown off by the small leadlight lamp by the bedside. The ceiling was high, with antique mouldings around the edges, and the walls were panelled tongue and groove. This room, being on a corner, had two sets of French doors: one leading to the verandah where they'd just been and the other to the section that wrapped around the southern side of the building. The flooring was the same wide timber boards used in the hallway, covered with a round, bright blue rug under the wrought-iron bed that dominated the centre of the room.

Jenny watched as Nick sat on the edge of the mattress, unbuttoning his shirt and throwing it aside, before pulling her to him with gentle hands on her waist until she stood between his legs. Her hands automatically went to his shoulders, his smooth skin warm and muscular beneath her fingers.

Her gaze held his silently as he worked the hem of her top up over her arms and head with agonisingly slow movements, leaving her standing before him in the pretty new lacy bra she'd thrown into her shopping trolley on a whim last time she went to Hamwell. She saw his eyelids lower as he took his time surveying what he'd revealed.

His fingers went to the waistband of her jeans, unclasping the button and lowering the zipper so she could shimmy her way out of them. Thank goodness she'd decided to add the matching bottoms to the bra—she couldn't remember the last time she'd purchased matching underwear, let alone remembered to wear each piece at the same time. Though, standing here before this man who seemed to be devouring her with his eyes, she'd never been so glad of a ridiculous impulse buy in her entire life.

Her eyes fluttered shut as his warm breath touched the swell of her cleavage and a delicious shiver ran up her spine. What was happening to her? How was she standing here, practically naked before a stranger, and not feeling the slightest bit embarrassed? This very situation had played through her mind on a loop ever since she'd started thinking about dating again. She had been positive she'd be mortified when it came to revealing her fifty-year-old body to a man for the first time. She'd only ever had sex with one man and every time she'd dared think about the possibility of meeting someone and doing . . . *this*, she could only imagine how awkward and uncomfortable it would be.

She swallowed a gasp as Nick's lips moved across her skin, the sensation sending a shiver of desire through her.

His hands slid up her sides and reached around to unclasp her bra, letting it fall to the floor. His eyes feasted on her bare breasts and still she felt no urge to cover herself and cower away. Her breasts were no longer as pert as they'd been in her twenties. They'd been working boobs, sustaining babies the way nature had intended. Unfortunately, nature hadn't returned them to their original condition afterwards and nowadays they were a little lower than they'd once been—although thankfully, still mostly rounded. She watched as Nick cupped them gently in his hands as though weighing them, then tipped her head back and released a ragged moan as she felt his warm breath upon them.

Her hands went to his head, her fingers running through his short hair, enticing a groan of encouragement from him that sparked one of her own in return.

Her internal babbling ceased and pure, unadulterated lust took over.

Twenty-two

Nick lay on his side in the dark, listening to the soft breathing of the woman tucked in front of him, and let his fingers trail along her arm. She was perfect. He'd never been one to use that term very often, but tonight it summed up everything. Together, they'd been explosive. He'd known he was attracted to Jenny ever since first laying eyes on her in the pub, but the intensity of the connection he'd just felt with this woman in his arms had surprised the hell out of him. He'd never experienced anything like it before in his life, and while he wouldn't say he was the man-whore a number of his mates were, he wasn't exactly a monk either and this had been . . . He was lost for words. Another first. Everything about Jenny stunned him. Her curves, her skin, the sounds she made, the smell of her hair—literally every bloody inch of her turned him on.

For the first time in who knew how long, he didn't know how he should proceed. He knew she wasn't asleep, her breathing was still too fast for that, and lying here in absolute silence was only going to make things weird, but he was scared he might say the wrong thing and send her scampering away. While she'd floored him with how uninhibited she'd been, he sensed now that she was rapidly retreating into her shell and that was the last thing he wanted. He wanted that woman she'd been in his arms only a few minutes earlier. The one with the slumberous eyes and pouty lips that had done things to him he'd never dared imagine her doing. He wanted the Jenny who'd matched him kiss for kiss and sent him over the edge of reason faster than he'd ever imagined possible.

'You okay?' he finally asked, cringing slightly. What he really wanted to know was, *Did that completely wreck you for all other partners the way it has for me?*

'Yeah. I'm fine.'

Fine? He frowned before deciding to feel out where she was at. 'That was pretty amazing.'

The small silence that followed had him holding his breath.

'It was,' she finally agreed, and he cautiously took that as a positive.

'Are you sure you're okay? I wasn't too rough or anything?'

'No. It was— I'm great.'

'You are,' he said, hoping that maybe lightening the mood might be the better course of action. 'You're amazing.'

Her sceptical laugh made him frown.

'I'm serious. That was incredible.'

He lifted his hand when she slowly pulled away. She sat with her back to him as she searched for her clothes. 'Hey?' he said, touching her back softly.

She stopped gathering the clothing but didn't turn to face him.

'Look at me,' he said gently and waited until, reluctantly, she did so. His frown deepened at the shuttered expression in her eyes. 'What's wrong?'

'Nothing,' she said, shaking her head quickly. 'It's late. I need to get home.'

'Jenny. Talk to me.' Christ, he'd just been daydreaming over what they'd shared like they were in some Disney movie and she couldn't wait to get away from him.

'There's nothing to talk about. I had a good time. You were great. It's just late.'

Was she seriously giving him the old one-night-stand brush off here? Okay, he may have used the same tone—hell, even the same excuse—a time or two, but never after the kind of mind-blowing sex they'd just experienced!

He sat up and stared at her back as she wiggled into her clothing, blinking as she turned and glanced at him.

'I'll call a taxi.'

'I'll take you,' he said, coming to his senses and moving from the bed to pull his own clothes back on.

'It's fine. Honestly,' she said.

'I'll drive you.'

A sudden tension filled the room with its uncomfortable presence and Nick let out a long sigh. 'Jenny, I'm sorry if I've done something to upset you . . . I thought we had a great time together.'

He saw her bite the inside of her lip as she risked a small look at his face before dropping her gaze to the floor. 'We did. You haven't upset me. You just . . . caught me off guard. I'm not sure . . .'

'Of what?'

'I'm not sure how I feel about it all.' She shrugged helplessly.

For the first time since she withdrew from him there was a glimmer of hope. 'It snuck up on me too,' he admitted carefully, deciding that he may as well throw all his cards on the table; he may not get another shot at it if he kept them close to his chest. Not with Jenny. 'I knew I was attracted to you, but I wasn't expecting the kind of sparks we gave off just now. That was intense.'

His spirits lifted a little more at the startled look in her eye and the fact she was holding his gaze timidly. Encouraged, he took a step closer, then another, until he was close enough to entwine one of her small hands in his.

'I'm not in this for a one-night stand, Jen. I've been attracted to you from day one, and it's never dulled. If anything, every time I've seen you, this need to get to know everything about you has kept growing. After tonight,' he said, shaking his head, 'it's only got stronger.'

'But the age thing,' she said.

'Isn't important,' he finished for her firmly. 'I don't have a weird fetish for older women or something. What I feel for you is simply a man attracted to a woman—a beautiful, intelligent, kind woman. I'm attracted to you as a person—not your age or anything else. Just you. That's it.'

He saw something shift in her then, and the glimmer of hope turned into something a little brighter. 'I don't know where this will go, but I do know that what we had just then isn't something that comes along every day. We'd be idiots to throw it away without giving it a chance.'

She held his gaze. He could see her processing and weighing something up in her mind before the conflict behind her eyes seemed to loosen and she relaxed a little.

'Okay,' she said simply.

'Okay,' he breathed, feeling as though he'd crossed the finish line of a marathon. He could work with an uncertain okay. He'd show her he was right and tonight wasn't some fluke. All he needed was for her to trust him a little. He leaned in and kissed her lips softly, feeling her own tremble beneath his, but restrained himself from deepening it, despite every fibre of his being urging him to do so. He had to prove he was worthy of her trust and he wasn't about to blow this chance. 'Come on, let's get you home.'

'Mum! I can't find my car keys!' Savannah yelled from the hallway the next morning.

'Are they hanging on the key hook?' Jenny hollered back.

'No. Why would they be there?'

Jenny gave a small tsk under her breath and closed her eyes briefly. *Of course not, it's far more entertaining to play a game of let's all look for Savannah's bloody car keys every damn morning.*

'I'm going to be so late!'

'Well, maybe if you got up when your alarm first went off and didn't stay in the shower for half an hour you wouldn't be late,' Jenny said.

'How is that at all helpful to point out right now, Mum?' Savannah snapped.

'About as helpful as you leaving a trail of stress and anxiety behind you every day when you tear through the place like a cyclone looking for your bloody keys!'

'I'm going to be fired if I'm late!' Savannah cried, and instantly Jenny's irritation subsided to go into comforting mode.

'We'll find them,' she said, picking up cushions from the lounge and checking underneath. 'Where did you go when you came inside last night?'

'Mum! Mum! Mum!' Sophie called out, interrupting and adding to the general bedlam.

'Shh, Soph. Just wait,' Brittany told her with a frown across at her younger sibling.

'I came in through the front door, through here to say hi to Britt and Soph, then up to my room.'

'Check your jacket pockets,' Brittany suggested from where she was wrestling her toddler into clothes for day care.

'I did.'

'Check the freezer,' Chloe called from upstairs. 'That's where I found my phone once.'

'Why would your phone have been in the freezer?' Jenny asked as her youngest daughter came down the stairs.

'I was getting ice cream,' she said with an offhand shrug as though it were completely logical.

Jenny bent down and picked up Sophie, who was now dressed but still fussing, and absently began rocking as she balanced the toddler on her hip.

'Hello, people? Still can't find my keys?' Savannah reminded them impatiently.

'Mum's right, you need to start taking responsibility for your shit,' Brittany said.

'Oh, right—like you're so perfect.'

'I know where *my* car keys are,' Brittany pointed out.

'Did you move them when you got home last night, Mum?' Savannah asked, after completing a slow turn of the room. 'I heard you stomping about down here.'

'I would have remembered moving them and told you,' Jenny said, putting the wriggling toddler back on the ground.

'I heard that too. It was like . . . after midnight. Were you only just getting home then?' Brittany asked, her eyes widening as she looked across at her mother.

'I don't know what time it was,' she said, eyeing the doorway and planning her escape from the sudden interrogation. 'I'm sure it wasn't that late.'

'So how was it?' Brittany prompted.

'Fine. Nice.'

'Uh-oh,' Chloe intoned with a doomed expression. 'What happened? Is he a dud kisser?'

'What? No,' Jenny denied quickly.

'So he was a *good* kisser, then?' Brittany surmised, nodding slowly.

'I didn't say—' Jenny started to protest before giving an impatient huff. 'Can we just find these stupid keys?'

'Okay, sheesh, calm down,' Chloe said, backing away.

'Muuuuuummmmmm!' Sophie yelled from across the room.

'What!' All four women turned and answered impatiently, startling the toddler, who stood beside her open doll house, holding up a set of car keys on a dream catcher key chain.

'I find,' Sophie beamed proudly.

'Good girl!' Brittany crooned with a proud smile.

'Oh, yeah, because she stashed them there—we'd have never found them,' Savannah snapped.

'Don't leave them lying around and she won't play with them,' Chloe advised, taking a condescending tone with her older sister that she seemed to enjoy.

'Shut up, Chloe.'

'Just sayin',' she said.

'Well, don't.'

'Come on, girls, just stop now. Savannah, hurry up and get to work. Chloe, can you do the dishwasher this morning and hang out the clothes in the washing machine before you leave the house, please?'

'I hung out clothes yesterday,' Chloe protested.

'You're the only one who isn't leaving the house this morning.'

'Well, that's convenient.' She pouted.

'Stop complaining,' Brittany cut in. 'You haven't had to do anything compared to when we were your age.'

'Oh, right,' Chloe scoffed.

'It's true! You're the youngest. You got out of everything.'

'I did not. Tell them, Mum!'

'She didn't get out of anything,' Jenny said wearily. God, she hated when they did this. How soon the older pair forgot the arguments and complaining *they* used to do whenever she asked them to do anything when they were teenagers.

'She did. All the time,' Brittany argued.

'It's true,' Savannah agreed. 'We had to do heaps more stuff around the house.'

'For goodness' sake,' Jenny muttered. 'Can we drop the drama and bickering? I seriously have not had enough coffee this morning to deal with this right now.'

'I'm not hanging out any of their stuff,' Chloe declared mutinously, which sparked a whole new round of how hard the older two had it growing up.

Jenny left the room without a backwards glance. She'd let them deal with it—they were supposed to be adults now. She'd buy a coffee on the way to work and sit in the car and drink it in peace.

As she passed the hall table, she noticed the bunch of flowers that Nick had brought over the night before had been placed in a vase. She'd forgotten all about them. She touched the petals of the delicate arrangement of pink and white carnations lightly then paused as she stared thoughtfully at the single pink hydrangea in the centre. It looked out of place, almost as though it had been added later.

She'd never told Nick she liked hydrangeas.

Twenty-three

Nick chuckled after she finished telling him about her morning, as they sat later that afternoon outside his room on the verandah. 'I envy the kind of relationship you have with your kids,' he said.

'Really? What's your family like?'

'I don't really have one.' He shrugged, and Jenny saw it as the deflecting gesture it was. 'My parents died in a car accident when I was serving overseas. There's only me and Susie now.'

'That must have been a terrible shock.'

'Yeah. It was.'

'So you and your sister aren't close?' she probed gently.

'Not really. She's older than me and had left home... well, had run away, by the time I came along. They had a pretty big falling out over it all. I didn't know her at all until I was about ten or eleven years old. That's when she finally came home. We've never had that typical sibling connection.'

'How old was she when she left home?'

'Fifteen or so, I think.'

Jenny tried to imagine any of her girls leaving home at that age and couldn't. They were still just babies. 'So there's a pretty big age gap between you.'

'Mum and Dad had given up on having kids when Susie came along. Then I happened and ruined any hope of retirement plans.' He chuckled. 'I think they were worn out by the time I arrived. Susie was a lot to handle as a kid and then they had to start all over again with me when most of their friends were ready to settle down and take things easier. I mean, older parents seem to be the norm now, but back then it wasn't as common.' He sent her a half-grin. 'I didn't realise we were a little different until I started school and the teachers used to think they were my grandparents.' He shook his head. 'As I grew up and came home from friends' places, I started to notice the difference in age. They didn't do parks or weekend sports. I don't think they wanted kids at all, to be honest. They weren't like you are with your kids,' he said, his smile softer. 'Neither of them were close with their own parents and siblings, so I didn't have much of a relationship with any of my extended family. Guess that's just the way they were.'

Jenny's heart broke a little at his words as she imagined the lonely childhood he was describing. 'And you and Susie never grew closer—as you got older, I mean?'

He shifted his arm slightly, getting comfortable. 'I wasn't exactly likeable as a teenager—I got into all kinds of mischief,' he said with a self-mocking smile. 'I think my parents were expecting me to end up in prison the way I was going.

I remember they tried to get Susie to talk to me at one point. You can imagine how well that went over with a seventeen-year-old smartarse. She moved back after our parents' accident and things were kinda different. I guess I'd matured a bit by then, but I wouldn't say we're close. I mean, we're all the family we have now.'

'So if you were a teenage delinquent, how did you end up in the army?'

'The Police Youth Club started a boxing session and I rocked up, ready to rumble, being the bad arse I thought I was, only to be knocked on my arse by this big, surly copper. He cut through the bullcrap and showed me where I'd end up if I kept heading down the path I was on. Before the police force he'd been in the army and, after a while, I kind of respected him. I joined the army because of him and here I am now.'

'He must have been a great guy.'

'He was.'

'Did you stay in touch with him?'

'Yeah. I used to drop in and visit him and his wife whenever I was home on leave. He still lives in Penrith. I haven't seen him for a few years, though.'

Jenny mulled over what he'd told her for a while. His life could have turned out so different if he hadn't had that positive influence intervening when it did, but she couldn't quite get past the whole siblings not getting along thing. 'You mentioned Susie was a silent partner in the pub? You must sort of get on to be business partners?'

Nick gave a short sigh. 'I had my parents' inheritance sitting in an account she managed. She was the executor of their will and they had a tight rein on me when it came to when I could access any funds. When I decided to leave the army, I had to go to her to get the money out, and when she realised I didn't have enough in my share, she offered to go in with me.'

'Well, that was nice of her,' Jenny said, feeling a spark of optimism at his words, till she saw the frown creasing between his eyebrows. 'Wasn't it?'

'I knew I was making a deal with the devil, but I didn't have much choice. The renovation costs went through the roof practically overnight with the whole Covid fiasco. I'd been putting a business plan together for a couple of years, had the thing polished to perfection,' he said with a sarcastic chuckle, 'then everything changed and suddenly it looked like it was going to be out of reach. So, I took her offer, even though I knew she'd want to pull rank whenever she felt like it. It wasn't the dream I had in mind.'

'It seems to be working out, though. You got it up and running.'

'Yeah—for the most part, it's okay.'

'Can you buy her out of her share down the track or something? If you don't like working with her?'

'That's the plan. It's just going to take a while to get the business to that point.'

'I had no idea your sister was Sussanne Angelopoulos until I saw the article in the food magazine the other day.'

For a moment he looked embarrassed. He shifted uncomfortably. 'Yeah. I don't really advertise the fact as a rule.'

'Why not? She must be an amazing woman.'

'I guess. I mean, don't get me wrong—she's famous for a reason and she's a brilliant businesswoman. We're just complete opposites in nearly every way.'

'Most siblings are. I mean, my girls all have different personalities and fight constantly—still,' she added dryly. 'But I know they'd be there in a heartbeat for each other if they were ever needed.'

'You've brought them up right, then.'

Jenny shrugged. 'I'm probably just lucky I had the opportunity to spend a lot of time with them when they were little, before I started nursing.'

'You love what you do,' he said and it was more a statement than a question.

'I do.'

'Did you always want to be a nurse?'

'No. Not at all, actually. I kind of fell into my profession. But now I can't imagine ever doing anything else.' The fact he wanted to talk about her job filled her with an unexpected warmth. So far she hadn't met any men, including her ex-husband, who'd shown the slightest bit of interest.

'You're good at what you do. I saw how you were with Dylan—working under stress. You were calm and able to keep everyone else around you focused on the job. That's leadership. You're a natural.'

His words surprised her. She'd never thought of herself as a leader—sure, at work, she was often the one who took the lead in situations but that was because she was usually the only one there and because she had to think outside the box to get things done thanks to the limited staffing and facilities.

However, she wasn't sure she could think of a single situation before nursing where she'd been a natural leader. 'I've been lucky that I've had some great training along the way and the job tends to throw situations at you unexpectedly, so you have to sink or swim. I do a remote clinic once a month and I soon found out that thinking on your feet was just something you have to do when there's people looking to you for help.'

'Sounds a bit daunting.'

'It was at first,' she agreed, 'but at the end of the day, it's the best feeling to help people and they really appreciate it, you know? I've got colleagues who work in the busy inner-city EDs, dealing with some of the worst of humanity, and I feel sorry for them. They go home at the end of a shift deflated and burned out,' she said, looking at him earnestly. 'I keep telling them, come out here or do a stint somewhere remote—find your worth again. But it's so hard to get doctors and nurses out to places like this and further. Even coastal rural towns struggle to get any medical staff—and they have the beach,' she said incredulously. 'No one wants to leave the cities.'

'I certainly see the potential,' he said, before tugging her close. 'And not just for the location.'

It was almost embarrassing how easy it was for him to reduce her to putty in his hands. Not that she was complaining. However, she did decide to see if her natural leadership transferred to out-of-hours things. She pulled away, tugging him towards the bed.

Maybe she did have hidden talents after all, she thought as his low groan of appreciation told her he was happy for her to lead the way.

'Not that I'm complaining about the fact you seem to be making it a habit of creeping into my bedroom after hours, or anything,' Nick said, running his palm up her arm as they lay in bed a couple of weeks later, 'but aren't you getting tired of all the late nights and early starts?'

'You don't finish work until late,' she said, and Nick felt a stab of male pride at the fact her voice sounded so lazily satisfied.

'Yeah, I know, but I could come to your place after work so you didn't have to wait up and drive over.'

'That won't work,' she murmured sleepily.

'Why?'

'Because of the kids,' she said, sounding a little more awake now.

'They're all adults, Jen. I'm pretty sure they wouldn't have an issue with their mother having her boyfriend sleep over.'

'They mightn't, but I do.'

'Really?'

He lifted his hand as she turned over to look up at him. 'This is still all too new,' she said, holding his eyes steadily. 'I'm not ready to make it . . . official yet.'

'But your kids know we've been seeing each other?' he asked slowly.

When she didn't answer immediately, he felt his frown deepen.

'Not since the first date, I haven't mentioned it, no.'

'Why not?'

'Because I just want to get used to it myself before everyone else makes a big deal about it.'

Nick pondered her comment. 'I know we said we'd take it slow, but do we really need to be sneaking around?'

'I'm not sneaking,' she said, almost indignantly. 'I just don't want everyone knowing our business. Is that so bad?'

'You're exhausted.'

'I'm fine.'

'This morning you left here with your shirt on back to front,' he reminded her.

'It was dark when I was getting dressed.'

'If I come to your place, you won't have to get up early and sneak out. You can sleep in . . . maybe even get lucky before you have to go to work,' he said, wiggling his eyebrows.

She chuckled lightly. 'You're insatiable.'

'Only where you're concerned,' he said, lowering his head.

'I'm just not ready,' she said with a small groan.

Nick stopped nibbling on her neck and lifted his head. 'Are you that embarrassed by me?'

'What? No . . .'

'You are,' he said flatly and leaned back on his pillow. He knew it was taking her a bit to get her head around the age difference, but he'd hoped she was getting over it. The fact she was uncomfortable about their relationship after all the amazing nights they'd spent together hurt.

'I'm not embarrassed,' she said more firmly, propping herself up on her elbows to look across his chest. 'Nick?'

He lifted his gaze to hers silently and weakened slightly at her distressed look.

'I'm not. It's just . . . I don't know. It's strange thinking about having a man in the house again.'

'I'm not saying I'll move in—I don't want to cramp your style that much,' he said, trying for a lighter tone. 'Is it how the girls will react that's got you worried?' he asked when she didn't smile.

'Sort of. I mean . . . they think their father with a younger woman is weird . . . I don't want them to think that about me.'

'I wasn't around when your ex moved in with Silicone Barbie,' he said and her lips did lift ever so slightly, 'but I'm pretty sure the girls' reaction is more about the fact he left you *for her*, not so much the age difference.'

She didn't look entirely convinced but at least she didn't argue.

'What if we break them in slowly? I could come over for dinner, take you out, take you all out, even? Just spend some time with them beforehand?'

His fingers itched to rub away the creases in the centre of her forehead—to take away everything that made her worry.

'Maybe you're right. Maybe we do need to tell them—or like you said, do it slowly.'

His spirits rose a few notches. This had been bothering him more than he cared to admit. He understood why she'd been hesitant about telling anyone—she was a private kind of person and he respected that. Hell, so was he, to an extent, but this relationship seemed so much more important than his care factor about who knew about them and who didn't. He didn't give a toss if people knew—he wanted to be part of Jenny's life and spend whatever time they had together.

'I'll leave it up to you to decide. If you want me there for moral support, I'm happy to come along.'

'I think I'll be okay.' She grinned. 'You're right,' she said with more conviction in her tone. 'It's probably time they knew.'

His hand rested on her hip and then slid lower, effectively distracting her from overthinking her decision. He spent the rest of their time keeping her too preoccupied to talk herself out of it.

Twenty-four

'You look tired, Mum,' Savannah said the next morning as Jenny leaned against the kitchen bench, waiting for her toast to pop.

Great. She'd have to cake on the make-up today. 'I couldn't sleep,' she murmured, grabbing the toast and buttering it.

'How come?' Chloe asked, and Jenny sent a swift glance at her youngest daughter. Her interest was odd.

'I just . . . didn't.' She was too tired to get into all this now but at the same time, she was sick of trying to make up any kind of believable story. Stuff it. She'd just tell them and get it over with.

'I'm seeing Nick,' she blurted and braced herself for the interrogation.

'It's about time you came clean,' Brittany said, putting her cup into the dishwasher.

'Came clean?'

'About spending pretty much every night over the last two weeks with him,' Brittany said.

'How did you know that—' Jenny started, gaping at her children, alarm etched across her face.

'Mum, we've known for ages,' Chloe informed her with a grin.

'What?'

'Hello, it's Barkley,' Brittany said blandly.

'What?!' She'd been so careful.

Brittany laughed. 'I'm messin' with ya, Mum. I found out a few days ago when Cassie saw you heading upstairs at the pub, after closing. Don't worry, she didn't say anything to anyone else. We just thought it was cute.'

Cute? Oh my God.

'I think it's great. Good on you,' Savannah said.

Jenny suddenly felt stupid all over again. Her kids thought it was cute that their mother was running around after some younger guy. This was a bad idea.

'Mum?' Brittany asked, sounding wary. 'Are you okay?'

'I'm going to end it,' Jenny blurted.

'What! Why?' they chorused in varying degrees of horror and surprise.

'Because it's—'

'It's awesome,' Brittany interrupted quickly. 'You're happier than you've been in a long time. We've all noticed.'

'He's barely older than you,' Jenny said miserably. 'He's closer to your dating bracket than mine.'

'Oh, please, he's what? Ten or eleven years older?' Brittany scoffed before screwing up her face. 'There's *no way* I would ever go out with a guy *that* old.'

'Forget the numbers—if he makes you feel good, who cares?' Savannah added firmly.

'Do you like him?' Chloe asked.

'Yes.' Jenny nodded and felt a tiny flame begin to flicker to life inside her at the thought. 'Yeah, I do,' she said, a little wistfully.

'Then don't worry about all the other stuff. The only thing we care about is if you're happy.'

Jenny's throat tightened and she blinked away unexpected tears. She really did have the best kids anyone could ever ask for. 'Nick wants to come around for dinner and meet you all, properly. I said I'd check.'

'If he's brave enough to enter the temple of oestrogen and put up with all of us, then I say he's already proving he's a keeper,' Brittany said.

'Okay, well, maybe tomorrow night?'

'I'll swap my shift at work,' Savannah said, grabbing an apple from the fruit bowl on the bench and kissing her mother's cheek. 'Don't forget the concealer this morning,' she added, peering at Jenny's face closely.

'I'll use the trowel,' Jenny promised dryly.

'See, I told you it wasn't going to be a big deal. Tomorrow night will be great,' Nick said when she called him.

'I hope you know what you're getting yourself into.'

'I'm a trained infantry soldier—I'm pretty sure I can handle a few hours with your kids.'

'Hmm,' Jenny murmured, saying goodbye and getting into her car to head off to work.

❖

Nick paused as he parked in the Haywards' driveway. Surely his hands weren't actually *sweating*? What the hell was this? There was nothing to be nervous about and yet now that he was here, his bravado seemed to have flown, leaving him with a sudden attack of nerves. This was stupid. It wasn't as though his and Jenny's whole future relationship depended upon making a good impression with her daughters or anything . . . Only, he realised, it probably did.

Freaking man up and get out of the car, he ordered himself. Everything was going to be fine. It was just a simple dinner.

Before he could knock on the door, it opened and Jenny's youngest stood in the doorway, looking him up and down.

'Hi. I'm Chloe.'

'Hey. Nick,' he said, feeling his pep talk fade away under her stern blue gaze, before she gave a tight smile and led him inside.

Jenny came out of the kitchen looking a little flustered before she paused to take a breath. She walked across to him and gave him an awkward hug. 'Nick, these are my two other daughters, Brittany and Savannah, and my best friend, Beth.'

'Nice to see you again,' he said, nodding at the women. He'd sort of met Brittany and Beth at the pub when they'd gone out to dinner with Jenny recently and Savannah at her party.

'Do you want a drink? Coffee? Beer?' Jenny asked.

'Is it too early for a beer?' he asked, holding her gaze and trying to send her a silent message that everything was okay.

'Hell, no,' Beth said. 'Follow me, I know where they keep all the good stuff around here.'

He did see Jenny smile then, and he was filled with confidence once more.

Later, as they were settled with beverages, a large, somewhat motley cat sauntered into the lounge room, stopping when it set its golden-eyed stare on Nick, who was perched on the front edge of the lounge. Nick dropped his hands and clicked his fingers to get the cat's attention, grateful for a distraction. The cat seemed to size him up thoughtfully with its cool, unblinking gaze before it slowly padded its way across the room to flop down on the carpet in front of him with a definite un-cat-like grace, exposing a fluffy white stomach.

'Go on, pat her on the tummy,' Savannah invited and Nick reached out to do so.

'No! Don't!' Jenny gasped from behind him on her way into the room with a tray of food.

He pulled his hand away quickly and sat back in the chair, noting the wide-eyed expressions focused on him from everyone else in the room. 'What?'

'Savannah!' Jenny snapped.

'Well, I didn't think he was actually going to do it,' Savannah sniffed.

'I was only going to pat her,' Nick said, still confused by the reaction.

'The last person who touched Fat Cat's tummy almost lost a hand,' Brittany told him.

'Lost a hand . . . to a cat?' he repeated doubtfully.

'They did not,' Jenny said, rolling her eyes.

'He had sepsis and almost died,' Brittany drawled.

'If only you hadn't badgered him about going to the hospital you could have saved yourself a whole heap of trouble,' Savannah said, shaking her head mournfully. 'It was Britt's ex,' she explained, seeing Nick's confusion.

'He was put on antibiotics and everything was fine,' Jenny cut in, trying to smooth over her daughters' dramatics. 'Fat Cat is just a little . . . temperamental sometimes.'

'Interesting name,' Nick commented, eyeing the animal, who continued to lay there looking like anything but the lethal weapon the rest of the family was describing.

'When we got her she was tiny, so we called her Little Cat, but then she developed some kind of food allergy and packed on the weight, so she ended up Fat Cat,' Chloe explained.

Maybe it was just him, but somehow it felt wrong to be fat shaming a cat. Still, he supposed they weren't really wrong. It was an extraordinarily fat cat. 'Hey, Fat Cat,' he said soothingly.

'Don't say it to her face!' Savannah gasped.

'You said that was her name,' Nick said, eyeing the horrified glances surrounding him.

'We don't actually *call* her that though . . . Jeez, what kind of monster says that to a cat?'

He sent a bewildered glance to Jenny, who briefly closed her eyes before giving him a reassuring smile. 'It's fine. They're only kidding. Girls, stop it.'

'Actually, we're not. If you want to call her, just say, "puss, puss,"' Chloe advised him and for the life of him, he couldn't decide if she was serious or not.

'Right. Sorry,' he muttered.

'Don't apologise to me—apologise to her,' Chloe said, nodding towards the feline spread out on the floor like some centrefold model.

'Sorry . . . Puss, puss,' he said obligingly, but felt like an idiot as Beth chuckled. What the hell had he gotten himself into?

Jenny lowered the platter of food to the coffee table and smiled weakly, her shaky confidence sending a pang through him. He gave her a reassuring grin in return. He could handle this. He had to if he wanted this thing between them to be more than a casual affair.

'So, what's it like having a famous sister?' Savannah asked, after reaching over to scoop some dip onto a biscuit. She leaned back. 'I've seen all those photos of her in the magazines, cruising on yachts in the Greek Islands and sitting in the audience at fashion shows. You must have had some pretty awesome holidays visiting her?'

'To be honest, I never visited her when she lived overseas.'

'What? Why not?' Chloe asked, looking shocked.

'We weren't that close when I was younger, and then I was in the army and it never really worked out to visit.'

'If I had a sister worth a gazillion dollars I'd have *made* it work out,' Chloe said.

'Chloe,' Jenny hissed, clearly horrified by her youngest daughter's observation.

'Well, it's true.'

'You don't just go and make assumptions about people's family like that,' she said, lowering her tone slightly.

'I wasn't. All I said was if Sav and Britt were rich, I'd be pretty much living with them.'

Nick chuckled, 'It's okay, Jen. I guess, if we'd have been closer growing up, I probably would have hung out with her more, but she'd already left home by the time I came along—she and my parents had a falling out and were estranged when she ran away, so I really didn't know her that well.'

'Her life must have been amazing,' Beth said. 'From a teenage runaway to a successful businesswoman. That's pretty impressive.'

'Yeah, she's always known what she wanted, apparently.' He shrugged.

Chloe pouted. 'Why couldn't either of you have married some filthy rich guy who owns a yacht?'

'Hey, there's still time,' Savannah said, flicking a crumb from her lap.

'Not if you never leave here,' Chloe shot back.

'Shut up. At least I've been out there and seen a bit of the world.'

'Then came back to Barkley.'

'To save up some money before I go again.'

'So you say. I don't see much money being saved when you go out almost every night,' Brittany said.

'You're just jealous because I *can* go out and party, while you have to stay home and take care of a baby. Consequences and choices, Britt, we all have to live with them.'

'Yeah, right, because I want to be still out there drinking and partying. That was fun when I was a kid. I chose to grow up.'

'You chose to get knocked up, you mean.'

'Hey!' Jenny snapped. 'Enough. Savannah, that was not called for.'

The blonde rolled her eyes and folded her arms across her chest as the two girls glared at one another. 'Sorry,' she eventually said, although to Nick, who had been trying to keep up, it sounded far from meaningful.

'It's okay, Mum. I have nothing to regret. Unlike some people, I grew up and got a job.'

'If growing up is becoming as boring as you, then no thanks,' Savannah snapped, before standing up.

'Girls,' Jenny sighed.

'Savannah's just being her usual dramatic self,' Brittany replied, ignoring her mother's mounting frustration.

'Whatever. I'm suddenly not hungry. Nice to meet you officially, Nick. I hope you're tough enough to handle this, because it's not all sunshine and lollipops around here,' Savannah said, before sweeping out of the room and throwing her older sister the finger as she passed.

Things were going well.

'It's okay,' Nick said quietly, catching the mortified look on Jenny's face and trying to reassure her. 'Seriously, you've seen my workplace . . . I deal with this kind of thing every day.'

Her smile, fleeting as it was, did not reach her eyes. 'Let's just eat.'

'Whatever it is smells great,' Nick said as he followed her out to the kitchen.

'It's probably not up to your celebrity chef's standards,' she said nervously.

'Hey, I still burn my toast—I think your cooking will be fine.'

'I'm sorry about all that back there,' she said. 'I don't know what gets into them sometimes. They can be ruthless.'

'It's all good. Hey,' he said softly, linking their hands, 'don't stress. There's nothing anyone can do to scare me away. You're stuck with me, okay?'

'I guess there're worse things to be stuck with,' she conceded, then grinned when he growled at her.

'Right! Dinner's ready. Let's do this,' she said with renewed confidence.

He wasn't sure if it was fake or not, but it sounded believable and for the first time in a long while, he felt like a part of a team. They'd get through tonight and any other hurdle that was thrown at them.

Twenty-five

Jenny found herself beginning to relax after the initial chaos of everyone finding a seat and reaching for food had settled. She looked at Nick and felt . . . relieved. He didn't look like a flight risk—in fact, he was swapping slang with Chloe as she quizzed him on life in the army, discussing the various names for things, which she found hilarious.

A surprisingly varied array of topics took them through the main meal, including, but not limited to, Nick's playing down of some remarkably hair-raising stories of stuff he got up to during his tour, most involving some less than by-the-book antics he and his mates had somehow managed to get away with.

'You make it sound like so much fun,' Chloe said once they'd stopped laughing.

'Some of it was. But there's a lot of not-so-fun times. The waiting around—there's lots of that.'

'You know, I think I'd like the army,' Chloe announced thoughtfully, then scowled at her oldest sister when she gave a hoot of laughter.

'You don't even like camping—not to mention you hate running,' Brittany pointed out.

'You *do* have to do a bit of that,' Nick agreed. 'But it's not as bad as it sounds. There's a lot more creature comforts nowadays compared to what it used to be. You should think about it,' he said, and Jenny watched her youngest daughter's eyes light up with interest once more.

'So, Beth,' Nick said after they'd finished dessert. 'I bet you have a few good stories to tell about things you and Jenny have gotten up to in the past?'

Jenny almost swallowed her spoon as she looked at her friend.

'Oh, yes, indeed.' Beth nodded gleefully.

'You so do not,' Jenny scoffed, raking her memory for anything potentially embarrassing she might think of repeating.

'What about the night we were supposed to go watch that movie but it was so stupid that we decided to leave half an hour into it and hit the town instead?'

Oh. She'd forgotten about that one.

'Hit the town? Gee that sounds ominous, Mum,' Brittany said.

'There just so happened to be a bagpipe convention in Hamwell that week,' Beth continued, her eyes sparkling devilishly across the table.

Oh. Crap. The bagpipe guy.

'Seriously?' Chloe replied, looking unimpressed and somewhat disappointed.

'Yep. Bagpipe bands. It's not even interesting,' Jenny cut in briskly.

'Oh, but it *so* is,' Beth said. 'We were walking along the street, deciding what we should do with ourselves since Jen had a babysitter booked till late, when we heard this God-*awful* sound coming from the pub.'

'It wasn't awful, it was the bagpipes.'

'Anyway,' Beth continued, rolling her eyes at Jenny, 'naturally we decided to go in and see what all the racket was about. Well . . . I'll be the first to admit that I was not expecting a bunch of bagpipers to look anything like the ones we found inside. Who knew men in kilts could be so hot?'

'I did,' Brittany said, putting her hand up. 'I watch *Outlander*.'

Beth nodded. 'Then you know what I'm talkin' about. So we decide to sit down and order a drink.'

'Would anyone like coffee?' Jenny asked, standing up quickly.

'Sit down, Jen. I haven't finished the story,' Beth said, flashing her a wolf-like grin.

'Yeah, Mum. Sit down,' Brittany echoed, obviously curious about her mother's reluctance to let Beth retell a story they hadn't heard before.

'So there we are, having a quiet drink, minding our own business, when a couple of men in kilts come over and ask if they can share our table. Of course, we said yes.'

'*You* said yes,' Jenny corrected.

'I was just being friendly to a couple of lads far from home. Turns out,' Beth continued, 'it was an international bagpipe thing so the place was filled with Scottish men. Anyway, we get talking and drinking and having a great time, then Jenny here, our timid little Jen, announces she'd like to learn how to play the bagpipes. So Collin and Angus run off to find a set of bagpipes and before you know it, there's Jen entertaining the entire pub with a rendition of "Thunderstruck".'

'Mum?' Chloe asked, staring at her mother, perplexed. 'Our mum got up in front of an audience and played the bagpipes?'

'Well, *played* is kind of a stretch,' Beth said, 'but she won a few hearts with her dogged determination. Apparently she has a natural ability when it comes to—'

'Okay, I'm making coffee,' Jenny interrupted firmly as her daughters choked on their laughter and stared at their mother with equal measures of disbelief and fascination.

'Mum!' Brittany chuckled. 'Who knew you could be so . . .'

'Fun?' Beth finished with a knowing smirk. 'I'll have you girls know your mother can be the life of the party when she puts her mind to it.'

'Our mum?' Chloe said.

'Yes, I know, hard to imagine the words "fun" and "Mum" in the same sentence. I'd had too much to drink,' Jenny said.

'We're just kidding, Mum,' Brittany soothed.

'I'm not,' Chloe said. 'What about all those lectures you give us about being sensible and not drinking too much in case you do something stupid that will come back to haunt you?'

'And this is exactly why,' Jenny pointed out. 'You could end up making an idiot of yourself in front of a bunch of bagpipe players.'

Nick had been silently laughing the entire time and Jenny looked at him sternly across the table, which seemed to only amuse him more. 'Sorry,' he said, wiping the corner of his eye. 'I really am, it's just that I'm picturing you jamming away on a set of bagpipes while playing AC/DC.'

'It sounded like a wounded pig screaming in agony,' Beth said, cheerfully. 'But she gave it a red hot go, did our little Jen.'

'You are hereby sacked as my best friend,' Jenny said, reaching for the empty bowls as she cleared the table and put an end to the humiliation.

'Aw, come on, Jen. You know you love me. Besides, I have way more stories to spill, so it's in your best interest to keep me around.'

'Spill!' Chloe said, leaning across the table gleefully.

One look at Jenny's face and Beth had the good sense to clamp her lips shut. 'Later,' Jenny heard her stage whisper to the girls as she carried the dishes into the kitchen.

'Are you okay?' Nick asked as she was stacking the dishwasher.

She glanced up and smiled; the truth was she'd forgotten all about that night. It *had* been fun. She'd been still married at the time, but Austin was away more than he'd been home and Beth had convinced her to take a night off and go out for a girls' night. It was supposed to be just a harmless night out at the movies, but it had turned into something far more entertaining. She couldn't recall ever being that spontaneous . . . Or drunk, she supposed, which was probably the reason she'd been so spontaneous in the first place. But that wasn't her. She was Jenny: mum, wife and nurse. She had to be the sensible, reliable one—not the bagpipe-torturing party girl.

'I'm fine. It was a good night—but if you ever tell Beth I said that, I'll deny it.'

'My lips are sealed,' he promised. 'But I think you should definitely show me how well you play those pipes,' he said, taking her into his arms and staring down at her with a mischievous look in his eye.

'I don't have a set of bagpipes,' she told him, smoothing her hands up his chest slowly.

'We don't need them,' he assured her, before the loud clatter of cutlery and laughter filled the kitchen as the others brought in the last of the dishes from the table.

Jenny eased out of his embrace but not before she heard him whisper, 'Later,' sending a flutter of anticipation through her.

'Thanks for the lift,' Jenny said as they pulled up outside the hospital the next morning. Her car wouldn't start. everyone else had left the house, and she was running late for her shift. Thankfully, Nick had decided to sleep over—another first for them that hadn't been anywhere near the big deal she'd been worrying it would be—so it hadn't turned into the nightmare morning it could have. She kissed him, then began to pull away, but he slid a hand up around the back of her neck, gently cradling it and drew her back for a much deeper one.

When he eventually eased back, Jenny found herself blinking like a stunned owl into a pair of smiling hazel eyes.

'That's so you don't forget how amazing you are.'

Jenny gave him a doubtful look, but a smile touched her lips. 'See you tonight.'

'Yes, you will.'

Jenny was still smiling when she walked inside, past reception. This was all still so new, but things had been happening so fast. Her kids all seemed fine with her new relationship—everyone had gotten on at dinner, and even Savannah, who'd appeared in the kitchen that morning, had apologised for the argument and given her blessing, saying Nick seemed okay . . . for an old guy.

The age thing hadn't really been on Jenny's mind lately—not when she kept getting distracted by how wonderful their time together was. Even when it was just doing something simple like watching a show on TV, she loved being tucked into his side and having his hand resting comfortably on her hip. He made her feel . . . special. Cherished. She was happy. It was only when she allowed the negative thoughts to invade while she was out in public that the age difference was still an issue.

Muffled giggles drew her gaze to the young admin girl and a trainee they'd had working part time. Her smile faltered as they averted their eyes before exchanging an amused look, which resulted in an outburst of raucous laughter. From the way they were avoiding direct eye contact with her, Jenny realised with a sinking heart that she was somehow the butt of whatever hilarious joke they were sharing. Her little bubble of happiness shattered into a million little pieces.

'They were laughing at me!' Jenny said, as she sat in Beth's workroom and helped pack up orders later that day. The heady scents of her friend's beautiful candle range filled the air and Jenny took a deep breath, willing the good vibes from the assortment of crystals laid out in bowls around the room to do their thing.

'They're immature little twats,' Beth said. 'Who cares what they think? They aren't the people who matter to you.'

'No, but they're the general public . . . They're only reflecting what everyone else in town is thinking.'

'That's ridiculous. The whole town does not care what you do in your private life,' Beth said, taking an olive-green box with a Lemongrass and Persian Lime candle from the shelf and gently packing it with some other items then taping the box securely.

'No, they just like to discuss it when they're out at the pub,' Jenny said disdainfully.

'They discuss everyone in the pub.'

'Well, I'm sick of it.'

'So, what are you going to do? Leave?' Beth finished addressing the parcel and added it to her growing pile.

'Maybe.'

Beth looked at her and Jenny blew out an irritated breath. 'No, I'm not leaving town. I just wish everyone would leave it alone.'

'They will. Someone else will do something even more scandalous and you and Nick will be yesterday's news. In time, none of this will even matter.'

'I just hate it. I hate people judging me.'

Beth tilted her head slightly as she considered her friend. 'You know, as much as all that gossip around you and Austin was uncomfortable, not once in any conversation I overheard or was told about, was anyone ever judging *you*. People here, they gossip about others because they feel like this community is their extended family. Families talk and pull apart situations and discuss stuff. This town was *outraged* on your behalf during the Austin/Christy fiasco. People were angry that someone had the audacity to hurt one of their own. They were rallying behind you. They still do.'

Jenny absorbed her friend's words. 'Maybe then but not with this. They're just laughing at me now,' she said, recalling the women at the hospital.

'The people who matter aren't. They're happy that you've found someone who makes you happy.'

'It's everyone *else* I'm frustrated with.'

Beth took down another scented candle and turned to face her. 'It's Barkley—it's a small town with not much excitement going on, so of course anything slightly interesting is going to get talked about. But the only ones who're saying anything snarky are the younger women who are insanely jealous that Nick is so clearly head over heels in love *with you* that they don't stand a chance. That man has been on the radar of practically every unmarried woman in town, not to mention a few married ones,' Beth said, lowering her voice and arching her eyebrows. 'The point is, people are going to gossip—it's a fact of life out here. You won't change that culture, but the majority of it isn't malicious—it's just people sharing news they think they're entitled to be sharing and they're happy for you.'

'I wish I could shake this whole hang-up I have. I don't want to feel like this, but it's always there,' Jenny said miserably.

'Give it time. The closer you two get, the stronger your relationship will be and you'll forget all about the age thing. Nick is crazy about you.'

Jenny still found it hard to comprehend, but her friend's words filled her with a fluttery warmth nonetheless. Maybe Beth was right. Maybe it *was* just going to take time.

Twenty-six

Over the next few weeks, life suddenly got very busy at work for Jenny. A new remote health clinic at a small place called Tallowhope had been in the planning stages for months, and Jenny had been doing the three-hour round trip out to the remote town, setting up the room for her fortnightly visits. She loved this part of her job—she loved lots of parts, but working in these clinics where no two days were ever the same was a highlight.

Today, on the drive out to the old hall they were using for the clinic, Jenny found herself thinking about how different her life was now. When it fit in with her shifts, Nick usually spent the night at her place and it was nice to wake up with someone—something she hadn't done for a very long time. She smiled as she thought about the simple things she looked forward to now: rolling over in the middle of the night and seeing Nick there, sleeping soundly beside her, one arm thrown over her hip or at least a leg touching hers, connecting them. She missed him when they went their separate ways to work and found herself counting down the hours until she saw him again.

So much for the strong, independent woman she'd always thought she was, she thought ruefully. Of course, she was still independent—they didn't do absolutely everything together, but the things they did do, she looked forward to. In this case, she didn't mind losing some of her independence. She *liked* being part of a couple again.

And it was almost like they were a real couple—this morning she'd left a note on the bench to ask Nick if he would take a look at the shower after she noticed it was making a strange noise whenever she turned it on lately. The only thing stopping them from being a complete couple was the full-time living arrangements, but it was way too soon for that. And yet when he was with her, it felt like they'd been living together forever.

She drove down the short main street of Tallowhope with its row of closed-up shopfronts—many of them looking like they'd been vacant for decades, their signs faded—before arriving at the clinic. The old timber hall had recently been painted a crisp white and its rusted tin roof replaced with a shiny new silver one. A plaque reading '1914' was secured to the front of the gable roof. Jenny could only imagine the stories the hall could tell. The town's war memorial stood outside the hall, the stone-built mound with the names of the area's missing and dead from both world wars managing to send a sting to Jenny's heart. *So many names*, she thought sadly. This very hall would have held dances and farewells to those men when they went off to fight, and all that was left of them now was a name etched in stone.

The population had clearly suffered due partly to the casualties, the families in town dwindling over the years that followed, until all that was left was a small grocery store, which also served as the post office, with the town's only petrol pump, a stock agent, produce store and a tennis court and children's playground alongside the hall. There were only a handful of houses in the town's three streets, so the majority of the people she'd see out here would be from surrounding properties.

Jenny unlocked the hall, put her bag away, switched on the jug and got started doing the equipment and drug check. With only time to down a rather tasteless cup of instant coffee, she was straight into seeing patients. She knew she had a full clinic today; they'd set up an online booking page and the appointments had been filled in the first few days. Already, depending on how well day one went, they were looking at adding an extra clinic day further down the track.

Jenny worked her way through the usual cases of patients needing repeat scripts for chronic conditions or a referral to a specialist, as well as a few vaccinations and some wound dressing changes, along with general check-ups.

The rest of the morning flew by and Jenny met a number of young mums with babies and small children, letting them know that she'd be doing a kids' health and vaccination clinic in the upcoming months as well as a women's health check. Everyone had been so appreciative and welcoming that she was almost sad to reach the end of her patient bookings.

It was a long day and the drive home seemed to drag. But all in all, it had been a great first day, and she had a feeling Tallowhope would be one of her favourite clinic days.

Nick sat up in bed and rubbed his hands across his face before reaching over and shutting off the annoying alarm, swearing as he realised he must have slept through the first three and was now running late. They'd fallen into a comfortable routine of finding as much time to spend together as possible, which was no easy thing when they both worked strange, long hours. The last few weeks had flown by and Nick felt like they'd been together almost forever. It was comfortable—it felt right, like nothing else before ever had. He threw off the covers, absently noting that Jenny wasn't home from work yet as he grabbed his clothes, tugging on his jeans without bothering to do them up. He carried his T-shirt towards the ensuite but skidded to a halt when he remembered the busted pipe he still had to replace. That left only one bathroom in the house. He headed out into the hallway and gave a quick knock on the bathroom door.

Hearing nothing, he opened the door and stepped inside.

It all happened so fast his half-asleep brain didn't react until he heard the gasp and registered that there was a naked woman in the shower in front of him . . . one that was not Jenny and was about to fall.

Savannah, having whirled around to find him standing there unexpectedly, slid on the slippery tiles and fell into his arms.

The shock that seemed to have held them both tightly in its grip suddenly let go, as common sense flooded back like a bucket of ice-cold water being tipped over his head. There was a wet, naked woman in his arms who was looking up at him with just as much surprise as he was feeling.

As he was scrambling to make his legs work and get the hell out of the bathroom, a third person appeared beside him.

He looked up to see horror on Jenny's face.

'What's . . .' Her question died on her lips as she slowly shook her head in denial.

Nick immediately put up a hand, in protest or as a gesture to wait, he wasn't sure, but Jenny was backing away and his own alarm suddenly gave way to confusion. Surely, she didn't think . . .

'Jenny.'

She didn't wait for further explanation, just headed to her bedroom, where she slammed the door.

What the actual hell had just happened?

'Nick! Get out!' Savannah was saying behind him, tucking a towel around herself and pushing at his back.

'Shit. I'm sorry. I knocked—'

'Out!'

Jesus. He'd barely had time to register he was awake and somehow he'd ended up in a horror movie.

'Jenny?' he called, tapping his knuckles on the bedroom door before opening it cautiously, half-expecting a vase to be thrown at his head.

'What the hell?' Jenny exclaimed, turning away from the window to face him.

He stopped midway across the room and watched her uncertainly. 'What the hell *what?*' he asked slowly. He had to be imagining the anger in her voice. It'd been an accident, surely anyone walking into that situation could see that? The blood seemed to drain from his face. She'd come home from work and walked past an open door and saw her half-dressed boyfriend and naked daughter in an embrace . . . *fuck.*

'Jenny . . . it was an accident.'

'You were *accidentally* naked with my daughter?' she replied, her voice rising an octave or two.

'I'm not naked—she was,' he pointed out, then wished he could take the stupid words back when she glared at him. Inwardly, he recoiled from the look. *Hang on, was she seriously thinking that somehow they'd been . . .*

'I walked in on her. *By accident.*' He reached out but she leaned away. The reaction felt like a kick to his gut. 'Are you serious?' he asked, frowning. 'You actually think there was something going on back there?'

He saw her return his frown as she seemed to be trying to find the words to whatever was racing through her mind.

'Okay, I can see how it must have looked—'

'Can you?' she snapped.

This wasn't happening. How could she think he'd do something like that . . . with her daughter? He was at a loss for words. Part of him wanted to continue to protest and make Jenny realise how wrong she was to even consider thinking what she saw was anything other than an embarrassing accident, while another part of him was just plain pissed off that she was.

'Okay. Fine. You jump to whatever conclusion you want then,' he said, stepping away and heading for the door. The more he protested, the worse it sounded. He wasn't going to stand there and beg for forgiveness for something he didn't do. He was hurt. She didn't know him at all.

He slammed the front door behind him and stormed to his car, arriving at the pub, barely recalling the trip. He climbed the stairs two at a time, passing Jeremy without stopping.

'So nice of you to turn up,' the chef said, but Nick didn't pause. 'We have a meeting remember?' Jeremy called irritably.

'Start without me,' Nick snapped, going to his bedroom and slamming that door as well for good measure. He needed a long hot shower to wash away this whole bastard of a morning and to hopefully wake up and realise it was all some weird, messed-up dream.

Twenty-seven

'Mum?' Savannah said, standing on the other side of her bedroom doorway. 'Seriously? You let him leave thinking you believed something disgusting just happened? Him and *me*? You think I'd *do* something like that?'

Jenny saw her daughter's worried face and felt her stomach drop. What was she doing? Why hadn't her first reaction been to acknowledge the embarrassing mistake for what it was? Why had she practically accused Nick and Savannah of . . . The idea was preposterous. She was an idiot.

'No. No, I don't. I don't,' Jenny said, crossing the room to reach her daughter. 'I don't know what just happened. I . . . Of course I don't think you'd do anything like that. It just . . . I wasn't expecting to walk in on . . . that.'

'Well, welcome to the club—it was somewhat of a rude shock to me too . . . but it was an accident. I slipped over and he saved me from breaking my neck. Of course, now I have to live with the mortification of my mother's boyfriend having seen me buck naked. Luckily I still have my psychiatrist on speed dial.'

'Oh my God. I don't know what I was thinking,' Jenny said, burying her face in her hands. 'I'm so ashamed.'

'Well, in your defence, it would have been the last thing you'd be expecting to see . . . Still, what the hell, Mum? I *do* have standards, you know. If I was going to make a play for some guy, it wouldn't be my mother's seconds. Please,' she said disdainfully, 'give me a little credit.'

Jenny's head was spinning. She replayed the entire horrible experience and cringed. Why hadn't she told Nick that she knew he wasn't capable of something like that? Why had *that* been her first reaction? She wouldn't blame him if he never spoke to her again.

'Just go and talk to him,' Savannah said gently.

'I can't,' Jenny said, shaking her head. 'I feel like such an idiot.'

'The same way he's probably feeling. You have to sort it out. It's only going to get weirder the longer you leave it.'

Savannah was right, of course, but the sting of humiliation still marked Jenny's cheeks, the skin hot beneath her palms. She just wished they could erase the whole horrible morning and start again.

Jenny sat in the car and took a few deep breaths. Nick deserved an apology, but she was scared he wouldn't want to see her. What if he threw her out of the pub in front of everyone?

Telling herself not to be so dramatic, she wrestled her nerves under control and climbed out of the car. *Just get it over and done with.*

Lifting a hand, she smiled weakly at Cassie before climbing the staircase and heading for the office. When she reached the top, she saw that the door wasn't open as was Nick's normal practice. That didn't bode well at all. Nervously, Jenny lifted her hand, giving the timber door a quick rap and holding her breath as she waited for him to answer.

When he eventually did, Jenny found herself swallowing hard. 'I'm sorry,' she blurted, biting her lip uncertainly as he stared at her. 'It caught me by surprise.'

'No shit, Jenny,' he growled.

'Well, put yourself in my shoes. It looked—'

'Bad. Yeah. I get it. But come on . . . it was your daughter. I was embarrassed enough without having you look at me like I was some kind of—'

'I know, I know,' Jenny groaned, closing her eyes briefly. 'I don't know why it happened . . . it's just that Austin had been in my head about the age gap before, worried about the girls living under the same roof—'

'Wait. Hold up,' Nick said, cutting in. 'Austin?'

'My ex-husband,' Jenny said slowly.

'I know *who* he is,' Nick said impatiently. 'But what the hell does he have to do with jumping to the conclusion that I'm some kind of sleazebag waiting to prey on your kids?'

'It was just something he mentioned ages ago at the party. Although I don't think he meant—'

'What exactly *did* he mean?'

Jenny detected the dangerously soft tone of his voice and knew she'd just made everything a million times worse. 'He made a comment about his daughters living under the same roof with you . . . It was before we even got together—he was hitting back at me because he saw us kissing . . . It was stupid—I didn't take any notice of it . . . It's just that it was somehow the first thing that flashed through my head this morning and I have no idea why. If you hadn't walked out, I would have come to my senses and explained.'

'Sorry if having the woman I love stare at me like I was just violating one of her kids was a tad too much to handle.'

The woman he loved . . .

'Just forget it,' Nick snapped.

'Wait. No. You're right,' Jenny said, shaking off the distraction quickly. 'It was unforgivable. You had every right to be angry. *Of course* I don't believe anything was going on . . . it was a shock and then everything kind of just imploded. Can we please just stop and talk rationally about it now?'

'I'd prefer never to mention it again. *Ever*,' Nick snarled.

'Well, too bad,' she said, stepping in his path when he went to walk past her. 'I'm here to apologise. I'll beg, grovel, publicly humiliate myself if you want me to. My reaction was totally inexcusable. I'm mortified that I made you feel as though you'd done something wrong. I can't even explain why I acted like that. All I can say is it was only for a moment and then I realised how stupid the idea was. I'm so, so sorry.'

'It's the fact that that was your first reaction *even for a second* that hurts the most.'

Jenny pressed her lips together tightly and stared at his wounded expression helplessly. 'I know. I . . .' She bit down hard on her lip when tears threatened to emerge. 'I understand how upset you are . . . I would be too. If you can't forgive me, I'll have to deal with that, but I hope you will.' She swallowed painfully and straightened her shoulders. 'That's all I came here to say.' *Just turn and walk away*, she told herself silently, *one foot in front of the other.*

She willed the tears not to fall. Not here. Not yet. But, one by one, they began to drop.

She'd reached the top of the staircase when a harsh voice called out, 'Wait.'

She paused, but didn't turn around, bracing for a hurtful parting shot.

'Don't go.'

Jenny turned and looked at him warily, swallowing hard.

For a moment they simply watched each other until he stepped forward and met her halfway down the hallway, pulling her into his arms as she threw her own around him tightly.

'I'm sorry,' she whispered.

'It's okay. It doesn't matter now.'

But it did. Somehow, she knew she'd broken an unspoken trust. She wasn't sure if it was something she could win back or not. Pain sliced through her chest at the thought. He'd said he loved her—was it now past tense, over before it'd even had a chance? Or was there still hope? She didn't know. All she knew beyond a shadow of a doubt now was that she never wanted to hurt this man like that again and, if it were within her power, she'd do whatever she had to in order to make sure she never did.

Twenty-eight

The days that followed fell into a heady routine of work, family and Nick. It was strange how well he'd integrated into her family. Once she thought she'd found peace and contentment and that life had been perfect, then Nick had come along and now she wondered how anything before had ever felt right.

The incident, as it was now known, had been put to rest, but only after the awkwardness of it all had been tossed about for a few days in order to defuse the ugliness of what had initially followed. Savannah—with her usual brashness—had taken great delight in bringing it up at the table, turning it into something almost hilarious.

'I'm going to head up for a shower now,' Brittany said, as she got up from where they'd all been lounging around watching a movie after dinner. 'Can you keep an ear out for Sophie in case she wakes up?'

'Nick'll be up in a few minutes to wash your back,' Savannah called as her sister left the room. It was followed seconds later by a chuckle as Nick threw a cushion at her.

'Funny,' he muttered, but Jenny saw the small grin that tugged at his mouth.

'I'm heading up too,' Savannah said, blowing them a kiss as she went. The room was quiet once more.

'Am I ever going to live that down?' Nick murmured into Jenny's hair as she sat tucked up against his side on the lounge.

'Probably not.'

She heard him grunt and settled in closer. A wry smile touched her own lips as she replayed the last few days. Embarrassing moments in this house tended to always become in-jokes—had done ever since the kids were little.

Nick's phone buzzed and he ignored it, until it sounded again and, with a muttered curse, he withdrew his arm from where it had been comfortably resting around Jenny's back on the lounge and reached over to pick it up.

When he let out a small groan, Jenny eyed him warily. 'That sounds like bad news.'

'It is. My sister's coming out here.'

'When?'

'Tomorrow.'

'Is that such a bad thing? It might be nice to catch up with her,' Jenny suggested, but one look at his scowl and she winced. Maybe not as nice as she thought.

'I don't imagine it's that kind of visit. More than likely she's just coming out to check on her investment—or more to the point, to criticise how I'm doing everything.'

'I don't see how she could criticise; you're doing a great job.'

He sent her a smile, before it changed into something more like a grimace. 'She'll find something.'

'Maybe just wait and see. She might surprise you this time.'

Nick gave a small chuckle before placing his phone back on the table. 'Okay, Miss Positivity. We'll wait and see.'

'Why do I feel like you're just humouring me now?'

'I have no idea,' he said, replacing his arm behind her and drawing her into his chest. 'But I can't wait till this movie finishes so we can go to bed.'

His voice dropping down an octave sent a small quiver of electricity through her. It was almost as seductive as when he whispered things in her ear in that gravelly, sexy tone that instantly turned her to jelly.

'We don't have to finish the movie,' she suggested as his fingers traced patterns across her hip.

He looked down at her with a lazy, almost wolf-like grin. 'I was hoping you'd say that.'

Somewhere behind the lust-induced haze in her brain, she realised this was Nick's way of disengaging from any further discussion about his sister and her impending visit, but she figured she'd let it slide. There'd be plenty of time to talk later.

To say the day at work had been hectic would have been a drastic understatement. Not only were they short-staffed, but it seemed every resident in the nursing home had decided today would be a great time for a number of urgent doctor visits, which had resulted in two transfers to Hamwell hospital.

Emergency had also been extra busy, which had further stretched resources. *It has to be a full moon tonight*, Jenny thought as she headed for her car. She'd just finished a long shift and was ready to fall into bed and sleep for a week. Only she couldn't, because Nick had left a message that his sister had arrived, and he'd asked her to drop in on her way home.

She'd tried to delay the meeting until she'd at least showered, but he had sounded a little stressed—and that was something she'd never experienced with Nick before. Jenny glanced at herself in the rear-view mirror as she checked behind her before reversing. *This is the perfect time to meet your boyfriend's only living family member for the first time*, she thought sarcastically.

She slid her sunglasses onto the top of her head as she walked inside the pub and waved as Cassie told her Nick was upstairs. With each step, her legs felt heavier. She eyed Nick's bedroom door and wondered if maybe she could just sneak in there and close her eyes for a few minutes first, but Nick came out of the common room and any chance of a detour was suddenly out of the question.

'Hey, babe, thanks for coming,' he said quietly as he drew her to him for a hug. 'I know you've had a huge shift, and I feel like a jerk asking, but I just wanted you here.'

'It's okay,' she assured him gently, breathing in his warm smell of fresh laundry powder and woodsy deodorant and snuggled a little closer, happy that she'd stopped by after all. She'd missed him; it was somewhat pathetic how much sometimes, but no matter how often they saw each other, whenever Jenny was away from him all she wanted to do was be back with him again. If it didn't take so much effort, she'd have rolled her eyes at how corny it sounded, but it was true.

'Come on, let's get this over with,' Nick whispered, before stepping back and taking her hand to tug her towards the common room.

Susie was perched on the edge of a wingback armchair and as they came in Jenny felt the weight of the woman's inspection. Jenny recognised Nick's sister from the photos she'd seen occasionally in magazines, of course, but in person, she looked a little different. There was less gloss, although nothing that took away from the fact she looked like she'd just stepped off a private jet after a Paris fashion show. She wore her honey blonde hair in an elegant chignon pinned neatly at the nape of her neck. Jenny resisted the urge to reach up and smooth her own hair, which she'd pretty much left it to do its own thing that morning.

'Jenny, this is my sister, Susie,' Nick said, his hand warm on Jenny's back. Comforting.

'Oh,' the blonde woman said, blinking as Jenny extended her hand. '*You're* Jenny?'

'I am,' Jenny said, forcing a smile. Something about the woman's unchecked surprise reinforced her earlier discomfort.

'Nick. Phone,' a young man called, sticking his head in through the doorway.

'Take a message,' Nick told him.

'I was going to but they said it was urgent.'

'Damn it. Okay. Be there in a sec.' Nick sighed irritably. 'Sorry, I'm going to have to deal with this. I'll be right back,' he said, taking his hand away, leaving Jenny feeling extremely vulnerable.

She breathed out imperceptibly and summoned a brave smile. 'It's nice to finally meet you. Nick's told me all about you.'

The woman across from her kinked an eyebrow as she held Jenny's gaze coolly before tilting her head. 'You're . . . not what I expected.'

Jenny's smile wavered. She felt awkward as the meticulously made-up woman seemed to openly dissect her. 'Well, I hope that's a good thing,' she said with false cheer. She took in the woman's expensive outfit and ridiculously high heels, her eyes falling on the unmistakable double G logo on the cream and gold handbag. That one item probably cost more than Jenny made in a month.

'Is this your first trip out to Barkley?' Jenny asked.

'Yes,' Susie said, glancing about the room without much enthusiasm.

'You'll have to take a look around town while you're here. There are some lovely little shops. Very quirky,' she said.

'Quirky,' Susie repeated doubtfully.

'But maybe that's not your thing.' Jenny wondered why she was so on edge with this woman. She dealt with all kinds of people in her job without allowing them to intimidate her in any way, yet Susie had her feeling inadequate and stupid all within the first five minutes of meeting her.

'No. Not really,' she said dismissively.

Jenny sent a glance towards the door Nick had vanished through earlier, urging him to reappear. 'We have some nice boutiques, too,' Jenny said, beginning to ramble. 'My daughters rave about them.'

'You have children?' Susie asked, her attention firmly back on her.

'Yes. I have three.'

'I can't imagine Nick with young children,' she said, and kinked an eyebrow in a superior kind of way that irritated Jenny more than her patronising tone.

'My eldest is nearly twenty-eight,' Jenny told her bluntly. 'They aren't exactly young children.'

This time the woman's expression mirrored something akin to horror. 'You have a nearly twenty-eight-year-old? How is that—'

'I started young,' Jenny shrugged, trying her best to dampen her growing irritation.

'So you must be—'

'Older than Nick. Yes,' Jenny said abruptly.

'Goodness.'

Jenny could literally see the woman mentally calculating the age difference as she stared at her. Every single insecurity Jenny had almost succeeded in sweeping aside over the last few weeks suddenly came rushing back.

'I had no idea,' Susie continued in a stunned tone as she stared at Jenny like she'd just sprouted a second head.

Where the hell was Nick? He needed to see this reaction—it was what she'd been trying to tell him: the age gap *was* an issue.

She couldn't stay here a minute longer. 'I actually have to get home. Could you tell Nick I had to go?'

'Of course,' Susie said, still looking at her oddly.

Jenny left the room, half-expecting to run into Nick returning, but he was still tied up with his urgent phone call and she was relieved that she didn't have to face him. He'd have made her go back in there with him.

The cool air outside hit her face and she felt twin flames of anger spotting her cheeks as she made her way to the car. How had she let him talk her into this? His own sister could see the ridiculousness of their relationship and clearly had an issue with it.

Fury mixed with despair as she reversed out of her carpark. Inside her, a gaping hole had begun to form where only recently hope and excitement had been unfurling. She'd been an idiot to listen to everyone assuring her that this thing with Nick was perfectly sane. It wasn't. It was crazy.

Twenty-nine

'Will Nick be here for dinner?' Savannah called from the kitchen as Jenny walked downstairs after managing an hour's sleep.

'No,' Jenny called back and wondered if her reply had sounded as panicked as she thought.

Savannah stuck her head around the corner. 'Everything okay?'

Apparently it had. 'Yep. His sister's in town. I think he'll be having dinner with her.'

'What's she like?'

'Different from what I was expecting.'

'Different good or bad?'

'Just different. I didn't really have much of a chance to talk to her.'

Her daughter pulled a 'whatever' face and disappeared into the kitchen to finish making dinner.

Later, once everyone else had gone their own ways—Brittany putting Sophie to bed, Savannah heading out to see friends and Chloe tucked away in her room on her phone—Jenny lay on the couch idly flicking through the offerings on her streaming service. Why was it you could never find anything you felt like watching when you literally had thousands of programs to watch? She'd been scrolling through every category for close to thirty-five minutes and absolutely nothing had snagged her interest. Bring back the good old days of watching whatever the hell the TV channel decided to play, she thought, before trying to figure out the specific point in time when everyone had gotten so caught up in all this pay-TV hype in the first place.

Her phone interrupted her pondering and she glanced down to see Nick's name on the screen. She'd figured he'd be calling at some point.

'Is everything okay? You didn't sound yourself in your text earlier.'

'There *is* no sound in a text,' Jenny pointed out logically. 'And yep, everything's fine. I figured you and your sister would want some time alone to catch up.'

'She's busy going over the books as we speak,' he said.

'Is everything going okay?'

'Define okay.' His voice took on a dry tone. 'Everything is exactly the way it usually is when Susie comes to visit.'

Jenny, who was normally a very open-minded and friendly person, could totally understand the underlying weariness in his meaning.

'Did Susie say something to you? Is that why you left in such a hurry?' he asked now, in a more serious voice.

'No,' Jenny said. Which was true. It wasn't anything the woman had said, it was what she *hadn't* said that had been the problem. 'But I got the feeling she wasn't impressed by your choice of girlfriend.'

'She wouldn't be, would she?' he replied with a dry chuckle. 'She didn't get to pick you out.'

'Your sister usually picks out your girlfriends?'

'Nope. But she reckons she'd do a better job of finding me someone suitable. And by "suitable" she means some career-driven, corporate imitation of her. Which is kind of not something I'm greatly turned on by, in case you were wondering.'

'Good to know,' Jenny said with a small smile, trying to imagine her Nick with a mini-me version of the woman she'd met today. *Her Nick . . .* The phrase sent a warm rush through her chest.

'I shouldn't have left you with her. I know what she's like but I didn't get time to warn you. Ignore anything she said. She'll get bored in a day or so and go back home.'

'At least she's trying to stay connected. That's kind of nice,' Jenny said, trying to put a positive spin on the situation.

'Kind of annoying, really. But I suppose you're right. I just wish she'd give me a bit more warning when she decides to drop in for an inspection.'

'I'm sure it's not an inspection. She probably just wants to see her baby brother.'

'And the books . . . and the invoices . . .' he listed without humour.

'At least it shows she's interested in your business.'

'Anyway, enough of that. Can I come over tonight?'

'Your sister just arrived in town.'

'She's fine.'

'I think her opinion of me is shaky at best, without me taking you away on her first night in town. I should get an early night while I can—I seem to be running on coffee and a handful of hours of sleep lately, thanks to you.'

'Who needs sleep when we have awesome sex?' he replied, his voice dropping a note to that husky, rugged sound that made her all tingly whenever she heard it—until she remembered how stupid she'd felt when his sister had looked at her when she found out how old she was.

'True. But I think I'll take some sleep while I get the chance all the same.'

He let out a long, extra dramatic sigh. 'Fine. I'll talk to you tomorrow?'

She smiled. 'Absolutely. 'Night.'

''Night, babe.'

Babe. She grinned as she disconnected the call. She never imagined hearing all the little endearments he came up with could make her feel so good. It was silly—he'd probably called a million women babe before, but somehow he made it feel special.

Jenny rolled her eyes and imagined what Beth would say right now—*You've got it bad!* She really did. A small sigh escaped as she got to her feet to head up to bed. This whole thing would be perfect if he was just . . . older.

A small voice inside her head gave a rude snort and she had to concede that maybe she was being a tad contradictory. Nick had come to mean a lot more than she'd initially been expecting. It wasn't just about the sex—it was how she felt around him, how he made her feel. She'd never imagined anyone could make her feel so important. She supposed she'd been important to Austin at one time—she was the mother of his children and the one who stayed home to take care of them, but that was a *practical* important. Nick made her feel like . . . She paused, trying to figure it out. He made her feel that without her, the sun wouldn't come up tomorrow and the world wouldn't be the same. Her heart gave an almost painful lurch. He made her feel loved.

I love him.

The realisation took her breath away.

She *really* loved him.

Thirty

Jenny heard her phone beep as she pulled up in the carpark of the pub. She opened the message from Nick and pulled a face when she reached the part about him running late. Well, she was here now. She'd worked a particularly long night shift, so waking up to Nick's earlier message and the opportunity to spend a few hours with him before she'd need to get ready for work again was an offer too strong to resist.

She walked into the pub and took a moment to allow her eyes to adjust from the bright sunlight outside. The scent of strong, delicious coffee pulled her towards the end of the bistro. She stopped when she spotted Susie at a table, talking on the phone while studying the computer screen in front of her.

Jenny waited for the woman to look up so she could say hello, but Susie's attention seemed to be solely on the computer and the clipped conversation she was having on the phone, so Jenny continued on to the bar and waited beside a couple who were talking to Amy, one of the daytime bartenders.

'It's like a completely different place, isn't it, George?' the woman, who seemed to be in her early sixties, was saying.

'Certainly a big improvement on the old pub,' George acknowledged.

'Well, I don't think it's fair to say it like that,' the woman said with a slight snap in her voice. 'Uncle Lionel was running a *country* pub, wasn't he? It's what pubs were back then . . . Nowadays they're all becoming . . . yuppified,' she finished with a small sniff.

'Maybe. But the old place was getting pretty run-down last time we were here.'

'Excuse me,' Jenny cut in, sensing the woman clearly didn't share George's opinion and hoping to defuse the situation in case Nick happened to walk in and cop an earful. 'Did you say *Uncle* Lionel? As in Gosson?'

'That's right,' the woman said slowly, eyeing Jenny suspiciously.

'You're a relative of the previous owners?' She had a feeling Nick might be interested in having a chat to these two if she could somehow soften the slightly huffy woman.

'Yes. I'm George's niece. We've been travelling and decided to drop into Barkley to take a look around.'

'Oh. How lovely.' Jenny smiled. 'Did you used to live here?'

'No, we're from Brisbane,' George said, 'but Sharon's family were out here and we visited from time to time.'

'The whole district has been undergoing a bit of a revitalisation. I'd imagine there've been a lot of changes you'd have noticed around the place,' Jenny said.

'Oh, we've noticed,' Sharon said, not bothering to soften her displeasure with a smile of any kind.

Change was sometimes hard and Sharon's wary attitude towards the changes around town was shared by a lot of people. But it irked Jenny that someone who hadn't even *come* from here was acting so offended.

'A few years ago things weren't looking that great for Barkley. As a local, I'm really glad things have turned around for us. I think most of the new owners of businesses in town have managed to keep the feel of the old Barkley, while just making it . . . better,' she said with a smile and a shrug.

'Well, I don't remember it being *that* dire,' Sharon insisted.

'We also haven't been out here for at least twenty years, love,' George reminded her.

'I suppose,' Sharon finally conceded, and Jenny was relieved to hear the defensiveness of her earlier tone had eased.

'I'd imagine seeing the pub for the first time in so long would be a shock when you have a personal connection to this place. But the new owner really has taken a lot of care when it came to keeping all the heritage as intact as possible. I know that meant a lot to him. Have you seen the dining room yet, with the huge mural of the original pub on the wall?'

'No. I haven't,' Sharon said, seeming to perk up a little.

'I'm sure he'd be happy to give you a tour if you liked?' Jenny offered, inwardly crossing her fingers that Nick would be okay with her volunteering him. But knowing how he loved the history of the pub, she figured he'd enjoy having a chat with some relatives of the old owner.

'You think so?' Sharon asked, now noticeably brighter. 'But we're meeting up with some travel buddies soon.'

'I'll have another chardonnay.'

Jenny turned, hearing Susie's voice further down the bar where Amy had been cleaning. Jenny resisted the urge to check her watch for the time. It was none of her business if Nick's sister wanted to drink in the early afternoon in the middle of the week . . . without any company. Nope, none at all.

'Nicole?' Sharon's confused greeting came out sounding more like a question and Susie automatically glanced up, wearing an impatient kind of expression. 'I thought that was you.'

'I'm sorry?' Susie asked, lifting an eyebrow dubiously at the woman.

'It's Sharon. Matthew's cousin,' she prompted, before continuing, 'it was a while back now, I guess . . .'

'You must have me confused with someone else,' Susie said, taking the drink Amy placed on the bar before her and turning away.

'I was sure that was her,' Sharon mused as she stared after Susie, who'd not returned to her table, but had instead headed upstairs.

'So, you reckon this new bloke would let us have a bit of a squiz around the place, then?' George asked, dragging Jenny's attention away from the staircase.

'Oh. Yeah. I'm sure he would. How long are you here for?'

'We've set up the van at the showground overnight. Thought we'd leave tomorrow sometime,' George said, scratching at the stubble on his chin.

'If you leave me your number, I can ask and let you know. Maybe you could drop by in the morning before you leave town?' Jenny suggested.

'Sounds good. What d'you reckon, love?' George added, turning to his wife.

'Tomorrow?' she repeated sounding a little distracted, before nodding. 'Yes, I suppose we could do that.'

Well, don't sound too excited, Jenny thought sarcastically, mustering a smile for George as the pair turned and left. Jenny ordered her coffee, adding a slice of lemon meringue pie, and made some general chit-chat with Amy, before sitting at a table to wait for Nick.

When he finally came in, dressed as usual in jeans and a T-shirt, Jenny realised she was ogling him before remembering she had a forkful of lemony tart halfway to her mouth. She quickly shoved it in.

'Sorry. I got stuck talking. Why are you sitting out here? You could have gone upstairs to my room or the office,' he said, stooping to plant a kiss on her lips. 'Hmm, you taste incredible.' His voice dropped an octave and her insides melted just a little bit more.

'It's the lemon meringue.'

'Mixed with you. Have you finished?' he asked, dropping his gaze to her mouth, making it suddenly difficult to remember how to swallow.

Managing a jerky nod, she pushed the plate away and to her feet, allowing him to lead her upstairs. Outside the door to his suite, he bent his head and kissed her, this time with far more urgency and a lot less care about who might be watching. Jenny snaked her arms around his neck and kissed him back. She would never get sick of kissing this man—ever. It was like a drug.

'Oh. Sorry.'

The words spilled over Jenny like a bucket of ice and Nick stilled, lifting his head to look over his shoulder at his sister.

'Don't mind me. Please, continue—I mean, clearly no one has a business to run around here or anything.' The fading sound of heels on the staircase filled the silence.

Jenny pushed against Nick's chest until he loosened his hold and she stepped away.

'Don't worry about her,' Nick said.

'She's right. It's the middle of the day!'

'So?'

Jenny knew she sounded prissy and, for some reason, Nick seemed to enjoy teasing her whenever she did. Now was no exception. That slow, cocky smile slid across his face with annoying attractiveness and she knew there was no way she was going to be strong enough to resist him.

'God, it feels like weeks since I've seen you,' Nick said later as they lay tangled in the sheets, the sounds of everyday life in the street below, muted.

'It's only been a day.'

'It's too long.'

She'd have liked to disagree and tell him not to be ridiculous, but the truth was it *had* felt like forever since they'd seen each other. It was crazy how much she missed him when she wasn't with him. But reality was beginning to raise its ugly head and she knew she needed to start getting ready for her shift.

'I really have to go,' she said, trying her best to sound firm but failing miserably as Nick continued to run kisses along her neck, making it near impossible to think straight, let alone summon the strength to leave.

'Take a sick day.'

'I can't.'

'Come on, the place is not going to fall down without you.'

'I wish I could say that was being overly dramatic, but it's actually not. We're dangerously short-staffed—have been for a while now.' Nurse-to-patient ratios were seriously out of proportion and staff were constantly having to cover extra shifts and stretch their resources in order to give their patients adequate care.

'But if the staff are burning out and can't even take a sick day here and there, what happens when you can't stretch any further?'

'I guess they'll shut down the hospital.' The loss of a vital service for Barkley would have dire consequences for the community. It was something that was always in the back of Jenny's mind. The elderly and their families who depended on the aged care facility would need to be relocated—something that many would find difficult, since they'd lived their entire lives in the Barkley area. Not to mention the difficulty many others would face if they had to travel to Hamwell for basic things like child and family services, community nursing and the various allied health services locals depended upon.

'Could they do that?' Nick asked, suddenly sounding more serious than he had before.

'If they found a way to save money somewhere, then absolutely. The bean counters are always looking to trim the fat wherever they can. That's why this revitalisation that's been happening in our area is so important. This is our chance to get people out here and show them what a lifestyle out here can offer. It's the first time in forever that an opportunity like this has presented itself and it's given a lot of people hope.'

'Fine, then. I guess I'll have to let you go to work.' Nick made a long-suffering sound before lifting his head and looking down at her. 'I love having you around the place.'

'I love *being* around the place,' she admitted with a soft smile. She really did. The old pub intrigued her with the secrets she imagined it hid within its walls. The history the old building must have witnessed—the comings and goings of fashion and culture and tiny glimpses of people's everyday struggles and triumphs. She loved listening to its gentle creaks and groans at night and through the quieter times of the day as she lay in bed or sat out on the verandah. Her skin tingled as she thought about the warmth of the dry timber boards under her bare feet on a sunny afternoon as she sipped a glass of wine and listened to the steady hustle and well, maybe not so much bustle, of the street below when she waited for Nick to finish working downstairs. The place was definitely growing on her.

'But I,' she said, finally able to concentrate now his lips weren't distracting her, 'have. To. Go.' She punctuated each word with a firm kiss on his mouth and backed away from his wandering hands and quickly dressed.

'Spoilsport,' he called after her.

She blew him a kiss from the doorway and chuckled at the pout playing on his lips.

Jenny was still smiling as she reached the bottom of the staircase, but then her gaze fell on the table where Susie sat. She forced herself to continue walking instead of turning to avoid her like she wanted to. She'd tried her best to like the woman and she felt terrible that she had to force herself to be polite—she was usually a great people person—but Susie made it so difficult when she barely hid the fact she didn't approve of Jenny and Nick's relationship.

When Susie glanced up and saw Jenny, she stiffened and clenched her jaw.

'I guess *now* I might be able to get Nick to focus on the business we're trying to run here?' she snapped as Jenny walked past.

'I don't know,' Jenny said with mock concern. 'He's pretty worn out. He might need a rest first.'

She hadn't meant to react, but Susie's self-righteous tone pushed her too far and her words had just slipped out. She took the tiniest bit of pleasure from the shock that passed over the woman's face, but it was soon replaced by a cool arrogance that Jenny immediately recognised.

'I guess I should be impressed—I'm not sure I could do such a large age gap, especially if I had children as old as yours.'

Heat began climbing up Jenny's neck at the insult and a fresh wave of shame filled her as old insecurities began to rise. Then a tiny voice spoke up inside her, reminding her of how she felt when she was with Nick, and that this thing between them wasn't some cheap, nasty fling to be mocked—especially by someone as cynical and cold as Susie.

'Maybe you should try it before you knock it,' Jenny said, channelling her irritation at the woman into casual disdain. Her gaze fell on the empty wine glass on the table and she suddenly remembered she'd forgotten all about telling Nick about the couple who wanted a tour of the pub. Then another thought occurred to her. 'That was pretty strange earlier—when the woman at the bar seemed to think you were someone she used to know. Are you sure you don't know who she was?'

The smugness in Susie's eyes vanished. 'Positive,' she said bluntly.

'She seemed pretty sure she knew you,' Jenny continued. She wasn't sure why she was pushing the woman, only that she knew, deep down, that Susie was lying. 'I forgot to tell Nick about them.' She turned to head back the way she had come. 'I said I'd ask him if he could give them a tour of the place.'

'Don't worry about it,' Susie said quickly, and Jenny stopped. 'I'll let him know. I'm heading up there now.' She gathered her computer and the bag she'd quickly stuffed the remaining paperwork inside.

Jenny watched her make her way up the staircase and narrowed her eyes. *That was not normal.* Something had shaken the unshakable Sussanne Angelopoulos and Jenny wished she knew what it was.

❖

Nick bit back a sigh and looked up warily as Susie walked into his office without knocking.

'Tomorrow I'd like to take a tour of this farm you're getting your beef from. I'm not convinced the outlay is justified.'

Nick sat straighter in his chair and stared at his sister. 'The expense is more than justified.'

'I've looked at the numbers.'

'I don't give a stuff about the numbers. I've built the whole concept of the restaurant on using locally sourced beef that we process on site. Without that, we're just another pub selling steak.'

'The costs would be cut considerably if you sourced your steak from a butcher or wholesaler.'

'That defeats the whole purpose.'

Susie made an indifferent expression. 'The figures are not suggesting this idea is making enough of a profit to justify the extra work and expense.'

'But it *is* making a profit,' he pointed out.

'There would be a *bigger* profit with some adjusting.'

'We are not losing the in-house processing.'

'We'll decide after I've been for a tour of the place tomorrow,' she said with an annoying finality that made him feel like a ten-year-old being scolded by an adult.

'Our agreement was you were to be a silent partner,' he reminded her.

'I can be a silent partner, but I can also withdraw any of the extra capital I laid out, which you and I both know you're depending on at the moment.'

Nick clenched his jaw and forced himself to rein in his growing temper.

'Oh, come on, Nicky,' she chastised, 'this is business. You need to learn to dissociate your heart from your head or you'll never make it.'

'Not everyone is out to make a fortune. I just want to build a life.'

'You won't be building anything if you go broke, though, will you? Do you have any idea how many businesses go bankrupt within the first few years of opening?'

'I'm sure you'll be happy to tell me,' Nick said, pressing two fingers to the bridge of his nose and closing his eyes. How many times would he have to hear this same doom and gloom lecture?

'Do you truly believe I want you to fail?' she demanded.

'I honestly don't know, Susie,' he said, dropping his hand and looking up. 'Sometimes I think maybe you do. Just so you can gloat and say, "I told you so." We both know what you really want me doing—and it's not running a pub in a place like this.'

'Of course it isn't,' Susie snapped, throwing her hands in the air. 'You could have any place in the world if you accepted the job I offered you—but instead you come to this run-down place in the middle of nowhere.'

'And that's the problem, isn't it? You're never going to accept that this is the choice I made—that this is what I want.'

'How can I, when I know you're making a huge mistake? Who in their right mind turns their back on making a fortune and instead takes on a . . . a pub?' she shot back, practically spitting out the word.

'This is what I want. This has been my dream for years. This is what got me through some of the darkest times in my life—why can't you just let me be happy?' he asked, trying to find the words to get through to her.

She looked taken aback as his meaning sank in, but then she lifted her chin. 'Because I don't believe this is where you belong. Is it such a crime to want you working with me? To see you succeeding in life—earning ten times the amount you'd earn doing this and without the worry and stress?'

'The fact you think doing what you do comes without stress or worry is exactly why I don't want any part of it. You might be able to switch off your humanity while you're dissecting businesses and making people unemployed all in the name of rebranding and selling companies off like scrap metal, but that isn't for me.' He'd had a brief taste of that life shortly after leaving the army, and being even remotely connected to any of it had made him feel like crap.

'If you'd stuck with the job long enough to give it a chance, you'd have realised that sometimes making those decisions actually saved those businesses in the long run. That maybe the directors of those companies had been avoiding doing exactly the same thing, which would have saved them from getting into the position where someone like myself had to step in and make those kinds of drastic changes. It's easy to make someone look like a monster just because they can see things practically, instead of through a pair of rose-coloured glasses. Not everything in life is clean-cut—you should understand that better than anyone. You were sent into places to do things so the rest of us didn't have to. It's no different from business.'

'And I got *out* of that to live a quieter life.'

For a second he thought her expression had softened slightly, but then it was gone and a flash of sadness moved across her face. 'I've only ever wanted what was best for you, Nick. Even when you haven't understood it.'

Nick hesitated at his sister's tone. For a moment, it sounded almost . . . vulnerable, which was absurd, seeing she was one of the toughest people he knew. Which wasn't really a compliment—not when tough could often be mistaken for cold or even callous.

'I know you believe that,' he said slowly, as he held her gaze, 'but it's not about what *you* consider to be the best.'

'Then for your sake, I hope that I'm impressed by what I see tomorrow with this beef-farming idea.'

Nick stared at the empty doorway for a long while after his sister had left, feeling a prickle of unease. He wished he'd never signed on with her as a business partner. He'd known it was going to come back and bite him on the arse—he just hadn't realised it would be so soon.

He couldn't lose his pub—not now. Not after everything he'd already poured into it.

Thirty-one

Jenny tucked her phone into her shoulder as she finished drying her hands on a towel and heard the dial tone cut off as Nick's deep voice answered.

'Hey, stranger,' Jenny said, as a wave of longing swept through her. Between her work schedule and his business, they hadn't managed to see each other since the other day in the pub.

'Hey, yourself. How was your day?'

'Pretty good. Busy. How about yours?'

'Same. I was out all day yesterday showing Susie all the ins and outs of the local restaurant sourcing, so today I was catching up on everything I had to do yesterday that didn't get done.'

'But that's a good thing, isn't it? That she's showing an interest?'

'Yeah, I guess. I mean, I don't know why now—she's never wanted to before. All she's really been focused on was the book side of the business.'

'Maybe this way she'll understand things a bit better?'

'Maybe. Anyway, what are we going to do about this other situation?'

Jenny frowned. 'What situation?'

'The situation where all I can think about is how much I miss you and that I need you in a bed beside me—any bed—I don't care whose.'

Her concern melted into a smile at his words. 'I'm sure between the two of us we can figure out a solution.'

She detected a muffled conversation then Nick said, 'Sorry, I've got to go downstairs and deal with something. I'll call you back later?'

'Sure,' Jenny said, hoping it wasn't anything too serious. She hung up, feeling the familiar pang of loneliness that always followed one of their goodbyes. Which was stupid, she reminded herself. She wasn't some thirteen-year-old pining for her first boyfriend . . . And yet, here she was.

She looked up as she heard footsteps outside her doorway and called out, 'Hey, Sav?'

Her daughter stuck her head into the room and raised an eyebrow. 'Yeah, Mum?'

'Come in here for a sec. Sit.' Jenny patted the edge of the bed.

'What have I done now?'

'Nothing . . . Have you?' Jenny asked.

'Not that I'm aware of,' Savannah said, eyeing her mother cautiously.

'I just want to touch base with you—I barely get to see you anymore. Have you made any decisions since the Bali thing fell through?'

'Oh, that?' she replied, scrunching up her nose a little. 'No. Not really. I'm actually glad I didn't go now. I've kinda been seeing someone.'

'What? Who?' Why was she only just finding this out now? 'When did this all happen?'

'Calm down, Ma, jeez. Firstly, you wouldn't know him, he's not from here. I met him on a dating site, and secondly, it's only just gotten serious lately.'

'A dating site?' Jenny asked, doubtfully. She still had the occasional flashback of awkward conversations and slobbery kisses and gave a small, involuntary shudder. 'If he's not from around here then where's he from?'

'He's in Canada.'

'Canada? Wait.' Jenny frowned, trying to understand. 'He's in Canada, as in, *in Canada* right now?'

'Yes,' Savannah said slowly.

'So, you haven't actually met him yet?'

'Not in person, no. But we've been talking every day and FaceTiming.'

'But . . . you said it's serious?'

'It is.'

'How can it be serious if you haven't met him yet?'

'Because it is. I haven't been interested in a guy this way for ages.'

'So, how's this going to work?' She should be happy—her daughter was interested in a guy who lived on the other side of the world, which meant an unplanned pregnancy would not be an issue. One less worry.

'I plan on heading over there as soon as I save up the airfare,' Savannah said with a carefree shrug.

'To Canada?' Jenny repeated.

'Yes, Mum, to Canada,' Savannah said, as though explaining it to a dimwit.

'But what about uni? I thought you were going to think about going back?'

'I thought about it, but it's not for me.'

Jenny rubbed her temples with her fingertips to try and stop herself from snapping, then took a slow breath in. 'Savannah, you need to start thinking about your future. I'm telling you, going back to school when you're older is hard. Get your degree now so you have it for later.'

'I don't want a degree. Why can't you understand that?'

'Because you're a smart kid and you're going to regret it. You can't just backpack around the world forever.'

'Why not?' Savannah asked, throwing her arms wide. 'If that's what makes me happy, then why can't I do it for as long as I want?'

'Because eventually you'll have to come home . . . you know, that annoying thing called a visa that made you come back before? It'll happen again, and one day when you come back, you'll suddenly realise all you'll be qualified for is a low-income job and you'll have nothing to show for all those years of travel, except a full passport.'

'Which most people would envy.'

'In theory,' Jenny agreed, 'but they'll be envying it in the house they bought and driving the car they own as they head off to the job that allows them to pay for it all.'

'I don't want to live like that. I don't want to be tied down to a mortgage and a job I don't like.'

'This boy in Canada? Does he have a job?'

'He's a professional snow-boarder.'

Jenny sighed and dropped her hands to her side. 'Of course he is.'

'There you go again, being all Judgy McJudgy,' Savannah snapped. 'You don't even know Randy.'

'Well, neither do you. Not well enough to risk travelling all the way across the world to live with him.'

'It's called making memories, Mum.'

'It's called practising for the next season of *To Catch a Killer*. This is exactly how most of those shows start off.'

'It's Canada, Mum. It's perfectly safe. I'm twenty-six years old. I don't need your permission to make decisions in my life. I just wish you'd be more supportive.'

'I have been supportive. But I think this is a mistake.'

'Then I'll learn from it,' Savannah said calmly. 'You always told us that's what mistakes were for.'

'Yes, but you don't have to deliberately make them. Just think about uni, okay? Before you make any more decisions about Canada.'

'I don't need to think about it. I'm not going back. I'm not interested in business, and I have no intention of ever using a degree. I'm going to bed. Love you.'

It was no use; she knew her daughter well enough to know the more she pushed about this, the more Savannah would dig her heels in and argue.

There was nothing as frustrating as standing on the sidelines and watching your kids make decisions that you just knew were going to end up hurting them.

The sun was out and Jenny admired the beautiful cloudless sky above. There was something special about a crisp winter day when the sky was so blue. She crossed the main street and noticed a couple coming out of the bakery, recognising them from the pub. George and Sharon. She'd forgotten all about asking Nick how the tour had gone, then realised it was odd that he hadn't mentioned it either. But then she remembered that he'd had to get off the phone quickly and she'd been asleep by the time he'd called back.

As she neared, the man looked up and Jenny saw that he recognised her as well, and offered a smile as she drew closer.

'Hello. It's nice to see you're still in town. Did you decide to stay a bit longer?'

'The people we're travelling with had some engine trouble in their motorhome, so we decided to set up camp for a few more days until they get back on the road,' George said.

'Did you get to look around the pub?'

'Yeah. The young fella behind the bar let us take a bit of a squiz,' he said.

'Apparently the owner didn't know anything about it,' Sharon said, pointedly.

'Really? That's strange. Susie, the lady you thought was someone else, was supposed to pass along the message,' Jenny said, feeling a need to point out she'd done her bit.

'Seems she didn't. Although I didn't make a mistake. When I knew her, she went by Nicole. She wasn't as hoity-toity as she is now, of course, but I recognised her straight away.'

'Are you sure it's the same woman? She seemed to think you'd gotten her mixed up with someone else,' Jenny said doubtfully.

'Oh, it was her all right. And she knew exactly who I was. We were good friends for a time till she disappeared without a word.'

Why would Susie ever have had a different name?

'You don't believe me?' Sharon challenged and Jenny realised the uncertainty must have been showing on her face.

'It's not that . . . Well, not really. It's just— I mean she said this was her first visit out here.'

The woman gave another scoff and Jenny was a little irritated now by her outright rudeness. If Susie said she didn't know Sharon then why was this woman so certain she was lying? Jenny wasn't sure when she'd decided to become an advocate for Nick's sister, but this woman was beginning to get on her nerves.

Sharon began digging through her oversized tote bag and withdrew a mobile phone. She started swiping madly. 'It's been bugging me ever since seeing her, so I had my daughter dig through some old photo albums at home and send me this,' she announced, triumphantly holding up the screen to show Jenny a photograph. 'Tell me this isn't the same woman.'

Jenny groaned silently. She really didn't want to get mixed up in all this . . . Then she looked harder. The image was of a young man and woman, possibly in their late teens. The boy was leaning against a fence railing, smiling, while the girl, dressed in a pair of cut-off denim shorts and a T-shirt, looked at the camera with a surprisingly familiar expression. There was a strange air of—Jenny wasn't sure how to describe it—almost arrogance?

She'd seen that exact expression more than once since meeting Susie. Sharon was right. The girl in the photo was *definitely* Susie.

'Who is she with?' Jenny asked, taking in the smug look on Sharon's face.

'That's my cousin, Matthew.'

Jenny noticed the pub in the background, in all its pre-renovation glory. Susie *had* lied. She'd said this was her first time in Barkley. Then Jenny noticed the girl had her hand resting on something. The photo was a little shiny; it looked like Sharon's daughter had snapped the shot directly from the photo album, under its plastic cover. But as Jenny peered closer, she suddenly realised it was a pram Nicole was holding and in it, the blurred image of a sleeping child.

'And that baby,' Sharon continued, as though reading her mind, 'that was their child that she abandoned when she took off and left town a few days after that photo was taken.'

Jenny's heart sank.

'I saw her again, you know,' Sharon said, taking back the phone. 'The other day, after I saw her at the pub. I was sitting at the cafe over there.' She nodded at the small takeaway shop across the street. 'She walked past and I tried to talk to her, but she got all hysterical and threatened to call the police.'

'Why would she do that?' Jenny asked.

'Because *she* knows *we* know the truth.'

'About what?'

'About who she really is. Who she was before she pretended to be some rich foreigner's wife and businesswoman.'

'I don't think she's ever hidden the fact that she came from middle suburbia,' Jenny pointed out, certain that she'd read an article about it somewhere.

'She didn't tell them the whole truth, though. But we don't care about any of that. All I wanted to do was find out about the baby. The family lost all contact after she took it away.'

'You just said she left *without* the baby.'

'She did, for about six months. She only came back for it after Aunty Ruth and Uncle Lionel tracked her down. It was after the accident, when Matt died. My aunty and uncle were getting on and they couldn't raise a baby and run the pub. So she came back, collected the baby and left again. That was the last anyone heard from her.'

A baby? Susie had *a child*? But that didn't make any sense. Nick hadn't mentioned a niece or nephew, and she was certain that he would have if he'd been aware . . . Nick said she'd run away from home as a teenager. Had Susie gone off and had a child unbeknown to the rest of her family, then put it up for adoption? The idea had merit. Nick could have a niece or nephew out there somewhere.

'Do you think you could find out?' Sharon asked, cutting into her racing thoughts and looking at Jenny solemnly. 'She's not going to talk to me about it, but maybe you could find out something? It'd mean the world to us. To know what happened to him.'

'*Him?*' Jenny repeated slowly. 'She had a little boy?'

'Yeah.'

Jenny had to stop the million and one questions zooming through her head to concentrate. 'When was this? How long ago?'

'Had to be—what? Forty years? No, maybe not that long . . . thirty-eight? Thirty-nine?' Sharon asked her husband, scrunching up her face as she obviously tried to calculate the time.

'Yeah, something like that,' George confirmed.

The same age as Nick. The ridiculous idea popped into her mind before she quickly shook it away. Surely not . . .

Jenny suddenly felt light-headed.

Nick's sister had a secret baby at the same time as Nick's mother had *him?*

She thought back to the conversations they'd had earlier about his sister. She'd run away before he'd been born. They hadn't grown up together. His parents had a falling out with her. *Stop it!* she told herself firmly. It was entirely possible that everything Nick had told her had been true. His parents had just had him late in life.

Somehow she knew deep down that she'd just discovered the shocking truth. Susie *wasn't* Nick's sister.

She was his mother.

Thirty-two

'Mum? Are you okay?' Brittany asked as they sat at the dinner table that evening.

Jenny wasn't okay. Her troubled thoughts had been eating away at her all day. She had to be wrong about it all. It was like watching an old rerun of *Days of Our Lives* or something. She had a soft spot for those old soapies—her nan had always stopped everything in the afternoon to watch her stories on TV when Jenny had been a kid. The memory gave her little comfort at the moment. Unlike the multiple scandals and far-fetched plotlines of those shows, this was everyday life; those kinds of things didn't happen to real people. And yet, they did. Far too often. Maybe not so much anymore, society had clearly changed a lot of the old rules. But Jenny understood that sometimes, when faced with traumatic situations, people made decisions based on fear. Whatever the truth was, Susie had been just a kid when she had her baby, and whatever choices she made back then, she'd probably made them because she was scared.

'I'm just not very hungry. I'll put mine in the fridge to heat up later. I think I might have an early night,' she said, smiling at her daughter as she finished feeding Sophie. Jenny felt a surge of gratitude. Britt was such a great mum and Sophie had so many people in her life to love her and protect her should anything ever happen. Susie hadn't had that. The thought made Jenny sad.

Jenny sat at the desk the next day at work.

She'd tossed and turned into the wee hours, the thought of bringing up what she knew with Susie off-putting, to say the least. Questioning her about something as private and sensitive as this was not going to go well; after all, Susie had threatened to call the police on Sharon and George.

The woman would have every right to tell Jenny to go to hell. It wasn't even any of her business; her theory was based on a couple of strangers' words and none of it had anything to do with her. She should just tell Nick and get him to deal with Sharon and George. But then, what if her suspicions were true? Regardless of what the truth was, finding out his sister might have had a secret child would be a huge shock and cause even more hostility between him and Susie.

On the other hand, if what Sharon and George said was true . . . If there *had* been a baby boy and his family wanted to know what happened to him, didn't they deserve some answers too?

❖

'Are you sure everything's all right? You don't seem like yourself,' Nick said. Jenny had dropped into the pub on her way home, hoping to figure out what to do about Susie. 'Yeah. Just . . . work stuff. And I have a headache,' Jenny said, which wasn't altogether a lie. She'd been in pain ever since being thrown into the middle of this horrible bloody fiasco.

'At least there'll soon be one less headache. Susie's leaving tomorrow.'

'Leaving?'

'Yeah. Thank Christ. She's been in an even bitchier mood than usual. And that's saying a lot.'

Jenny could understand why. It was no doubt a little unsettling to have people from your past hounding you about things you probably didn't want to have brought up. 'Do you think she's got something going on?' Jenny asked carefully.

'Going on? Like what?'

'I don't know. Could something be worrying her? Maybe you should try and find out what's going on in her life. If she's worse than usual, it could be because she's going through something.'

'I'd be the last person she'd tell.'

'You're her family,' Jenny said. 'You should be the first person she'd come to if she had a problem. Maybe that's why she came out here? You said her visit was unusual.'

He seemed to consider the idea before giving a twist of his lips. 'I reckon she'd have a team of therapists on retainer to handle any of her problems, and knowing my sister, they wouldn't be personal, they'd be financial. She lives and breathes business—she doesn't have time for personal crises.'

Jenny didn't understand families like this. She just didn't. They were supposed to be there to help each other, not treat one another like business partners. Still, if Susie was intending to leave, there was no more time to put off whatever she was going to do.

'Babe, I gotta catch the sales rep before he heads out. I'll see you later?' he asked, kissing her lips quickly as she nodded absently. 'She's up in her room if you want to say goodbye,' Nick said over his shoulder as he left.

Jenny let out a long breath as she eyed the staircase. She *should* go and say goodbye. This was Nick's sister—or possibly his mother—and if she and Nick were going to be in a committed relationship, then she would have to at least try and get on with any family he had left.

She didn't have to bring up the baby thing, she reminded herself as she walked down the hallway and stopped at the door to Susie's bedroom.

Lifting her hand to knock, she heard the clip-clop of heels on the timber flooring before the door swung open to reveal an impatient Susie on the phone, staring at her expectantly.

'Oh. Sorry, I didn't know you were on the phone,' Jenny started, before the woman raised her finger and silenced her abruptly.

'No, Jonathan. That's not good enough. I don't care that you had personal reasons for the delay. You're a professional. I expected that contract to be on my desk and it wasn't. If we've missed out on signing up this client you'll have being jobless to add to your issues. Get that contract sorted. Today.'

Wow.

Susie swiped the disconnect button and looked at Jenny with a bored expression. 'Can I help you?'

The woman was a tyrant. Jenny fought to hold on to her compassion. Tyrant or not, she'd also once been a frightened fifteen-year-old.

But the woman in front of her was as far removed from that helpless girl as a person could get. There was nothing vulnerable or scared about her now. She was a fortress.

'I heard you were leaving. I came to say goodbye,' Jenny finally said.

'Checking to make sure I was packing?' Susie asked, arching an impeccably manicured eyebrow.

'I don't know why we got off on the wrong foot—'

'Because you are not who I want for Nick.'

Okay. To the point it is, then. 'Why would you care who Nick is with?' Jenny asked.

'Because if he gets involved with you, he'll never leave this place and do what he should be doing. He has the potential to work for, and one day own, a multibillion-dollar business. Do you seriously want to deny him that? Just to stay here and run a pub in a backwater country town with absolutely no future?'

'Nick's a grown man. He's worked hard to make his dream a reality. I would think that you'd support him instead of trying to manipulate him.'

'Manipulate him? That's rich coming from a woman old enough to be his—'

'Mother?' Jenny suggested. Jenny hadn't meant to bring it up—she honestly hadn't. She'd decided to keep her mouth shut and mind her own business, until Susie went and brought up the age thing—again.

A flash of horror crossed Susie's face briefly, before it was replaced with a look of disdain.

'Well, in theory at least . . . although it would be more believable if there'd been fifteen years between us instead of twelve.'

Whenever she'd thought about this moment, she'd never been sure exactly what would happen in the split second after she confronted Susie, but it hadn't been this deathly, shocked silence. The stillness was far more unnerving than if the woman had yelled and screamed.

'I bumped into Sharon and George again the other day. They showed me a photo. It was of you and Matthew Gosson. You lied about never being here before.'

'That woman is delusional. She's attempting to blackmail me.'

'Why would you not tell Nick that you knew the previous owners of this pub?'

'I told you, she's lying. She's fabricated the whole thing to make trouble.'

'And the baby?' Jenny asked, and this time the flash of pain on Susie's face was something that struck at her heart. 'All they want to know is what happened to him.'

Susie gave a bitter laugh and turned away.

Jenny wasn't sure what to do, but she couldn't leave Susie alone after dumping all these questions on her, so she cautiously followed her into her bedroom. Susie poured herself a glass of liquor from a bottle on the bedside table and frowned. The healthcare worker inside Jenny noted just how much Susie seemed to drink. Sure, even *she* liked the occasional drink after a hectic day, and yes, she'd been guilty of drinking to drown the odd sorrow or to erase the after-effects of a crappy date or two, but maybe Susie used it for something completely different.

'The caring, concerned Gosson family,' Susie sneered.

'Is it really so hard to believe they'd want to know what happened?'

'It is, considering not one of them stepped up to offer to help at the time,' Susie snapped.

'So what *did* happen to him?' Jenny prodded when the silence threatened to linger too long.

'I think you already know, don't you, Jenny?'

Despite suspecting the truth, hearing her if not admit it, then at least not deny it, still felt like a brick dropping in Jenny's stomach. Nick was Susie's son.

'You think you're so clever.' There was no hiding the slight slur to Susie's words as she poured herself another glass.

'I didn't ask to get involved in this. It wasn't anything to do with me.'

'And yet here you are, smack bang in the middle of it. Enjoying every minute.'

'That's not true. I don't enjoy other people's misery,' she said, honestly.

'Unlike me? Is that what you're saying?'

Well, if the shoe fits, sunshine. Jenny's mind briefly wandered to the phone call a few moments earlier and poor old Jonathan.

But no, she told herself sternly. *That's beside the point. Focus on the issue.* 'I didn't come here to call you out on your behaviour. I truly feel for what you must have gone through back then. It can't have been easy.'

'You honestly think I need your sympathy?'

'It's not sympathy.' As a nurse, Jenny had often come across unlikeable people, but she always managed to stay professional and do her job. This particular person, though, was a different matter. She was just so . . . unpleasant. And yet, there was something about her—a feeling Jenny had that, deep down inside, this woman wasn't the Godzilla she tried to present to the world.

'Well, whatever it is, it's annoying. Stop it.'

Deep, deep, deep down inside, Jenny corrected as she watched Susie swig the last of her drink. 'Fine. Have a safe trip home.' She sighed and turned away. This had been a complete disaster.

'What are you going to do? Run back and report to Sharon?'

The question stopped her at the doorway and she turned back slowly. 'Nothing. Like I said. It's none of my business.'

'And Nick? What are you going to tell him?'

Despite the caustic tone, Jenny suspected there was real concern not too far under the surface. 'I don't know enough of the story to tell him anything. But you don't seriously think you can keep this from him forever, do you?'

'Worked so far.'

'Until Sharon decides she wants to take it further. Once she meets Nick, she's going to put two and two together, just like I did, and figure it out. Do you really think he deserves to hear it from a stranger instead of you?' Jenny realised that was why Susie had been so keen to get Nick out of the pub—in case Sharon and George came back for that tour and met him.

'That nosey cow.'

'Surely you had to realise in a place like Barkley there'd be someone who might remember you?'

'None of the Gosson family I knew was still alive or still in town.'

It had to be some pretty unfortunate luck that Sharon had been visiting for the first time in decades at the same time Susie was here and that they'd bump into each other.

'Nick being drawn to this place wasn't just an accident, was it?' The thought had only just occurred to Jenny. 'He lived here with his father and grandparents. In the pub.'

'He was too young to remember any of it,' Susie dismissed bluntly. 'But I couldn't believe that, of all the places he could choose to buy, he'd pick this one. That had to be some cosmic joke, aimed at me.'

It was a little too specific to be some kind of accident, Jenny thought. The subconscious was a mysterious thing. Maybe Nick's childhood memories had been stronger than anyone had thought.

Susie sank down in an armchair by the window and stared out morosely.

'Why did you leave him here?' Jenny hesitantly asked.

'I met Matt in Sydney. He promised me all kinds of things—I was fifteen and living on the streets and he felt like some knight in shining armour,' she said. 'We were two kids head over heels in love. He had a job and a flat. I was going to go back to school so I could go to university. I thought life was finally about to start going right. Then I got pregnant. He just left. Left me to try and raise a baby alone. I was trying to study and work and take care of a child but I was just a kid myself. I couldn't do it anymore, so I came out here to find him.'

Jenny inwardly debated whether it was wise to continue prodding or not, but the alcohol seemed to have loosened Susie's tongue and she appeared to be in a generous mood. 'What happened when you found him?'

'He freaked out and gave me a fistful of money to catch the train back to the city. So I came here, to the pub, and I told his parents who I was and introduced them to their grandson. They insisted Matt step up and be a father. We tried for a few months, before we both realised it wasn't going to work. I couldn't become a domesticated housewife. I had plans and I couldn't do any of them out here. I knew I couldn't give a baby the life it deserved, either, so I left him here. With them.'

'It must have been hard to leave your child,' Jenny said, and meant it. She could only imagine the pain of making that kind of decision—and at such a young age.

'You have no idea what I had to do in order to survive with a baby in the city—the places we had to live. I didn't have your life—the luxury to be a stay-at-home mummy and do crafts all day. I had to work. I did what I did for Nick's own good.'

'I don't doubt that for a minute,' Jenny said calmly, trying to dissipate the woman's hostility. 'So Nick was brought up here in Barkley?'

Susie's anger seemed to have settled slightly when she eventually answered. 'Till he was two. Then his father died. His grandparents couldn't cope with a toddler after that, so they found me—I still don't know how. I was with Gino by then, and they threatened to tell him everything if I didn't come and get the baby. So I did.'

The news shocked Jenny. Clearly Susie's life had turned around by then if she was with her wealthy husband. 'You didn't go back for him once you were married?'

Susie looked out the window once more and, for a moment, Jenny thought she wasn't going to answer.

When she did, it was almost as though she was telling a story she'd rarely spoken about.

'I'd always had a plan—from maybe twelve or thirteen years old. I saw how my mother was: miserable. Defeated. Living a life that was mediocre at best. And I knew I never wanted that for myself. I'd vowed to leave and make my mark on the world as soon as I could.' She made a harsh sound in her throat and all traces of her earlier vulnerability vanished.

'How did you meet your husband?' Jenny asked.

For a moment Susie looked at her like she hadn't been aware Jenny was still there. 'It was very romantic,' she said in a dry tone that reminded Jenny of the one Nick often used. 'I was working in a jewellery shop—a very high-end jewellery shop,' she added. 'He was there to buy his wife a birthday present.' Susie sent her a somewhat condescending smirk, waiting for her outraged reaction.

'Oh,' Jenny said, blinking uncertainly.

Susie shrugged. 'Anyway, we got talking, he invited me out for drinks. Long story short, he gave me the thirty-thousand-dollar bracelet that night and I was his mistress for the next year and a half before he divorced his wife and married me.'

Jenny was stuck on the thirty-thousand-dollar bracelet. Who paid that much for a piece of jewellery?

'I've shocked you?' Susie asked, bluntly.

'It sounds all very . . .'

'Scandalous?' she supplied, widening her eyes sarcastically.

Jenny was getting tired of this woman treating her like she were some naive, small-town hick, incapable of understanding someone so worldly and sophisticated as her. 'No, actually, I was going to say it sounds like something out of one of those midday movies bored people sit and watch at lunchtime.'

She got a moment of satisfaction from the flash of disappointment that crossed the woman's face, and wished she'd never bothered to ask about her stupid marriage.

'We were married for twenty-five years,' she said, holding Jenny's gaze with a triumphant glint. 'He never had another mistress after we were married.'

Oh, well done, Gino. The man sounded like a dick, but then she realised just how messed up this whole affair must have been. Susie was an eighteen-year-old being seduced by a middle-aged man. Albeit a man she'd been married to for a very long time. 'It must have been hard when he died. Losing someone you'd been married to that long.'

Susie's face lost all expression once more and she cleared her throat quickly. 'It was. Although it's been somewhat . . .

liberating, too. He could be quite demanding. Set in his ways,' she added with a dismissive wave of her hand, almost as though she hadn't meant to get that personal. 'Our life was very different from anything back here.

'Gino didn't want children. Not his own, not anyone else's. He made that very clear in the beginning. I had no choice. I couldn't have Nick with me—at least, not then. Once I was secure in my marriage—once I had my own money and I knew I could support him if anything happened to Gino, then I could bring him back.'

'But you didn't.'

'No. I . . . The lifestyle wasn't fit for a child to be part of. I took him to my parents. I ate my pride and went back there. They agreed to raise him if I sent back money for his care and never told him who I really was to him. They didn't want him being confused later.' She shook her head. 'They kick their daughter out of home at fifteen then act all moral and high and mighty.'

Jenny was stunned. She stared at the woman before her, completely lost for words. Her thoughts jumped from one detail to another in a desperate attempt to try and understand everything Susie had just revealed. Poor Nick. He was going to be devastated by this—his whole life had been a lie.

'Nick must never know,' Susie said harshly.

'Nick has *every right* to know! You've lied to him all this time.'

'How dare you judge me? You have no idea what my life was like back then,' Susie snapped, and shame momentarily poked at Jenny's conscience.

Judgement played no part in her professionalism as a nurse. She dealt with people from all walks of life and situations that often defied logic or common sense, but each person was treated with dignity and respect—no matter what Jenny's personal opinion may be. A patient was a patient. However, Susie was *not* her patient. She was the sister—or rather mother—of the man she loved and she'd turned her back on him and left him for others to raise and care for. As a mother herself, Jenny couldn't wrap her head around any of those decisions.

'You're right, it's not my place to judge you. However, Nick deserves to know the truth about his life—and who you are,' Jenny said calmly, despite the emotional upheaval that was battling inside of her. 'It would be better that it comes from you.'

'Meaning that if *I* don't tell him, *you* will?' Susie asked with a snarl.

Jenny's eyebrows lifted slightly in reply.

'Wow, you sure know how to hide that devious streak behind the wholesome Mother Earth persona.' Susie gave a dry chuckle before narrowing her eyes. 'I guess this is one way to get rid of someone who doesn't approve of your relationship.'

'This isn't about Nick and me. Or our relationship.'

'And yet, how convenient that you'll be on hand to pick up the pieces while I'll be cut from his life completely.'

Jenny shook her head. 'You don't know that. But regardless, this is about you telling him the truth.'

'Telling him the truth about what . . . exactly?' Nick asked, stepping into the room, eyeing them warily.

The look on Susie's face, the complete and utter fear, made Jenny's heart sink. Dread crept its way up her spine. Yes, Nick deserved the truth, but it wasn't going to be a calm, rational discussion. Despite what Susie believed, Jenny felt for her. She wouldn't wish this situation on anyone.

'What's going on?' This time there was something more than just a slight twinge of apprehension on his face. His eyes had hardened and his mouth tightened into a straight, no-nonsense line. He held Susie's wide gaze.

'I'll leave you to it,' Jenny murmured, taking a step towards the door.

'No. Stay,' Nick commanded. 'I want to know what's going on.'

'Nick, you and your . . . you and Susie need to talk.'

'About what?' he demanded, then eyed Susie sharply. 'What did you say to her?'

'It's not like that,' Jenny cut in swiftly.

'She's upset because I told her the truth,' Susie snapped, losing that terrified look and returning to the confident businesswoman she'd been before. 'The age difference matters. I should know, I was married to an older man.'

Jenny gaped at her, but Susie had already turned on her heel and was headed for the door.

'Don't say I didn't warn you.'

Then she was gone, and Jenny was left trying to figure out how the tables had not only turned but flipped completely over. *That bitch!* She could almost applaud the absolute cunning of the woman. This was why she was so good in business—the ability to think on her feet and seize an opportunity.

'Whatever she said to you, don't listen to her. This is what she does—makes a huge scene and then leaves the building.' He sighed, shaking his head. 'She's always been the same. At least she's gone now and probably won't be back for another year or so, if we're lucky.'

Jenny could only continue to frown, speechless at Susie's audacity. Was she seriously just going to walk away from this like nothing happened? It was crazy. It was worse than crazy—now Jenny was stuck in the middle, left to pick up the pieces, and it wasn't even *her* mess to pick up after!

Nick's arms circled her from behind and he rested his chin on the top of her head. 'I'm guessing that the chat wasn't particularly friendly?'

He took her silence for acknowledgement. In truth, Jenny was still trying to figure out if she should tell him exactly what the conversation had been about, but she couldn't bring herself to find the words. This was not her story to tell, and yet, it was Nick's story to hear. She bit back a frustrated groan.

'Forget about her. I was coming to tell you about the meeting I just came from. We've been selected to feature on that TV show, *Take a Break*.'

Jenny took one look at the excitement in his eyes and all thoughts of breaking the news about Susie quickly disappeared. Nick was happy. Maybe she was just being a coward, but she didn't want to watch that excitement be replaced by shock and anger, and she *really* didn't want to be the one on the end of it, as the messenger. So instead, she kissed him and smiled as he told her all about the new plans, nodding and making all the appropriate gestures in all the right places and pushed away the little voice that warned her about putting it off.

But that night all her misgivings returned, louder and more persistent and with a prickle of foreboding that this was going to end badly.

Thirty-three

Jenny tipped her head back and closed her eyes behind her dark sunglasses, enjoying the caress of the warm sun on her face. The courtyard of the little heritage cafe was a recent addition the new owners had just finished, adding to the vintage appeal. The cobblestone-look pavers, potted shrubs and black wrought-iron fencing was a vast improvement over the vinyl gingham tablecloths and faded plastic seats that had been crammed into what used to be known as Mrs McConnley's Tea Room. The cafe was now known simply as 46 Main Street, and it all felt very fancy for Barkley. Not that Jenny was complaining.

'Oh, please.' Beth's droll tone interrupted Jenny's moment of solitude and she opened her eyes to look up at her friend.

'What?'

'You,' she said, pulling out a chair. 'Looking exhausted from all that hot sex you've undoubtedly been having.'

Jenny sat straighter in her seat and hoped no one nearby had overheard as she slid her glasses onto the top of her head and reached for the menu. 'Would you stop it.'

'Hey, I'm your best friend and I'm living vicariously through you at the moment since my husband is away, so deal with it. Most of us only dream of having some hunk sweep us off our feet and chain us to the bed for endless hours of *toe-curling* sex.'

Jenny gave a strangled chuckle as she shook her head. 'Sorry to disappoint, but there are no chains involved.'

'But there *is* toe-curling sex,' Beth said, eyeing her with a shrewd look and nodding slowly. 'I knew it.'

Jenny sighed irritably. 'Can we just order?'

'What's the matter?'

'Did it ever occur to you that maybe I'm getting sick of everyone making fun of my love life?' Jenny snapped, then felt bad when she saw her friend's grin slip and a flicker of hurt cross her face. 'Sorry. I didn't mean to snap. I'm just tired. I didn't sleep very well last night.'

'Why? What's going on?'

'I've just . . .' Jenny stopped and let out a sharp breath. 'I've been put in a position where I have information about someone, but it's really not my place to say anything.'

'I see,' Beth said, tilting her head slightly, studying her friend. 'But this information is important, and the person it relates to has a right to know about it?'

'Yes,' Jenny said, tracing her finger along the edge of the table.

Beth shrugged. 'Then you should tell them.'

'Yeah but . . . it's huge. Like, life-changing huge.'

'Okay,' Beth said slowly. 'Well, put yourself in their position . . . Would *you* want to be told?'

It sounded so simple when someone else said it out loud, Jenny thought wearily. But it was the same conclusion she'd come to last night. Nick had a right to know—he had *every* right to know—only she didn't want to be the one who dropped the bomb on him.

'Yeah, you're right,' she said.

'So who's having the affair with whom?' Beth asked in a low whisper as soon as the waitress took their order and left.

'It's not that.' She smiled at her friend's crestfallen face.

'Come on, I'm your best friend, you can tell me. I need some distraction in my life if you're going to stop filling me in on your sex life from now on.'

'It's complicated.'

Beth frowned. 'Is it serious then?'

'It's pretty huge.'

'I think if I had to hear some bad news, I'd rather you be the one telling me,' Beth said solemnly, before her eyes widened. 'Wait. It's not me you need to tell something bad to, is it?'

Jenny shook her head and gave a tired chuckle. 'No. It's not you.'

'Phew. Thank goodness. Thought my whole day was about to get ruined.'

'Nope, not yours.'

But someone else's she cared about was. She couldn't risk putting it off any longer. She wouldn't survive many more sleepless nights like the one she just had.

❖

Nick finished organising the long list of jobs that would need doing before the film crew arrived in two days' time to film the segment for *Take a Break*. The show's audience was mainly aimed at people who were looking for places they could visit for a long weekend so it was exactly what the pub needed to lift their exposure and Nick had been going over the entire place with a fine-tooth comb to ensure they were ready.

Things had settled down a lot since Susie's visit—he wasn't sure if it was connected or not, but Jeremy's shitty mood and the chip he'd been carrying on his shoulder since arriving seemed to have improved. Not completely, of course—he was still an arrogant dick—but he was at least speaking to the staff better and had even surprised Nick today with an idea for a new signature dish he'd been working on.

The visit hadn't all been positive, though. He was still worried about whatever he'd walked in on with Jenny before his sister had stormed out. The dramatic exit wasn't his concern—it was almost Susie's trademark move—it was the tension she'd left behind. He'd tried to get Jenny to talk about it later but she clearly hadn't wanted to discuss it so he'd left it alone, but *something* had happened. They'd barely had time to touch base since then—he'd been distracted by all the TV show preparations and Jenny had her clinic visit—but he made a mental note to make some time to get to the bottom of it as soon as they could wrangle a free night alone.

He had some calls to make to double check times for the TV crew to head out and film at the farm to showcase their beef and was on the stairs when he heard his name being called. He hung his head to swear softly, before turning around to go back to the bar.

'Nick, there's some people waiting to see you in the front lounge.'

'Okay.' He'd get this dealt with, *then* make the phone calls . . . and go to the bank and go over that inventory issue with Jeremy, and smooth over things with the supplier Jeremy swore at last week . . .

A man and woman rose from their seats as Nick approached. The man gave Nick a brief, firm handshake while the woman openly stared.

'Nick . . .' she said, barely above a whisper, making him eye her a little more closely.

'Can I help you with something?' he asked, shifting his gaze from the woman, with her faded and grey-streaked hair, to the man.

'I'm George, and this is my wife, Sharon,' the man said, breaking the awkward silence.

'And I'm your father's cousin,' the woman blurted.

'My father?' Nick replied, slowly. 'Reg?' He hadn't been aware his father had any cousins left. He'd certainly never heard of any.

'No, sweetheart,' the woman said gently, 'Your *real* father. Matthew. Matthew Gosson.'

Clearly the woman had him mistaken for someone else. 'I'm sorry, the Gossons were the previous owners. I've recently bought the pub. I'm Nick Mason.'

'The Gossons are my family,' Sharon continued, but it was the way she was speaking—in that slow, careful tone people used to break bad news to someone—that caught Nick's attention. 'Your family, too,' she said with a weak smile. 'I know this isn't probably the best way to do this, but I'm not sure there's an easy way. So I'm just going to tell you. Your father was Matthew Gosson. Lionel Gosson was your grandfather. And this was their pub before you bought it.'

He had enough on his plate right now without adding whatever the hell this crazy woman was trying to sell him. 'Look, I think you have me mixed up with someone else. I'm not a Gosson. I'm no relation to the previous owners. I'm sorry, I can't help you with any more information—I don't know anyone out here. Maybe a few of the old-timers who come in later might be able to help you track down whoever you're looking for, but right now, I need to make a heap of phone calls, so I gotta get going.' He turned back to the stairs.

'Your sister isn't who you think she is,' Sharon called, stopping him in his tracks, before he turned back to face her. They may not be close, but Susie was family and if someone ever tried to threaten her, they'd have to deal with him first.

'What's my sister got to do with this?'

Sharon stood beside her husband, wringing her fingers as she determinedly held Nick's gaze. She lifted her chin slightly, almost as though readying herself to face battle, before her voice hardened.

'She's not your sister.'

For Once In My Life

Jenny felt the weariness of a long day lift as she spotted Nick's car parked out the front of her house when she turned into her driveway. The trip home from Tallowhope had seemed even longer after a full day of clinic but Nick's unexpected visit had rejuvenated her and she climbed out of her car with far more energy than she'd climbed into it with earlier.

'Hey,' she said, heading over to where he stood, leaning against his car. 'Did you only just get here?'

'No. I've been here a while.'

'Why didn't you go inside?' Jenny asked, coming to a stop in front of him and noticing his taut expression for the first time. 'What's wrong?'

'I had a visit today from a woman who told me my whole life was apparently a lie,' he said bitterly. Jenny felt her heart drop. 'I woke up this morning thinking I knew exactly who I was and where I was headed, and by lunchtime, I had nothing but a bunch of lies as my past, and no idea who I am.'

'Oh, Nick.' Jenny sighed and reached out to hold his hand. 'I'm so sorry.'

For a moment she saw confusion cross his face before it turned into disbelief and her heart sank even further.

'You aren't even surprised? You *knew about this*?'

'I—' She couldn't seem to make her brain and mouth work together fast enough before he began to back away.

'This was what that argument with Susie was about, wasn't it? The day she left and I walked into the room. I knew there was something off about it all.'

'I'd only just found out.'

'I can't believe you knew about it and didn't tell me.'

'Susie was supposed to tell you,' she blurted. 'Only she took off!'

'Then you should have stepped up and done it. Instead, you hid it from me—you're no better than she is.'

'Now hold on,' Jenny said stiffly. She had *not* been the one who'd abandoned a baby. She was not even in the same league as his sister . . . or mother . . . or whatever the hell she was. 'That isn't fair.'

'Really?'

'Nick, I know you're hurting right now, and probably in shock—'

'You think? You should have told me, Jen. I can take being lied to from anyone else—but not you. You, I trusted.'

'I did *not* lie to you.'

'You've had all this time since finding out, yet you haven't said a word.'

'I didn't . . . I wasn't sure how to . . .' God! Bloody Susie! This was all her fault. If Jenny hadn't witnessed first-hand the terror in the woman's eyes that day when Nick had walked in the room, she'd swear she'd planned all this as a way to make some serious trouble between them. It was even more infuriating that this was some kind of happy accident for Susie.

Jenny took a calming breath and tried for a civilised tone. 'Susie left me to do her dirty work. I wasn't prepared for it—and I've been sick ever since, knowing that I *was* going to have to tell you and how that would affect you. I didn't hold back the news to hurt you. I just had no idea how I was going to break it to you.'

'You should have told me as soon as you knew,' he said quietly.

'I know. You're right. I should have. I'm sorry.' There was no point being angry that he was blaming her—she already knew he was just lashing out at the only person available, but that was easier said than done, and his anger still stung.

She reached out to take his hand again but he stepped away.

'I can't do this right now, Jen. I just need some time and space.'

'*Time and space?* Okay. Any idea how long we're talking?'

'Honestly, Jen?' he said quietly. 'I'm not sure.'

His empty tone stabbed at her heart—a sharp, white-hot pain that momentarily stopped her breath.

Jenny watched him walk around the car and get in without a word and drive away.

Thirty-four

Nick uttered a long string of profanities that he hadn't heard or used since his days in the army and thumped his steering wheel with enough force that a shot of pain raced up his hand into his forearm and made him swear again.

He was exhausted. Not in a physical way, but emotionally. He felt empty, drained of every emotion, and he was pretty sure he'd been through them all: shock, denial, anger, outrage, betrayal and everything in between. It was like he was trapped in some weird reality TV show—like *Jerry Springer* meets *Bad Moms* or something equally as crazy. This couldn't be really happening. His sister was his ... *mother*? God, even thinking the words made him want to cringe. How was this even possible?

He'd gone back to the pub after leaving Jenny's house and packed an overnight bag. Left instructions for Cassie to hold down the fort for a few days, and started driving. He thought about how many people had lied to him through his life. His parents—no, they were really his *grandparents*. He rubbed a hand across his tired face. He couldn't even deal with this right now. He just wanted to sleep. But he knew he wouldn't be able to—not without Jenny beside him. He never slept the long, peaceful, deep kind of sleep he slept with her if she wasn't there.

His mood darkened even more. She'd known. She'd found out Susie's secret and she hadn't told him.

It was that part he hated the most. Everyone he'd ever loved had lied to him—had known the truth and never said a word. He was the only one who hadn't been in on the joke. It hurt. Even Jenny had been in on it. Maybe not to the extent of his parents and Susie, but right now, when he was still so angry and hurt, the fact she'd been hiding this secret felt like a betrayal.

The highway signs flashed past but they barely registered. Driving in his condition, fuelled only by anger and caffeine, probably wasn't the smartest thing to do, but he needed to confront Susie face to face. This wasn't something he could do over the phone. He had no idea what he was going to say to her, but he'd use the hours of empty driving to figure something out—or at the very least calm down a bit.

It was going to take a long time before he was anywhere near calm again.

Twelve hours almost to the dot later, Nick leaned out his car window and pressed the intercom button at the front gates of Susie's posh house in Toorak and waited. He rubbed his hands across his face and felt the stubble under his palms. He could only imagine what he looked like: blood-shot eyes, unshaven and still in the same clothes he'd been wearing the day before. He didn't care about any of it. All he cared about was making Susie look him in the eye and tell him the truth.

He pressed the buzzer again and glared up at the security camera impatiently. If she was in there, she would more than likely already know why he was here.

He kept jabbing at the button until the loud click of the front gate sounded. He watched the large gates glide open with a low mechanical whirr and withdrew his hand from the button to drive through.

He'd only been here once before, and that was when Susie had first moved back from overseas after Gino died. He ignored the long winding lane lined with an impeccably kept hedge bordering a lawn that most bowling green groundskeepers would envy and pulled up in the circular driveway. A wide stone staircase led into the twelve-bedroom, ivy-covered, English manor–style home.

As he reached the top of the steps, the door opened and Susie stood there, watching him warily, but also with a kind of resigned defeat that somehow made her look older, more frail than he ever recalled seeing her. Wordlessly, she turned and led the way inside.

Her heels click-clacked across the black and white checked tiles of the large entry into which his entire bedroom, bathroom and possibly office space could have fitted. He followed her through a set of tall doors into a luxurious sitting room that overlooked the garden and pond outside.

'Drink?' she asked, going to a sideboard. She reached for a crystal decanter containing an amber-coloured liquid.

'No, thanks. I'm guessing you know what I'm here for?' he said after she filled a square glass and took a seat on one of the elegant cream couches.

'To take me up on that offer of a job?' she asked, kinking an eyebrow almost lazily.

'Enough!' Nick yelled.

Susie startled and spilled some of her drink. He was relieved to see she'd at least lost that smartarse, cold exterior he'd always detested.

'No more of these sick, twisted games, Susie. Tell. Me. The. Truth.'

'I'm surprised it took you this long to get here. I suppose perfect Jenny couldn't wait to tell you all about it as soon as I left.'

'I didn't hear it from Jenny,' he said stiffly and saw the news surprised her.

'So who told you? Oh. Let me guess . . . Sharon,' she said darkly.

'I want to hear the truth from you.'

'No doubt you've already heard the whole story.'

'I want you to tell me.'

'I don't see what the point is when you aren't going to like it . . .'

'Tell me, Susie! At least have the decency to explain what you did to my face. You left me on the doorstep of a bunch of strangers and then pretended to be my sister my entire life—who the hell does something like that? *Why* would you have done something like that?'

'Because I wanted more from my life than to be some teenage mother living on the dole,' she snapped. 'Is that what you wanted to hear?'

'I just want to hear the truth.'

'Well, that's it. That's the truth. I was a selfish, immature kid who didn't want a baby dragging me down.' Her voice quivered a little. 'All of it's true. Everything they would have told you.'

Nick thought his feelings couldn't be hurt any more than they already had been. He was wrong. Her words were like armour-piercing bullets and they ripped through the shield he thought he'd had firmly in place to protect him.

'I want your version,' he persisted, even though his heart was warning him that he'd got the answer he came here for. And yet he wanted to hear her say she was sorry and that she regretted it . . . Anything to give him a reason to somehow, if not forgive her, then at least understand her motives.

He watched her take a sip from her glass. Her hand wasn't as steady as it should be.

'You know what Mum and Dad were like,' she started, breaking the long silence that had fallen between them. 'They were strict and unrelenting about appearances and reputations. They went to church and were involved in fellowship groups and Bible studies—the lot. They didn't know what to do with a rebellious daughter who refused to conform to all the ridiculous, over-the-top values they had, and they blamed me for becoming an embarrassment to them in front of all their churchy friends. By the time you came along, they'd mellowed. They were outcasts from their church and had stopped going.'

Nick frowned at that. He remembered his parents reading the Bible and always saying grace before dinner. And Easter was always a big deal in their house, but he'd never seen them interact with anyone from a church or even go to one.

'They were hypocrites—the whole lot of them. They went to church and listened to some minister telling them how they should love their neighbours and take care of the less fortunate, then in the next breath they were standing by watching the same minister beating the devil out of me with a strap—literally. That's the justification he gave them: the devil had to be beaten out of me.'

Nick stared at her. No. That wasn't possible. Sure, his parents were strict and they were a bit odd, but he'd always put it down to them being from an older generation. Surely they wouldn't have let something like that happen to one of their kids?

'Why do you think I ran away from home? Why do you think I couldn't go back?'

'Susie . . .'

'You don't have to believe me, but you said you wanted the truth so I'm giving it to you—warts and all,' she said and wiped at her eyes quickly.

That action alone took Nick by surprise. He'd never seen Susie cry. Ever.

'I was living on the streets for a while, doing stuff I never imagined I'd be doing just to eat, then I met a guy. He was a few years older than me, and he swept me off my feet. His name was Matthew Gosson. He was fresh out of the country and had a job as an apprentice builder. He seemed so reliable and made me feel normal for the first time in forever. He took me in and gave me a home and we were happy. Then I found out I was pregnant, and at the same time Mum and Dad found out where I was and threatened to call the police on Matt for sex with a minor—I hadn't exactly corrected him when he thought I was older than I was,' she admitted. 'So he freaked out and left. Mum and Dad were still in the church at this point—barely. Apparently giving up on a devil-child was a sign of weakness so they were obliged to find me, but when they discovered I was pregnant and wouldn't get rid of it—*you*,' she said, and paused briefly, 'they said they were done with me for good.'

'If I'd caused so much trouble, why didn't you just get rid of—' Wow, this whole conversation was blowing his mind. *He* was the baby they were talking about getting rid of. The thought that he potentially may not have ever *been* was a lot to take in.

She shrugged. 'I don't know. I know you want me to say it was because, deep down, I wanted to keep you, but the fact is, at that stage, I was probably keeping you just to spite my parents.' She looked at him then and must have read the gutted expression he was wearing. 'You were the pawn in this whole sorry saga,' she said quietly. 'It wasn't fair. But whether you want to believe it or not, I was thinking of what was best for you when I left you with your father. The Gossons were a family—a normal, decent kind of family. I knew your dad wouldn't turn you away and you'd be taken care of.'

'But then he died,' Nick said. He hadn't had time to really process all of that yet. That was for later—right now, wrapping his head around this part was enough.

'Yes.' There was sadness in her eyes as she answered, but not sorrow—not like she'd lost the love of her life. Not like when she'd been grieving Gino.

'But you came back to take me to Mum— to your parents,' he corrected quickly. 'After everything they'd done to you, you decided to leave me there?'

'By then they were out of that crazy church. I didn't have any other choice. I'd planned on telling Gino about you once I felt like we were in a good place, but then . . . he . . .' She stopped and let out a sharp sigh. 'I had my own issues. Looking back, I think I knew he'd throw me away if he found out about you, and I was so emotionally screwed up at the time—so desperate to hold on to the relationship—that I couldn't risk jeopardising it.'

She paused then chewed her lip uncertainly, holding his gaze with an openness he'd not experienced from her before. 'I am truly sorry for the way everything happened. Our life wasn't . . .' She searched his eyes for a moment as though trying to figure out how to put whatever it was she was attempting to say into words. 'There were often things going on around us . . . I'm not proud of it, but it was what it was. There were drugs and too much alcohol, and in those early days the parties were out of control—money was no object to the people we did business with. It was no place for a child.'

'It still doesn't excuse why you didn't tell me later. You've had thirty-eight years.'

'There didn't seem much point. Why upset the applecart?'

'Because I had a right to know!' he said, raising his voice again. Christ, why couldn't she understand what a huge deal this was to him?

'It wouldn't have changed anything.'

'You don't know that.'

'I do. For years I've been trying to get you set up in business—prepare you for taking over the company—and you've wanted nothing to do with it. Would being the woman who gave birth to you instead of being your sister have made any difference?'

'No. But it's got nothing to do with the business. I had a right to know who you really were.'

'There was nothing to gain by telling you I was your mother because I wasn't. I gave birth to you. I didn't raise you. Mum and Dad did that. For all their faults, they at least kept their word and raised you as their own. I was barely a sister to you, let alone a mother.'

Some of his initial anger seemed to have faded since they started talking, but the lack of sleep and exhaustion was finally kicking in, draining him of the last of his energy.

'I'll show you to a room where you can sleep. After you've rested, we can talk some more if you like.'

He was dead on his feet and couldn't be bothered to argue. He'd come to hear the truth and he'd got it—regardless of how empty it had been. He wasn't sure what he'd been expecting, maybe some sort of closure? But at the moment, he had nothing. He still felt angry and betrayed and somewhat stupid that he hadn't figured any of it out for himself. He hoped that things might make more sense after a sleep, because right now, nothing did.

His whole life felt like it belonged to someone else.

Thirty-five

It had been three days since she'd heard from Nick and Jenny couldn't remember the last time she'd felt so miserable.

She'd tried calling and sent messages, but he hadn't replied to any of them and after the second day she'd stopped trying to contact him. She knew he would be hurting and he clearly needed some time alone to process everything, she just wished he hadn't left the way he had. She understood why he was so angry, but at some point he had to realise that she wasn't the one he should be blaming.

Work usually took her mind off her problems, but even there she found herself worrying about him, and the extra energy needed to concentrate with each shift was mentally draining.

'I don't get it,' Beth said, over coffee the next day. 'He just left?'

'He obviously had something to do.'

'Do *what* exactly?'

'Deal with whatever it is he has to deal with,' Jenny said, fighting to keep her own frustration in check.

'What was the fight about?'

'I told you, it wasn't a fight. It . . .' Jenny closed her eyes wearily. 'It's not my place to say anything.'

'It was Nick, wasn't it?' Beth finally said, leaning back in her seat. 'The day you were struggling over whether to tell someone something, it was Nick you were talking about.'

Jenny didn't bother denying it, she just sent her friend a level look across the table.

'Is he sick or something?' Beth asked quietly, concern etched in her dark Mediterranean eyes.

'No,' Jenny assured her, 'it's nothing like that. Please, Beth, don't ask. He wouldn't want everyone knowing this.'

'I'm not exactly *everyone*. I *can* be trusted to keep a secret, you know,' she said with a small sniff.

'I know. And I would trust you with mine completely. But this isn't mine to tell.'

'You're a good egg, Jenny Hayward,' Beth said after a few moments silence as the women sipped their coffee. 'I hope he knows what a good woman he's got.'

Jenny gave her friend a small smile. He didn't think she was terribly great the last time they spoke. Had he had time to cool down and reassess that opinion over the last few days? Or would he come back and treat her like a stranger? The thought of that was almost too terrible to think about. How could she go back to thinking of him as just the guy who owned the local pub after loving him all this time?

Damn it, she'd just gotten over the whole age-gap thing too!

When she got home, she headed upstairs and had a shower, hoping to wash away some of her glum mood, before dressing in her daggiest pyjamas and going downstairs to retrieve the ice cream she'd bought on impulse on her way home.

Seated on the lounge, watching a rerun of *McLeod's Daughters*, she glanced up when Savannah entered the room. Her daughter's eyes were red-rimmed, she was dressed in a mismatched pyjama top and tracksuit bottoms and her hair looked like it hadn't been brushed in days. Wordlessly, Jenny passed her the ice-cream container.

'Everything okay?' she asked after the third spoonful without any indication of Savannah handing it back.

'Randy is seeing someone else.'

'Oh.' *Yay!* part of her wanted to cheer, but another part was sympathising with her daughter's broken heart. 'I'm sorry, bub. I know how much you cared about him.'

'Men suck,' Savannah declared, digging the spoon into the ice cream rather aggressively.

Not so very long ago, Jenny would have agreed with her. 'Some do,' she said, smoothing her daughter's tangled hair like she used to do when she was five. 'But the right one doesn't. He's out there somewhere, waiting for you.'

'Well, it would be nice if he decided to be a bit more proactive and come and find me.'

Jenny's lips twitched and she held her hand out for the ice cream.

'What's going on with you and Nick? He hasn't been around lately.'

Jenny shrugged. 'He's just dealing with some family stuff.'

'But you guys are okay?' she asked, eyeing her mother closely.

'Yeah, sure.' She had no idea.

'I've decided to look into uni,' Savannah announced, after they'd been watching TV quietly. 'But,' she said, holding up a finger in warning, 'before you get too excited, I'm not going back to do business.'

'You're not?'

'No. I'm going to do travel and tourism. I figure I love to travel and I have heaps of experience and know about a lot of different places, so I may as well put it all to use and get paid for it.'

'I think that's great,' Jenny said calmly, and Savannah had no idea how hard she was containing the urge to jump to her feet and let out a cheer. Finally, little by little, all the bits of her life that had been worrying her were falling into place. Now, if only she could fix her love life, her little world would be darn-near perfect.

Later that night, alone in her room, Jenny kicked off the covers, staring up at the shadows of the trees on her ceiling. A small blip announced the arrival of a message and Jenny's heart momentarily skipped a beat as she reached for her phone. For the briefest of moments hope seemed to spin madly like a coin on its edge—unsure if it was happy or disappointed by the sender's identity. Then her heart rate kicked up a notch.

Caffeine_Addict
Are you awake?

Jenny stared at the screen before answering.

Florence_71
Yes. I haven't heard from you in a while. How are you?

Caffeine_ Addict
I've been better, to be honest.

Florence_71
Is everything okay?

Caffeine_Addict
Have you ever wondered why it is we haven't exchanged phone numbers?

Florence_71
I figured because you were shy.

Caffeine_Addict
Can't say I've ever been called shy before. No. That's not the reason.

Florence_71
Then how come? Oh, no . . . don't tell me. You're married?

Caffeine_Addict
No.

Florence_71
It's because of your job, isn't it? You really are a spy and you avoid personal relationships because your fiancé was murdered right before your eyes by an

> arms dealer in some foreign country and you swore you'd never again risk someone's life.

Caffeine_Addict
Wow. You should think about a career change to writing novels.

Florence_71
Okay. I have no idea.

Caffeine_Addict
Would you like to meet in person?

Florence_71
When?

Caffeine_Addict
How about right now?

Florence_71
It's almost eleven o'clock.

Caffeine_Addict
Come out the front.

Jenny's heart did a strange little flip-flop as a smile danced on her lips. She crept downstairs quietly and stood behind the closed door, fighting back the sudden rush of emotion that seemed to be drowning her. A mix of anticipation, excitement and longing. She slowly opened the door and lifted her gaze to the tall man standing outside, patiently waiting.

'Surprise,' Nick said, sounding almost hesitant.

'Not really,' Jenny answered, resting her head against the door jamb as she soaked him in. She knew she'd missed him, but until this moment—so close that she could breathe in the smell of him and feel his warmth—she hadn't realised just how much.

'You knew it was me?'

'Not at first. But I was wondering how long it would take you to come clean.'

'I didn't set out to deceive you. It wasn't supposed to go on as long as it did. I was just curious about finding out who you were and why you were dating all those morons.'

'You were the only thing that stopped me deleting that whole stupid app.'

'When did you figure it out?'

'You have the complete collection of *McLeod's Daughters* DVDs in the bookcase in your bedroom.'

'That was it?' he asked doubtfully.

'There was also the flowers on our first date. You couldn't have known pink hydrangeas were my favourite flower unless I'd mentioned it. The timing was always a little conspicuous too.'

Nick gave a surprised little grunt-like sound. 'So why didn't you call me out on it?'

'To be honest, I kind of liked the mystery man thing. But I like the real version much better.' Jenny sobered. 'Are you and Susie okay?'

'I think we will be . . . in time. I'm not sure how I really feel about it all. It's been a struggle to think of the woman

I've always known as my sister as my mother. I'm not even sure if I *can* make that switch.'

'There's no rush. It's probably something that will take a long time to come to terms with.' Jenny swallowed nervously, shifting her weight against the door jamb. 'I'm so sorry for not telling you earlier. You were right—I should have told you. No matter how hard it was. It should have been me who broke the news, not some stranger.'

'I was in shock that day . . . I shouldn't have blamed you. Susie should have told me years ago. I was just lashing out at the one person who didn't deserve any of that anger. So, *I'm* the one who's sorry. Can you forgive me?'

'There's nothing to forgive,' Jenny said softly. 'I just . . . I've been worried about you.'

'I know. I shouldn't have shut you out like that.'

He stepped closer and Jenny breathed deeply. God, she'd missed him.

'I had time to think through a lot of things while I was away,' he said, and at the first touch of his hand against her hip, Jenny thought her heart might burst through her chest.

'Oh? Like what?'

'Like the fact I don't ever want to be away from you for a single day, ever again,' he said softly. 'That I know beyond a shadow of a doubt that I am, completely and utterly, head over heels in love with you, Jenny Hayward.'

His lips touched hers and sent a spark of white-hot fire through her body.

She wasn't sure how long they stood there for, lost in each other's kisses, but the sound of a car engine slowing down as it passed the house made Nick ease away and look down in concern.

'I think that was Mervyn, the taxi driver,' Nick murmured. 'It'll be all around town by morning that he spotted us making out at your front door.'

Jenny felt a smile spread across her face. 'I don't care,' she said calmly. 'In fact, let's give 'em something to talk about,' she said, and she reached up to pull his head back down and kiss him deeply.

And the truth was, she really didn't care anymore who knew they were an item. She loved this man more than she'd thought possible.

Acknowledgements

A big thank you to Judy Ward, Kaitlin Blakemore and Lyn Mattick. Mitchel Ward, chef extraordinaire and brainstormer of kitchen accidents. Leanne and Renae, my amazing cousins and super nurses, always on hand to answer the weirdest questions. Anything that doesn't add up is purely my error, for which I'll plead author's prerogative to slightly bend facts to fit a plotline! My Google search history—I've definitely left instructions for *you* to be destroyed upon my passing . . .

My daughter, Jessica, who I somehow left out of my last book's acknowledgements and who has held it over my head ever since—I'm sorry! And I'm adding you to these ones!

MAREE